THE VOICE OF KALI

Praise For

The Green Spider by Sax Rohmer

"Fine, creepy stuff."
—*MysteryScene*

"Not to be missed."
—Dispatches From the Last Outlaw

OTHER VOLUMES IN THE SAX ROHMER LIBRARY FROM BLACK DOG BOOKS

The Green Spider and Other Forgotten Tales
of Mystery and Suspense

The Leopard Couch and Other Stories of
the Fantastic and Supernatural
With an introduction by F. Paul Wilson

The Romance of Sorcery—The Complete
Occult Writings of Sax Rohmer

SAX ROHMER LIBRARY
VOLUME 3

THE VOICE OF KALI

THE EARLY PAUL HARLEY MYSTERIES

Sax Rohmer

With an introduction by William Patrick Maynard
author of *The Destiny of Fu Manchu* and *The Terror of Fu Manchu*

Selected and edited by Gene Christie

2013
Normal, IL

COPYRIGHT

Citations of first appearances of the works in this volume may be found on page 204.

ISBN 978-1-884449-39-0

Editing: Gene Christie.
Additional contributions made to this volume by: George Locke.

Black Dog Books, 1115 Pine Meadows Ct., Normal, IL 61761-5432.
www.blackdogbooks.net | info@blackdogbooks.net

Publisher's note: These stories are a reflection of the time period and accepted ideals of the era in which they were written. This book may contain language and opinions that some readers might find objectionable.

Contents

INTRODUCTION

Paul Harley's unlikely debut was a mere passing reference in Sax Rohmer's 1912 novel, *The Sins of Severac Bablon,* where he was identified as one of the three greatest "practical investigators" in the world. Anyone familiar with the stalwart protagonist of the Fu Manchu series knows that Nayland Smith bore more than a passing resemblance to Sherlock Holmes. When Rohmer began chronicling Harley's cases in 1920 with the short story, "The Man with the Shaven Skull," it became obvious he intended to make good on his promise of shaping a detective worthy of being Holmes' successor.

Two more adventures for Mr. Harley followed in rapid succession, "The White Hat" and "The House of Golden Joss." By the end of 1920, Paul Harley had made the transition from short story to novels with two full-length efforts, *Bat-Wing* and *Fire-Tongue.* Both books were fraught with problems for Rohmer.

Bat-Wing encountered publishing difficulties as the magazine that had begun to serialize the novel folded and a substitute had to be found at short notice. Several years later, the book was plagiarized as a Sexton Blake novel, *The Black Skull* (1929). Rohmer opted not to file suit. The situation with *Fire-Tongue* proved even more challenging.

The author was about a third of the way through the novel when he was stricken with writer's block. More specifically, as a thriller writer unaccustomed to plotting traditional mysteries, he found he had painted himself into a corner and was unable to resolve the story satisfactorily. The main cause for alarm being that *Fire-Tongue* (as with most of Rohmer's novels) was serialized before the manuscript was completed. The author had a contract to finish the novel and could not work out how to do so. It was Rohmer's friend, the legendary escape artist, Harry Houdini who suggested he insert a flashback that allowed Rohmer to escape from this trap of his own plotting.

Paul Harley returned to the short story format with "The Dyke Grange Mystery" in 1922 while the novelette, "The Black Mandarin" appeared later that year. "The Black Mandarin" was unique in containing strong continuity references to several of Rohmer's other stories and novels. The involvement of the deadly Madame de Medici (see Volume Two in the Sax Rohmer Library, *The Leopard Couch* for more of this delectable *femme fatale)* would also link the Paul Harley series to the world of Rohmer's fiery Irish detective, Red Kerry. "The Black Mandarin" also brought Paul Harley back to Chinatown for the first time since "The House of Golden Joss."

Harley made the transition to the stage when Rohmer's play, "The Eye of Siva," opened in August 1923 with future Sherlock Holmes star Arthur Wontner playing Harley. Rohmer reworked the play as the novella, "The Voice of Kali," which followed closely on the heels of the stage play. Both the play and the novella bring Harley closer to the type of fantastic pseudo-scientific thrillers one associates with the author's Fu Manchu series in sharp contrast to the more realistic style of the earlier Harley mysteries.

A more traditional Paul Harley adventure, "Red Mist" would follow in 1924. The short story concludes the present collection of the early Paul Harley stories. It would be nearly six years before the character made his next appearance in the story, "At the Palace da Nostra" which linked Paul Harley with another of Rohmer's series detectives, Gaston Max.

The final three Paul Harley tales were written in 1937, yet only "The Death of Boris Korsakov" found its way to print that year despite all three titles being snatched up for publication. "Skull Face" (a thinly rewritten version of "The Man with the Shaven Skull" whose title suggests a cheeky acknowledgement of Rohmer's influence on Robert E. Howard) and "The Treasure Chest Murders" (a reworking of the earlier Morris Klaw mystery, "The Case of the Tragedies in the Greek Room" which may be found in Volume Two of this series) were not published until the collection, *Salute to Bazarda,* saw print in 1939.

Collectors may wish to note that the character of Malcolm Knox, who often played Watson to Harley's Holmes, also appeared on his own in two Chinatown stories, "The Pigtail of Hi Wing Ho" (1916) and "The Hand of the Mandarin Quong" (a 1922 rewrite of "The Hand of the White Sheikh" which appeared in Volume Two of this series). The character's surname, incidentally, was also the maiden name of Rohmer's wife.

Those interested in further bibliographical detail should seek out copies of the late Dr. Robert E. Briney's excellent fanzine, *The Rohmer Review,* or visit Dr. Lawrence Knapp's award-winning Page of Fu Manchu website, its online successor. Further insights and speculative research may be found in the works of the eminent Wold Newtonian scholar and author, Rick Lai. The work of all three men will enrich your appreciation of Rohmer's superlative gifts as a story-teller. As always, keep your eyes peeled for more from the essential Sax Rohmer Library courtesy of the fine folks at Black Dog Books.

William Patrick Maynard
Northeast Ohio

William Patrick Maynard's lifelong passion for writing and love of detective and thriller fiction was rewarded when he was licensed by Sax Rohmer's Literary Estate to continue the Fu Manchu thrillers. *The Terror of Fu Manchu* was published by Black Coat Press in 2009 and *The Destiny of Fu Manchu* followed in 2012. His articles and short fiction have been published in numerous magazines and anthologies. He is a former weekly columnist for The Cimmerian and is currently a weekly columnist for The Black Gate. His work has been nominated for a Rondo and a Pulp Factory Award. He makes his home in Northeast Ohio with his wife and children.

THE VOICE OF KALI

I
A Man Unknown

The coroner's jury, their unpleasant task concluded, filed out of the extemporized courtroom and with almost military precision filed on into the bar parlor of the Three Fishes Inn.

It was near to sunset on a perfect summer's day. High up in the elms at the back of the ancient inn there was much busy chattering from the feathered colony, as though already they were discussing their southern journey. Rooks cawed unmusically and a red glow spread further and further, right and left of the wood on a neighboring hill, beyond which the sun sank gloriously to rest.

A group of farm laborers, homeward bound, had collected in the porch of the old inn to gather news of the excitement that had come to stir the life of this sleepy Norfolk village. The jurymen, conscious of their prestige, nodded distantly to acquaintances and entered the bar parlor to drink the traditional pint with the landlord. Curious glances were cast at the only stranger present.

This was a leanly built, brown-faced man whose air of eager vitality must have told even the most inexperienced yokel that here was no ordinary personality. He had listened attentively to the recent proceedings, closely studying all the witnesses. And now, looking about him for a moment, he singled out a florid-faced individual whom everybody else treated with the utmost respect and who seemed to be fully conscious of the fact that he deserved it.

"Ah, Inspector Gorleston," he said, "I thought you had gone."

"No, sir," replied the inspector, "not yet. I wanted another word with you. You see, my professional reputation is at stake, if you follow me."

"I quite understand your anxiety, inspector. A whisky and soda?"

"Thanks," said the inspector, leaning on the counter. "I can do with it. This thing has rattled me." He glanced about him and then bent forward confidentially. "You see," he whispered, "when Mr. Burton van Dean applied to us at Scotland Yard for protection, we did our best. We had a special man put on duty at his place—the Abbey. What happened?" The inspector took a drink and answered his own question. "Scotland Yard instructs us to take him off! And what's the result? Here's this poor fellow the coroner's just been sitting on, comes and dies right there in the Abbey shrubbery!"

"Quite true."

The inspector glared in choleric fashion, as if highly irritated at his companion's quiet acceptance of his concluding statement.

"Well," he demanded belligerently, "he wouldn't have died if Jones had been on duty, would he?"

"Oh, I see the point!" murmured his acquaintance. "As you've just heard, the verdict was 'death from natural causes, man unknown.' But was it my fault, sir?"

"Not at all."

"Some half-starved tramp he was," continued the inspector bitterly. "Yet, since it happened, Scotland Yard has ordered us not to come within a mile of the Abbey!"

The other nodded sympathetically.

"They think we're country jossers because we live in Norfolk. And because a tramp dies in my district, I'm told I'm unfit to look after a gentleman whose life is in danger."

"Then you really think Mr. Van Dean's life is in danger?"

Inspector Gorleston bent more closely forward and, with a fat forefinger, he tapped his acquaintance confidentially on the shoulder.

"I've got two eyes, sir! Two good eyes! And there's something funny about that house."

"About the Abbey?"

"About the Abbey, sir. Funny lights have been seen there. Also, the figure of a monk. Funny noises have been heard."

"What sort of noises?" asked the other.

"Well, sir, as you're staying there, perhaps you've heard them yourself. A kind of piping, for instance?"

"Oh," said the other, and his rather grim face relaxed in a quick smile, "that is caused by Wu Chang, Mr. Van Dean's Chinese servant. What other noises?"

"Well, sir, you heard two witnesses speak of the fact that a sort of wailing sound was heard the night that this unknown man died there in the shrubbery."

"Yes, I took particular note of this evidence. You see, I had not arrived at the Abbey at the time of the man's death." And the speaker's glance became introspective, as though he were contemplating some new idea that had just occurred to him.

"Altogether, it's a funny house," continued the inspector. "Of course, Mr. Van Dean is an American gentleman, and very eccentric. But how Mrs. Moody can go on living there beats me. Still, I'm here if I'm wanted. I expect to be wanted very soon."

His companion seemed to have lost interest in the conversation, however. And shortly afterward, bidding the inspector good day, the stranger left the Three Fishes and set out along the dusty road, a lean, active figure in his well-cut blue serge, swinging an ash stick and puffing so vigorously at his briar that a positive wake of tobacco smoke spread out behind him as he went.

Curious glances followed him, for few strangers visited the inn, but Inspector Gorleston pompously announced that the gentleman was a guest staying at the Abbey, and this minor interest soon became swamped in the greater one of the tragedy that day investigated by the coroner.

Nevertheless, the worthy sensation-mongers in the Three Fishes would have found their interest revived had one of their number been curious enough to follow the stranger for three hundred yards along the road. At a ragged gap in a blackberry hedge, he paused. He knocked out his pipe on the heel of his shoe and looked cautiously around him. Then, "Are you there, Wessex?" he asked.

"Here I am," replied a voice from someplace beyond the hedge. "Any instructions?"

"Yes. Where have you left the bike?"

"In the lane at the other side of the meadow."

"Then fly back, I'll walk slowly in order to give you a good start."

"Good," replied the voice.

Came a sound of moving foliage, of stumbling footsteps; and then silence.

Probably it would have conveyed nothing to the local worthies assembled at the Three Fishes had they been informed that the distinguished looking visitor who had so closely followed the coroner's inquiry and who now was proceeding once more along the dusty road was none other than Paul Harley of Chancery Lane, London.

Affairs of state, involving possibilities of war, had more than once been entrusted to his experience. East and West, he was known as the confidential agent of the highest powers. But here, in this forgotten corner of Norfolk, he was known merely as a guest of Mr. Van Dean, the American millionaire traveler who had leased the Abbey, one of the county's historical properties.

Paul Harley, however, was no seeker of notoriety. The nature of his profession rendered it inadvisable that he should attract public attention.

Now, as he paced along the narrow road with the rays of the setting sun behind him, he became aware of an unaccountable chill, despite the genial warmth of the evening. That is to say, he experienced a chill which would have been unaccountable in another, but which, in himself, Paul Harley had learned to recognize as a sixth sense. This abrupt lowering of the temperature had often before advised him of the nearness of hidden danger.

It had come to him, that sense of danger, at the moment that Inspector Gorleston had spoken of the wailing sound, which, according to two witnesses, had been heard at about the time that the unknown tramp must have died in the shrubbery of the Abbey.

Possibly, this sixth sense was the product of a trained imagination. But experience had taught him that it was closely allied to clairvoyance. Therefore, he felt that he must follow up the clue of this wailing sound. It was in some way associated with the extraordinary affair that had compelled him to abandon every other interest and to set out hotfoot for Norfolk,

He came to the end of the lane, but, before crossing to the stile opposite, which gave access to a footpath, he paused, listening intently. Far away on the right, through the summer evening stillness, he heard the purring of a motor bicycle.

He crossed the stile and began to walk briskly along a path that would lead him to the tree-shaded lane encircling the northern part of the Abbey grounds. On his left was a wood, romantic in the growing dusk; on his right a sea of grain splashed with the red of the poppy, was a peaceful enough English landscape, but, persistently, that uncanny sixth sense spoke of danger. He stood still again, listening.

It seemed a perfect summer's evening, but long experience of the tropics told Harley that there was a hardness in the blue of the sky and a quality in the red sunset foreboding a storm. Faintly, he detected the rustling of the higher leaves. His suspicion became a certainty that there was a thunderstorm brewing.

He pressed on, crossed the stile at other end of the meadow and entered the shadowed lane below the rising Abbey grounds. On his right lay the nettle-grown gully where once had been the waters of the moat, in the days when the Abbey was a monastery.

He came to the gate, opened it and crossed the bridge. There was no one in the lodge beyond, and as he walked up the drive, arched over with ancient trees, he experienced anew that foreboding chill. He came at last in sight of the beautiful old house, surrounded by lawns and well-kept beds of flowers. His gaze, however, was directed toward an open first-floor window.

II
Kali

Burton van Dean had certainly changed the atmosphere of the Abbey. In the spacious library, with its paneled walls and oak-beamed ceiling, the influence of the American Orientalist manifested itself in the form of numberless Eastern relics and curiosities which seemed strangely out of place; for memories of the monastery clung more tenaciously to this room than to any other in the old Abbey.

At about the time that Paul Harley was passing the lodge, Mrs. Moody sat in the library, knitting. Her expression was as sweet and as restful as usual as she bent over her work, so that no one could have suspected the gray-haired old lady of any thought more important than the number of her stitches. But Mrs. Moody was a conscientious housekeeper. Actually, she was listening for some sound that should enable her to locate the whereabouts of Parker, the new gardener. Guests were expected to dinner; and cook had forgotten to arrange with Parker about the fruit salad. There came a discreet rap upon a door.

"Come in," said Mrs. Moody.

A tall, handsome Oriental entered and inclined his turbaned head in a salute at once dignified and respectful.

"Parker is not in the orchard, *memsahib,*" he reported.

"Oh, dear," said Mrs. Moody, "how annoying. Do you know where Miss Joyce is?"

"I will inquire," replied the dignified servant; and, repeating his curiously Eastern salute, he turned and left the library. This was Mohammed Khan, the Indian butler, and one of the several innovations introduced by Burton van Dean.

Mrs. Moody sighed gently and resumed her knitting. She had only taken up two or three stitches when a girl crossed the terrace and came into the library, pulling off thick gardening gloves. She was good looking in her open-air, English fashion, fresh complexioned and bright-eyed. Her brown hair was as the wind had left it, and she had a swinging carriage that was nearly, but not quite, aggressive.

"Hullo, Mumsie!" she called, and, running down the steps, she perched on the side of the chair and threw her arms around Mrs. Moody. "Stop knitting and tell me how to get rid of Jim. He's become a perfect pest."

"What's that?" inquired a drawling voice.

Both the ladies turned their heads as a tall, athletic-looking young man, the habitual expression of whose tanned face was one of great gloom, came slowly down the steps into the library. His hands were thrust deep in the pockets of his dazzling golf knickers.

Mrs. Moody laid her knitting aside.

"Is Joyce being rude to you again, Jim?" she asked sympathetically.

"Rude!" echoed Jim. "Well, rather! I've been trying to talk seriously to her. What with chaps dying in the shrubbery and all that sort of thing, it seems to me there's something funny about the house. Old Inspector Gorleston has got a yarn about a monk, or something or other."

"Don't be funny, Jim," admonished Joyce.

"I don't know about funny," drawled Jim. "It's my belief that old Van Dean, with his funny servants and squatting idols and what not, is haunted."

"Jim, dear!" exclaimed Mrs. Moody. "Haunted!"

"He's a haunted man," persisted Jim. "There are lots of haunted houses; why not a haunted man?"

"Poor Jim!" muttered Joyce.

A muffled sound of barking proclaimed the presence in the house of a dog somewhere quite near. Jim glanced guiltily in the direction of a door approached by a short open stair in the fashion of the Tudor period of architecture.

"Good dog!" he muttered.

"You see, Mumsie," explained Joyce, who was Mrs. Moody's stepdaughter, "Jim brought Rex over from the Warren."

The sound of barking was renewed.

"Oh, Lord!" muttered Jim, "Shall I let him out, Joyce?"

"Well, not unless I can find a key," was the reply; and Joyce crossed to a writing table and began to search among the many objects which littered it.

Mrs. Moody, who had been looking from one to the other, round-eyed, expressed her gentle remonstrances.

"Surely, Jim," she said, "you haven't locked a dog in Mr. Van Dean's study?"

"Well," replied Jim, standing first on his right foot and then on his left, "old Rex kicked up such a row when we bumped into the livestock—"

"Which means," interrupted Joyce, "that Rex took fright when he met Mr. Van Dean's tame cheetah in the grounds, and so we had to lock him up to keep him quiet. No, no key here."

Composedly, she crossed and rang a bell beside the deep-set fireplace.

"But, my dear!" murmured Mrs, Moody, "in the study! Mr. Van Dean's new book is there, a frightfully important book. Suppose the dog has eaten it!"

"Rough on me, Mumsie," retorted Joyce; "considering I typed it!"

Mohammed Khan entered, inclining his head in dignified salute.

"Mohammed," cried Joyce, "will you go up to my sitting-room and see if I've left a key on my desk."

The butler bowed, turned, and was approaching the door when there came hurrying in from the terrace a gaunt-faced man. He wore horn-rimmed glasses and a Stetson hat with the brim pulled down over his eyes. His tweed suit was untidy, as was his whole appearance, and there was something at once furtive and nervous in his manner.

Jim Westbury saw him first, and, "Oh, Lord!" he muttered. "Here's old Van Dean!" and glanced guiltily in the direction of the study door,

Van Dean, however, had his glance fixed on Mohammed Khan.

"Mohammed!" he called sharply.

Mohammed Khan turned.

"Sahib."

"Make an early inspection of the grounds, tonight. Test all the connections and report to me with the keys before dinner. That clear?"

"I understand, *sahib."* He saluted and went out.

Jim exchanged a significant glance with Joyce. Then: "Anything wrong, Van Dean?" he asked. "You look hot and bothered."

"No, no!" The famous American traveler threw his hat upon a settee and, going to a side table, poured out a glass of water. "Nothing to worry about. My nerves aren't too good these days."

His hand shook as he raised the glass to his lips.

"Haunted!" whispered Jim, intending the words for Joyce's ears alone. "I knew it!"

"Well," declared Mrs. Moody. "I must say, Mr. Van Dean, that *I* have a dreadful sensation, sometimes, of being watched."

"Nonsense, Mumsie," said Joyce, sitting on the arm of her chair and taking her hands. "Don't say you're going to get nervy, too. You've been so wonderful."

Jim, who had been curiously watching Van Dean, now took him aside.

"What's up, Van Dean?" he asked.

Burton van Dean glanced in the direction of the two women.

"I thought I heard a faint voice a while ago, as I came through the shrubbery," he replied in a low tone.

"Near where the dead man was found?" said Jim.

"Yes. Say no more about it. It was probably imagination."

He turned, staring hard in the direction of a strange-looking jade image, on a carven pedestal which stood immediately to the right of the French windows.

"Mrs, Moody," he called, "do you know why no one has come

to remove this thing?"

"No," replied Mrs. Moody. "I understood they were coming this afternoon."

"I wish they had!" cried Joyce. "The horrible thing gives me the creeps. But, oh—!" She hesitated. "I'm giving away secrets!"

"No, no, Miss Gayford," protested Van Dean. "You are not. You have been an ideal secretary. But—" his nervousness became more apparent—"I feel I owe your mother an explanation. I had hoped it might not have been necessary. Tonight, I know it is. Mrs. Moody, when I leased the Abbey, I knew my life was in danger." He turned almost pathetically to the elder lady.

"Then why," she exclaimed mildly, "did you allow Joyce and myself to remain?"

"Because your brother made it a condition of the lease, a condition I have never regretted. But I think you ought to know that, before I came here, I had been in the East for close on seven years. I was reported missing, counted as dead. Your daughter knows where I was. There's no further reason why you should not know also. I was away up on the borders of Tibet. It was there I learned—" he pointed to the jade image—"what *that* stands for. I blundered onto a secret up there beyond Khatmandu. A horror! A thing which—you—" His voice broke. "Well, I got away," he added, "maimed, but alive. Here, in the heart of peaceful Norfolk, I thought I should be safe."

Mrs. Moody's eyes were growing more and more round.

"Safe? From what?" she asked.

"From the Voice of Kali!" he replied, but in so low a tone that the words were barely audible.

"But," exclaimed Jim, "I can't cope with the thing! What has the voice of Kali got to do with this funny-looking image."And what *is* the Voice of Kali?" asked Mrs. Moody.

"It is a summons," replied Van Dean, "used by an organization which regards the days of the world's white races as numbered!"

"A summons to what?" asked Joyce eagerly.

"To death!" replied Van Dean.

The two women stared at him, expressions of horror growing on their faces. Jim continued to regard the image on the pedestal. And then, "What is this thing, Van Dean?" he demanded.

"The emblem of the Indian goddess, Kali!"

III
The Locked Door

For a while, there was silence in the big library. The sound of a lawnmower could now be heard in the garden. Joyce was the first to speak.

"Is what you have told us the reason the government has sent Paul Harley down?" she asked.

Van Dean slowly nodded his head.

"Yes. No white man, myself may be excepted, knows so much of this secret danger to us and all other civilized countries as Paul Harley of the British Foreign Office."

"I'm beginning to grasp the idea of the barbed wire in the moat," announced Jim, "and the case of small arms and the burglar alarms, and what not."

"I assure you," said Van Dean, "that they are necessary." He turned and advanced in the direction of the study stair. Before the French windows, he paused for a moment, looking out. "We're in for a storm," he murmured. "I wonder if Wu Chang has locked up the cheetah. He will have to be moved, tonight, as we are expecting visitors. He is always uneasy during a storm."

Three pairs of eyes watched him as he hesitated and finally went out by way of the door flanked by bookcases.

No one noticed that the sound of the lawnmower had ceased, and no one observed the approach of a bearded, surly-looking man wearing a battered straw hat, who slowly crossed the terrace and stood looking into the room.

Finally, Mrs. Moody, heaving a great sign, turned in his direction.

"You wanted me, madam," said the bearded man.

"Oh, yes, Parker," she replied, "I wanted to speak to you about some peaches for tonight. Joyce, dear—" she turned to her step-daughter—"will you see about it?"

"Certainly, Mumsie, Get a basket, Parker," she instructed. "I'll join you in a moment."

Parker nodded and retired as Joyce dropped down again on the arm of Mrs. Moody's chair.

"Dear old Mumsie isn't really worried, is she, about all this bogey stuff?" she asked affectionately.

"Well, dear," confessed Mrs. Moody, "it *is* rather disturbing."

There was a rap at the door and Mohammed Khan came in.

"Pardon, *memsahib,*" he said to Joyce, "there is no key on your desk." He turned to Mrs. Moody. "There will be, tonight, how many guests?"

Mrs. Moody, whose expression had now settled into one of bewilderment, replied, "Let me see: Mrs. and Miss Westbury; Captain Latham and—oh, Jim, you will never have time to dress!"

"Eh!" said Jim, who had been staring intently at the image of Kali. "Just time to buzz back to the Warren and change."

"Oh!" replied Mrs. Moody doubtfully. "Four besides ourselves, Mohammed."

The Oriental bowed and retired.

"Uncanny chappie, that," muttered Jim. "This place is full of funny people, funny noises, threats of sudden death and what not."

"I quite agree," murmured Mrs. Moody; "but I think—at least I hope—that Mr. Van Dean exaggerates."

"I don't know, Mumsie," said Joyce. "The Foreign Office would never have sent such a big *sahib* as Paul Harley down if there hadn't been something important doing. I should say—"

Suddenly, from somewhere in the house, came the sound of a loud crash, followed by that of a whining that died away in a manner curiously horrible. Mrs. Moody clutched at Joyce convulsively.

"Good Lord!" said Jim. "What's that?"

Mrs. Moody stood up.

"I'm almost certain it was in the dining room," she said. "Joyce, do come with me!"

The old lady hurried out, calling for Mohammed. But Joyce hesitated, looking at Jim.

"Jim," she said, "that was in the study!"

"The dog!" muttered Jim guiltily. "I'd clean forgotten him!"

"So had I. I'll go and look for the key myself."

She ran out. Jim was standing, peering awkwardly in the direction of the locked study door when Paul Harley strode briskly across the terrace in the growing dusk, and into the library. Jim turned with a start.

"Hello, Harley!" he cried. "Anything wrong?"

One quick glance Harley gave him.

"Yes!" he snapped, and ran up the stairs to the study door.

He tried the door and snapped his fingers irritably when he found it to be locked.

"Westbury!" he ordered. "Run 'round the garden to the study window. Quick, man!"

Jim stared for a moment and then, turning, ran out of the library, crossed the terrace and disappeared. His footsteps could be heard upon the stone stairs as Joyce came hurrying back. On seeing Harley standing on the landing, she paused in confusion.

"Oh, Mr. Harley," she cried, "I can't find the key!"

"What key?" snapped Harley grimly.

"The key of the study. Rex, Captain Latham's dog, is locked in there!"

"Ah," muttered Harley. "Is that so? How long had you been in the library?"

"About ten minutes."

"Anyone been up these stairs?"

"Not a soul."

"Sure?"

"Positive, Mr. Harley."

A door was flung open and Van Dean came in.

"Quick!" said Harley to him before he could speak. "The key of your study, Van Dean!"

Van Dean ran up the stairs, fumbling for and producing his keys.

"What's wrong, Harley?" he asked. "What's all the disturbance?"

"I don't know," was the reply, "yet." Paul Harley took the key handed him and fitted it into the lock of the study door. "You haven't been in your study during the past ten minutes?"

"Why, no," returned Van Dean. "I never use the other door. It's kept locked. You don't think—"

"No time," interrupted Harley, "to think." He opened the door cautiously and entered, Van Dean following him.

"Good God!" muttered the latter as he recoiled.

Joyce had been following up the stairs.

"Oh, what is it?" she cried. "Mr. Van Dean, tell me!"

Van Dean turned, holding up his hands. The expression upon his face terrified her.

"I'll tell you in a moment," he said. "Stay there."

"Oh!" whispered Joyce. "Is it Rex?"

Paul Harley came out on the landing and closed the door behind him.

"It is Rex, Miss Gayford, An accident."

"Dead?" whispered Joyce.

"Yes," said Harley. "I wonder if you would send Mohammed Khan to me here."

"Yes, Mr, Harley," the girl replied, "But what does it mean? Who could have—"

"Later, Miss Gayford!" interrupted Harley sharply. "All in good time."

Joyce, dimly recognizing that there was more in this than either man had declared, turned and walked slowly out. As the door closed behind her, Van Dean clutched Harley's arm in a vise-like grip.

"Merciful God!" Van Dean whispered. *"He is here!"*

Harley rested his hand upon Van Dean's shoulder. They came down together into the library.

"Keep a grip on your nerves, Van Dean," Harley said firmly. "There is more to come. Someone, never mind names at the moment, entered your study a while ago."

"But," whispered Van Dean, "the doors were locked!"

"There's the window,'" retorted Harley, "and the north wing is covered in ivy. Oh, there's no room for doubt! I saw something moving up there as I crossed the lawn below. He found Latham's dog in the room. The poor brute went for him, and—"

He ceased speaking as Jim Westbury, looking rather sheepish, came in by the French window.

"I say," he inquired, "can I dismiss? Not a soul about."

"Of course," replied Harley in preoccupied fashion. "Sorry. I was afraid you would be too late to see anything." He turned to Van Dean. "If you have no objection, I should like a word with Mohammed Khan and Wu Chang. I have satisfied myself about the other servants."

"As you like, Harley," replied the American. "It's up to you. God knows, I'd trust them both. But, all the same, I—"

There came a rap on the library door and Mohammed Khan entered.

"Mohammed," said Van Dean, "Harley *Sahib* wishes to speak to you."

The Oriental bowed. Paul Harley crossed and stood just in front of him, looking him up and down with his penetrating gray eyes.

"You have seen military service," Harley said. "When and where?"

At that, a trace of uneasiness disturbed the serenity of the Oriental's countenance.

"I serve under the Gaekwar of Baroda, *sahib,"* he replied in his musical voice, "from the time I am twenty, for five years."

"Why do you claim to be Rajputanan?"

"I was born in Rajputana, *sahib."*

"What town?"

"Shahabad."

"And after Baroda?"

"I go to the Madras Presidency in the service of Colonel Forrester."

"As what?"

"As butler."

"Next?"

"He comes to England; I come also. He meets with misfortune, but the colonel *sahib* gives me a good name at the agency, and I am engaged here."

A little longer the steel gray eyes challenged the glance of the dark brown ones.

"Very good, Mohammed. You may go. Send Wu Chang to me in Mr. Van Dean's study."

Harley's glance followed Mohammed's departure across the library. Then, with not a word to Van Dean or Westbury, he turned, mounted the stairs and disappeared into the study.

"Good Lord, Van Dean!" Westbury burst out. "What's it all about? I always thought you brought Mohammed Khan from India and all that."

"No, Westbury," replied Van Dean. "When I was forming my household here, I advertised for an Indian butler. He came from the Anglo-Indian Association in London. His references were above suspicion."

"Then—" began Jim, and paused.

Unheralded by any knock, a little, stooping Chinaman entered the library, silent in his padded shoes. He glanced neither to right nor left, but shuffled across to the study stairs, mounted them, rapped on the door and went in, closing it behind him.

IV
The Mandarin

Latterly, an odd sense of unrest had come to the household at the Abbey. Bates, the chauffeur, had formerly lived at the gate lodge, where, later, Parker, the gardener, had also slept.

But latterly, by Mr. Van Dean's orders, accommodation had been found in the main building for both of these.

An indefinable air of mystery had begun to manifest itself from the time that the wealthy and distinguished American traveler took up his habitation there. Several servants had left, but had been replaced by others sent down from London. Mohammed Khan, the butler, and Parker, the gardener, were comparatively newcomers; and to the dignified Mohammed fell the duty of inspecting the grounds every night at dusk, particularly with regard to the efficiency of certain electrical burglar alarms which Van Dean had installed early in his tenancy.

Where once, in ancient days, the moat had flowed was now a stagnant, nettle-grown ditch. This had been rendered impassable by the introduction of a quantity of barbed wire, many thousand feet of which had been delivered at the Abbey, giving rise to sensational rumors in the neighborhood. Once the gates had been locked by Mohammed Khan, it would have taken a clever man to gain access to the Abbey grounds; for these gates were not only formidably protected, but were incorporated in the alarm circuit in such a way that anyone attempting to scale them would set bells ringing in the study.

The tall, white-clad figure of Mohammed Khan seemed most singularly out of place in these old English gardens and shrubberies as he made his rounds from point to point this evening. Once, at a door in an ancient brick wall, he had paused, listening. Then he stood aside as Parker came out, carrying a basket of peaches.

The surly gardener gave him no word of greeting; indeed, scarcely glanced at him, but proceeded up the sloping path in the direction of the house. Mohammed Khan passed through into the orchard, closing and locking the door behind him with one of the keys from a considerable bunch that he carried. He made his way round through the kitchen garden to the north wing of the house; and there he paused, looking in at a barred window.

A dull, crooning sound could be heard. The place was a sort of outhouse, connected by a covered way with part of the servants' quarters; dimly visible within, Wu Chang crouched upon the floor, caressing the wicked looking-head of a lithe, cat-like creature whose black-spotted coat of gold gleamed through the dusk. It was Van Dean's Indian cheetah; although fairly tame, it was at times a dangerous pet. However, the Chinaman was crooning to it like a mother to her baby. Out of a cage on the wall, two little monkeys peered, chattering.

Indeed, not the least of the distinguished American's eccentricities was this minor menagerie that he had installed at the Abbey, practical zoology being one of his hobbies.

Mohammed Khan proceeded round the wing of the house and finally entered the library through the French windows. The room was empty and the tall Oriental stood for a moment listening. Dimly, he could hear voices proceeding from the study upstairs, among them that of Mr. Van Dean.

In the study, a small room so laden with relics of Van Dean's unusual travels that it resembled the apartment of a very untidy antique dealer, Paul Harley, leaning against the edge of the writing table, was speaking to Jim Westbury. Van Dean sat near him in a revolving chair, his elbow on the table, his chin resting in his hand.

"I asked you to come up here, Westbury," Harley was saying, "because you might as well know the truth about what's happened. But there is no occasion to upset the women."

"What has happened?" demanded Westbury.

"Well," said Harley, "whoever gained access to the study just now took nothing; probably hadn't time."

"Poor old Rex disturbed him?"

"Exactly. I told Miss Gayford that Rex's death was an accident. Here's the truth."

From his pocket, Harley took out a long, slender dagger with a hilt richly encrusted with jewels, conspicuous among them being a large green stone that glittered eerily. One startled glance Westbury took at the thing.

"Good Lord!" he muttered. "There's blood on it!"

"Naturally," said Harley dryly. "The poor brute was stabbed to the heart. This thing was stuck fast between his ribs."

He paused abruptly, placing the dagger behind him on the table as a sound of rapping came upon the study door.

"Come in!" cried Harley.

The door opened and Mohammed Khan entered. He bowed to Van Dean.

"Everything is in order, *sahib,"* he reported. "The gate, I could not lock until your guests had arrived."

Paul Harley watched him intently while he spoke, but the man's handsome face was quite expressionless.

"Very good," said Van Dean, "you may go."

Mohammed Khan gravely retired. Harley thoughtfully relighted his pipe before resuming, the others watching him anxiously.

"Look!" he said, again exhibiting the dagger. "The sign of the Group!" He pointed to the green stone on the dagger's hilt.

"The mark of Kali!" whispered Van Dean.

Westbury glanced at him, not comprehending.

"What is this?" he asked, "An emerald?"

"No," replied Harley, "a green sapphire; and beneath it is an inscription. Roughly translated, it reads, 'He who is summoned by the gods, listens and dies.'"

"The Listening Death!" said Van Dean hoarsely.

"But," cried Westbury, "I can't fathom this thing. I mean to say—"

"Westbury," Harley interrupted sharply, "you don't realize what stakes we are playing for. You don't know that there is a great seething out there in the heart of the East, the surface indication of a threatening mystical fanaticism of such horribly devastating probabilities as the world has never witnessed nor heard of before. I must inform you, Westbury, that this house is the focus of a great conspiracy which may be backed by anything up to four millions of people."

"Good heavens!" gasped Westbury. "But what are they after?"

"They are after *me!"* answered Van Dean.

"And, incidentally, myself as well," added Harley. "Van Dean, we are right up against it. Without any shadow of doubt, you have been traced. We must be ready for anything. I'm only sorry that there will be ladies here tonight."

"But you're not suggesting," said Westbury rather wildly, "that we're in for a siege or something?"

"Hardly that," replied Harley, "but this knife bears the crest of the most dangerous criminal in the whole world. I can give him no other description."

"Who is he?"

"He is known as the Mandarin K. One of the secret council

termed 'the S. Group.' Their symbol, Westbury, is the mark of Kali, and those who fall foul of them die."

"A strange death," whispered Van Dean, "strange and horrible."

"For over a year," continued Harley, "I have been searching for the nameless mandarin, the genius behind the mark of Kali, with all the power of the British Empire to back me. In India, in China, in the Near East I have had news of him, have met with his handiwork."

He paused again, listening intently. A sound of someone playing on a reed pipe made itself audible, a weird dirge, rising and falling monotonously, Westbury turned startled eyes on Van Dean.

"What's that?" he demanded.

The American smiled rather wanly. "It is only Wu Chang," he replied. "Have you never heard him playing before?"

"Phew!" said Westbury. "No, I haven't! It quite startled me. Go on, Harley."

"I am coming to my point," resumed the latter. "Knowing what I know, that this man is a menace to the world, I would give all I possess to trap him. I thought that I alone stood between him and his monstrous ambitions, until—"

"Until," Van Dean continued, "an inquisitive American blundered even further into the secrets of the S. Group! With the result that the Mandarin K—"

"Is in England?" demanded Westbury excitedly.

Harley stared in silence at him for a moment, then: "Unless I am very much mistaken, was, tonight, *here!"* he corrected.

"What! In the house?"

"Yes, either the Mandarin K. in person or one of his agents."

"But what on earth for?"

"For Van Dean's book," replied Harley. And again he paused, listening.

From somewhere, miles away, perhaps from over the sea, came the dim rolling of thunder. Paul Harley nodded grimly. The storm he had foreseen was approaching; but Van Dean buried his face in his hands and groaned.

"I shall never live to see it published!"

"Pull yourself together, man!" cried Harley sharply. "There, in that safe, lies material which, when it is made public, will wake up the white peoples of the world to a peril of which they have scarcely dreamed. Yet it grows and grows, like the storm over yonder. One day, if we fail, it will burst on the white races like a second deluge. Remember, nothing to the women."

From his pocket, he took out a revolver and tossed it to Jim Westbury. The latter, though obviously startled, succeeded in catching it.

"Loaded!" snapped Harley. "Keep it handy. Directly Captain Latham arrives for dinner, I want to see him alone. I should be obliged, now, if you would grant me the freedom of your study. Van Dean. I want to make a few inquiries."

"Surely, surely," said Van Dean, speaking in a weary voice and standing up. "Here are my keys." He laid them on the table. "Westbury and I will leave you."

Westbury, turning the revolver over in his hand as though it were some rare curiosity, preceded Van Dean from the study. In the doorway, the latter turned.

"I don't think I ever funked a danger I could see, Harley," he said, "but this invisible watching—"

"I understand," replied Harley sympathetically. "But, whatever you do, Van Dean, don't lose your nerve. The climax is yet to come."

V
Scientific Murder

Immediately Paul Harley found himself alone in the study, he proceeded to lock the door. Then, seating himself in the chair that Van Dean habitually occupied, he closed his eyes and endeavored for a moment to concentrate upon this new development in the case.

It was characteristic of Westbury, of whom Joyce Gayford had said that he "had a magnificent drive, but intellectually was negligible," to lock an Airedale terrier in this room of all others. Here, so far as he could judge at the moment, lay the hub of the mystery. Here, in this room, was the explanation of why the S. Group had turned aside temporarily from its gigantic intrigues and had detailed no less formidable a personality than the Mandarin K to do—what? Presumably, to recover from Burton van Dean something of such value to their schemes that no crime was too great to deter them in its recovery.

Sitting thus in reflection, his pipe, long since cold, clenched between his teeth, Paul Harley became suddenly aware of that odd lowering of the temperature which unfailingly advised him of evil activity. He opened his eyes and looked sharply about him. The body of the dog had been removed by his orders, but there was a bloodstain on the carpet not far from his feet, where the animal had lain.

He endeavored to reconstruct the events that had led up to the death of the dog. Someone, by using a duplicate key to the door that opened upon the corridor of the north wing, or by means of the ivy, which formed a natural ladder from the shrubbery beneath to the open window, had entered Van Dean's study that evening.

The intruder, he must conclude, had been unaware of the presence of the dog. The animal, with the instinct of its breed, had attacked instantly. Recognizing detection to be imminent, the unknown visitor had stabbed the dog to the heart and decamped, probably by the same route by which he had come. So far, it was clear enough.

His leaving so valuable a clue as the jeweled knife might be accounted for by panic. It is easier to drive a keen blade into a thorax than to withdraw it. The explanation did not satisfy Harley, but it sufficed for the moment. Clearly, then, a member of the S. Group had been in the Abbey that evening. Came the unanswerable question: For what?

He had been through Van Dean's notes; he had examined in detail every tangible record of his dreadful sojourn on the borders of Tibet. The importance of his discoveries it was impossible to minimize; and, unless the death of the man who held such dangerous knowledge were the object of the organization, to what other end had the S. Group made this house the focus of a dangerous part of its activities?

Again presuming the death of Van Dean to be their object, why had the unknown visitor penetrated to the study that evening, when it must have been evident from an outside survey that Van Dean was not at his table?

Harley found himself baffled. The safe had not been tampered with. Indeed, so far as he could learn, nothing had been disturbed in the room. Yet, that he was near to the heart of the mystery, that queer sixth sense of his insisted urgently. It was all very baffling. He mentally reviewed his recent interview with Mohammed Khan, the Indian butler, and that, less satisfactory, with Wu Chang, Van Dean's Chinese servant.

The American's eccentricities irritated him. For a man who knew himself to have incurred the enmity of a powerful Eastern group to retain in his household a native of Rajputana, and one of Canton, was not in accordance with common sense. But eccentricity must be excused, he reflected, in a man distinguished alike by his intellect and his millions. Harley stood up, knocked out his pipe in an ashtray and reloaded it thoughtfully.

That inner prompting of his higher imagination spoke to him no more, but, intellectually, he was alert. These isolated incidents were rapidly leading up to some crowning event; and for this, he must be prepared.

When he came down from the study to go to his room to change, for he had had little enough time before dinner, he discovered Wu Chang engaged in drawing the curtains before the French windows. He had not yet lighted up, however, and, beyond the terrace, Harley had a glimpse of an angry sky, although, save for that distant rumble, the brewing storm so far had failed to proclaim itself.

As Harley left the library, the Chinaman, his task completed, turned and, tucking his hands into the sleeves of his blouse, stared up at the study door with half-closed eyes. No man could have read anything from the expression of that shriveled, yellow face, nor have improved his knowledge of the psychology of Wu Chang by studying the curious shrug which he presently gave ere shuffling across to the door beneath the balcony and leaving the library.

Almost at the same moment, a car came purring up the drive, and Mohammed Khan, opening the door, admitted a pretty, rather fragile-looking girl, curiously unlike, yet in some way oddly like, her gloomy brother, Jim. She was accompanied by a man so deeply bronzed as to tell of recent exposure to tropical suns. His neatly groomed black hair, short regulation mustache and upright bearing all spoke of the soldier. He carried a suitcase, and as Mohammed Khan opened the door of the library and turned up the lights, he directed, "Take this suitcase to Mr. Westbury."

Mohammed Khan bowed.

"Van Dean *Sahib* presents his compliments and will be with you in a moment," he said.

"Oh, thanks," murmured the visitor and followed his companion into the library.

"Harry, I'm frightened!" said the girl at the moment of the butler's departure. "I'm sorry now we came. There was something strange about that telegram."

"Hush," returned the man, "there's someone coming. Don't let your imagination run away with you, Phil."

"But," she protested, "I have always been frightened in the Abbey. And lately—"

She paused as Mrs. Moody, dressed for dinner, entered with beaming face.

"Phil, darling!' she called from the open doorway. "You look perfectly sweet." She turned to the man. "Don't you think she looks perfectly sweet?"

"Perfectly," he agreed. And he spoke with sincerity.

"So glad to see you again, Captain Latham," Mrs. Moody said, "before your leave expires."

Torrential rain had begun to descend, pattering up from the terrace onto the library windows.

"Brute of a night, isn't it?" said Latham. "We've just dodged it. But I shall miss every spot of that dear old rain when I'm back in Rangoon."

"But I thought you liked Burma," exclaimed Mrs. Moody.

"Well," said Latham, glancing at Phil, "it may not be so bad, at times."

"But, my dear!" cried Mrs. Moody in turning to the girl. "Where is your mother?"

"Well—" Phil Westbury hesitated. "She had a queer telegram." She stopped, as if at a loss for words, and Latham continued, "Yes, Mrs. Moody, the family solicitor is coming down to see her tonight. Urgent affairs, I gathered. Asked us to apologize."

Just then came an interruption. Jim Westbury, in an ill-fitting dressing gown, his face lathered and a shaving brush in his hand, peered in through the doorway.

"Phil! Phil!" he complained to his sister. "You've brought the wrong waistcoat!"

Latham, smiling whimsically, stared at the lathered face in the doorway.

"Jim," he said, "in the name of decency, don't discuss your wardrobe before ladies. You, my host, disappear after lunch from the clubhouse, owing me a return round, and reappear now in a semi-clothed condition. Go away, Jim. I'm offended."

"Oh, is that so!" drawled Jim Westbury gloomily. "Well," he waved his shaving brush, "cheerio, everybody." And he departed.

"I like people to make themselves at home," smiled Mrs. Moody. She turned again to Phil Westbury. "Come, and leave your things in my room, dear. I know you'll excuse us, Captain Latham. The men will be in in a moment."

As if to confirm her words, Harley, dressed for dinner, met them in the doorway.

"Good evening, Miss Westbury," he said. With a bow, he closed the door after the ladies and turned to Latham.

"Ah, Latham," he said. "I wanted to see you."

"Good," was the reply. "Is there any news, then?"

Harley dropped into an armchair facing the speaker.

"Yes. Bad news," he replied. "But first a question. Did you by any chance see the body of the man who met his death in the shrubbery here recently?"

Latham stared hard at the speaker for a while.

"Yes," he presently replied. "When I heard of the tragedy, I thought the man might be the same who called recently at the Warren—Phil was with me at the time—and asked for work. Therefore, I applied to see the body; but it was not that of the same man."

"Ah," said Harley.

"Did anything occur to you at sight of him?" asked Harley.

"It did," replied Latham, staring harder than ever. "You may remember that curious epidemic in Burma early in '22—the series of mysteries which became known as the Listening Death."

"Ah!" Paul Harley jumped up and banged his fist on the table. "So *you* noticed it?"

"Look here," said Latham, looking badly puzzled, "I wonder if we're driving at the same thing?"

"Listen!" Paul Harley's face grew very grim. "Were you stationed in Burma during the affairs you speak of?"

"Yes, Moulmein. The district superintendent put the deaths down to fanaticism, to some dodge of the devotees of Kali, sort of wishing a man to death."

"Quite!" snapped Harley. "They were found with that horrible expression of listening upon their faces?"

"Yes, and no marks of violence. There was nearly a panic. Talk about Kali calling for victims! When I saw that poor beggar's face the other day, I had an awful shock."

"You recognized the Listening Death in peaceful Norfolk?"

Latham smiled unmirthfully. "Of course, it was a delusion," he said.

"It was no delusion!"

"What?"

Paul Harley shook his head grimly.

"The Listening Death," he explained, "is not peculiar to Eastern people. And now I am coming to my point. Do you recall Dr. Ulric Ernst?"

"Yes," Latham answered, closing his eyes and speaking musingly. "The Swiss electrician, inventor of the Ernst Trajector, much discussed but never demonstrated."

"That's the man," snapped Harley; "he died abroad, and—well, the voice of Kali is a far-reaching voice!"

"But, damn it all, Harley!" exclaimed Latham. "The voice of Kali doesn't kill folks in England!"

"It does!" Harley's expression grew more grim than ever. "The man you saw died of the Listening Death!"

"My dear fellow!" Latham's tone was almost incredulous. "What is it? A disease? Hypnotism? Magic?"

"No," snapped Harley. "Scientific murder! Listen!" He stood up and looked from door to door as if expecting eavesdroppers. "That 'tramp' who was found to have died 'from natural causes' by a local jury was really here to protect Burton van Dean."

"What!"

"He was Detective Sergeant Denby of Scotland Yard! Oh, we gagged the press, but Denby was murdered. That is why I am here!"

"Good God!" whispered Latham.

"Another victim was sacrificed this evening, old man," Harley continued. "I'm sorry to have to tell you, but Rex, your Airedale that Westbury brought over, was killed in Van Dean's study."

"Rex!" cried Latham, standing up. "Rex! *Here?*"

From a pocket of his dinner jacket Harley took that jeweled knife.

"I found him with this through his heart," he said. He returned the knife to his pocket once more. "The women don't know the truth, yet," he added. "Remember."

VI
The Light on the Tower

Immediately after dinner, Paul Harley slipped away to his room. An unpleasant tension had characterized the gathering. There were several things that puzzled Harley, particularly the acute nervousness of Phil Westbury. Over and over again, he had caught her exchanging mysterious glances with Latham, and he intercepted silent looks of reassurance from the latter. It might be, of course, that she knew of the menace that overhung the Abbey and its occupants. But this explanation did not entirely satisfy him. He determined to take an early opportunity of questioning Latham respecting the telegram that had detained Mrs. Westbury.

On entering his room, he did not turn up the light. But, groping his way to the window, he raised the blind and looked out. As is the fashion with such midsummer disturbances, the storm that had been threatening all the evening now hovered to the west, blackly. Distant peals of thunder there had been during dinner, and two short but intense showers of rain, but no lightning; and now, although angry banks of clouds were visible in the distance, the sky was cloudless immediately overhead.

He softly opened the window, inhaling the fragrance of moist loam and newly wetted leaves. Away on the right, he had a view of a corner of the terrace; directly before him, the ground dropped steeply to a belt of trees bordering the former moat; beyond, it rose again, and two miles away, upstanding weirdly beyond the distant park, showed a ruined tower, one of the local landmarks and a relic of Norman days. It actually stood on part of the Westbury property, although it was half a mile or more from the Warren.

At first, his survey of the prospect was general and vague; indeed, he had opened the window more to enjoy the coolness of the evening air than for any other reason. He had wanted to reflect; but now, suddenly, his entire interest became focused upon the ruined tower rising ghostly above surrounding trees.

Clearly visible against the stormy backing, a little point of light high up in the tower appeared and disappeared like a winking eye!

Paul Harley clenched his teeth, craning out at and watching

intensely. A code message was being transmitted from the tower! For a while, he watched it, a sense of triumph hot within him, only to realize, to his mortification, that it was in some code unknown to him. Instantly upon recognizing this, he acted.

The geography of the neighborhood, which he had made it his business to memorize, told him that this message could only be intended for someone at the Abbey. Neglectful of the fact that the leaves were drenched with rain, he quickly got astride of the ledge and began to climb down the ivy to the shrubbery beneath. He had used this route before and was moderately familiar with it.

He dropped into the wet bushes without other mishap than the saturating of his evening clothes and, keeping well within the shadow of the building, he began to work his way round in the direction of the terrace. He passed the dining room, glancing up at the rooms above it, and, proceeding, noted that the library was illuminated. Below the terrace, he paused, looking again toward the distant tower.

The top remained just visible above the trees; and there, still coming and going, was the signal light. He stepped out further from the building, cautiously looking upward and to the left.

"Ah!" he muttered and, dropping down upon the sloping lawn, the grass wet from a recent downpour, he crept further northward until he could obtain a clear view of the study window.

The study was in darkness, but the curtains were not drawn. A light, probably that of an electric pocket torch, was coming and going, dot and dash, in Van Dean's study!

Harley came to the end of the terrace and, taking advantage of a bank of rhododendrons, crept yet further away from the house until he could see not merely the reflection, but the actual light being operated in the room.

Faintly as it glowed in the darkness, he could detect the figure of the one who held it. And at first he was loath to credit what he saw, believing that certain words of Inspector Gorleston, which he had considered curious, must be influencing his imagination. But one thing he could not doubt, nor ascribe to his drenched garments, nor to the comparative cool of the evening. This was the premonitory chill, the awakening of his sixth sense. Intently, he watched, crouched behind the bushes until the unintelligible dots and dashes ceased.

The man signaling to that other on the distant tower, for a man he assumed the signaler to be, was wrapped in a sort of *cowl,* his head so enveloped in the huge hood that in the dim reflection of the torch it was quite impossible to detect his features.

"Good God!" muttered Harley. "What does this mean!"

Stooping below the level of the bushes, he turned and regained the shelter of the terrace, and ran for twenty paces. Then, leaping into the shrubbery, he located the thick branch of ivy that was a ladder to his window and began to climb up to his room again, his heart beating very fast and his thoughts racing far ahead of his physical effort. So that, ere he drew himself back over the ledge and regained his bedroom, he was, in spirit, in Van Dean's study, confronting the cowled man.

His room regained, he was about to run out into the corridor when long habits of prudence came to his aid. He paused, turned, lowered the blind and, opening the wardrobe, contemplated the garments there, wondering what explanation he could give for changing from evening dress into tweeds at that time of the evening, for he had no other dress clothes with him. But he fully recognized the folly of giving his unknown enemy a clue to his recent movements.

He finally decided that a change of shoes, the service of a hard clothes brush and a hasty wash would render him sufficiently presentable to pass muster. Two minutes later, he walked into the library. Latham was there with Phil Westbury, but no one else.

"Where is Mr. Van Dean?" asked Harley sharply.

"In the drawing room," replied Latham. "At least, I left him there."

Harley nodded and ran up the stairs to the study. He rapped, and as there was no answer, opened and looked in. The room was in darkness. He quickly depressed the switch and glanced around. The study was empty. He tried the further door, but, as usual, it was locked; then turning, he came down again into the library.

"How long have you been in here, Latham?" he asked.

"About ten minutes, I should say."

"So long as that? Are you sure?"

"Why, I should think for quite ten minutes," answered Phil Westbury, that unaccountable expression of fear coming again into her eyes, "But why do you ask, Mr. Harley?"

"If you have been in here for ten minutes, you can tell me if anyone else has entered or left the room during that time."

"No one," replied Latham blankly. "Not a soul."

Harley stood irresolute, looking about him; then, turning, he went out and crossed to the drawing room, but contented himself with looking in at the open doorway.

Van Dean was there, talking to Joyce Gayford. Mrs. Moody was knitting and Jim Westbury was turning over some music by the piano. Hearing footsteps behind him in the darkened corridor, Harley turned. Mohammed Khan, carrying a tray bearing coffee and liqueurs, passed him and entered the drawing room.

Harley proceeded in the opposite direction, finally opening a door communicating with the covered way. As he did so, the sound of a reed pipe came to his ears. He paused again, but finally went forward. He came to the outbuilding, which was the home of the miniature menagerie, walked around it and looked in through the barred window.

The cheetah was in its cage; the monkeys were huddled close together in theirs, fast asleep. Seated on a mat, in a corner remote from the window through which Harley was peering, was Wu Chang, the Chinaman, with expressionless slanting eyes that stared straight before him. His wrinkled, yellow fingers rising and falling rhythmically, he played upon a Chinese pipe, a plaintive, wailing melody, monotonous and unpleasantly weird.

For a while, Harley watched him. Then, turning, he retraced his steps; and as he came again into the main building and closed the door, the sound of piping became inaudible. In its place, from the direction of the drawing room, came the strains of a very modern foxtrot. He returned along the corridor and met Mohammed Khan coming out of the drawing room.

"Mohammed," he said.

Mohammed Khan paused and inclined his head gracefully.

"Is the outer gate locked?"

"It has been locked for an hour, *sahib.*"

"Good," said Harley shortly. "That is all."

Mohammed Khan bowed and departed

VII

The Shadow of a Cowl

After, in the library, there was a curious development. Harley had been seeking for an opportunity of a chat with Latham, but it had not presented itself. Burton van Dean had brought Phil Westbury in to exhibit some of the strange curios that were housed in this room. But Harley had not failed to notice her reluctance and the manner in which she constantly glanced in Latham's direction.

"Really, Mr. Van Dean," said the girl, "I hate to mention it, but mother will be worried to death. You know, I should love to stay. But, really—" She looked once more at Latham.

"Miss Westbury," interrupted Harley, "I regret to cause you any inconvenience, but I don't want anyone to leave this house tonight."

His words created a momentary silence of stupefaction.

"Hang it all, Harley!" replied Latham, *"our* lives aren't in danger."

At that, Van Dean stood up and laid his hand paternally on Phil Westbury's arm.

"Miss Westbury," he said, "I quite understand and I apologize right from the bottom of my heart. I'm going to say that you don't grasp all the facts. Harley is right. Harley knows."

"I know part, but not all," replied Harley. He pointed to the image of Kali upon its carven pedestal. "One thing I don't know and cannot understand is why you give that thing house room. It's an image, I know, but the symbol of a dreadful danger."

Van Dean shrugged his shoulders.

"It was sent down by one of my agents, Harley," he replied. "It is very old and probably unique, so, for a while, I tried to stifle my feelings about it; but I had arranged for its removal today. There's been some hitch."

During the latter part of the evening, he had recovered something of his self-possession, but now his voice shook nervously. Turning to Phil Westbury, he said, "Really, you mustn't go tonight."

Jim Westbury, whose face wore its most gloomy expression, had listened dully to this conversation.

"I wonder if I dare take a pull at the old pipe?" he inquired. "Anybody mind me smoking a pipe in the library? Van Dean?"

"The ladies are used to it," was the reply.

"Cut it out, Jim, for a minute," Joyce interrupted. "I want you to try that new step with me. Come along, you can smoke in the drawing room, if you like. We've got a lot of new gramophone records you haven't heard."

The two withdrew. And Harley, crossing to Latham, whispered, "I want a word with you. Come up to the study."

Latham exchanged a quick glance with Phil Westbury and then followed Harley up the stairs to the study. Switching on the light, Harley closed the door and faced the other.

"Tell me, Latham," he said quietly, "what's the mystery about the telegram which detained Mrs. Westbury?"

Latham started and then smiled rather unnaturally.

"Well," he replied, "it was rather queer, Harley. It was worded in such a way that the sender obviously intended to detain not only Mrs. Westbury, but Phil and myself at the Warren tonight."

"Hm!" muttered Harley. "By the sender, you mean Mrs. Westbury's solicitor?"

"I doubt it!" was the reply.

"What do you mean by that?"

"I mean that I feel dreadfully guilty to have acted as I have acted. But I think it was a fake! Phil thinks so, too, and she's rapidly getting in a panic about it."

"You mean," suggested Harley, "that this telegram did not come from the solicitor?"

"That's my meaning," replied Latham. "Someone, for an unknown reason, wanted to prevent us coming to the Abbey tonight."

Harley stared at him curiously for a moment. "That being so," he asked, "why did you come?"

"I might as well be frank with you, Harley," Latham replied. "Phil and I are engaged, but Mrs. Westbury doesn't know! Oh, you haven't met her, Harley! She has ambitions for Phil far higher than a poor Indian Army officer. My leave expires on Thursday and, to tell you the truth, we bolted just in order to be alone together for the evening, or, at least, away from Mrs. Westbury. But in the circumstances, for there was something very mysterious about that telegram, Phil is naturally anxious to get back."

"I see," said Harley, and held out his hand. "Let me congratulate you, Latham. You have solved a minor point that was worrying me. But, frankly, although I am sympathetic, no one must leave this house tonight. You are probably correct in your surmise that the telegram was not genuine. This makes it all the more important that you should not venture out of the grounds of the Abbey tonight. I have something to tell you. Not long ago, I saw a signal being flashed from the tower on the hill."

"The tower in the grounds of the Warren?"

"Yes. It was distinct. The night's as black as the Pit; there's a devil of a storm brewing. I couldn't read the message; it wasn't in plain Morse. But I do know that it was intended for someone here in the Abbey

"How do you know?"

"It was answered."

"Answered! By whom?"

Harley lowered his voice.

"By someone in this room!" he replied. "Someone who was in this room at the time that you and Miss Westbury were in the library below!"

"Good God!" muttered Latham, "Are you sure?"

"Certain. I saw him."

"Who was it?"

"I know it sounds like a nightmare," he replied, "but it was someone enveloped in a cowl and hood! Oh! It appears preposterous, but there may be common sense behind it. There is a tradition that the Abbey is haunted by a monk. Anyone meeting such a figure in the passages would maybe not be likely to query his identity. Do you follow me?"

Latham stared hard for a moment.

"Yes," he replied. "I do. It's someone who would be recognized?"

Harley nodded grimly.

"Latham," he said, "for many nights past, someone has come into this room and the library after everyone else was in bed. Yet, never a bell of the alarm rings. There was someone in Van Dean's study earlier tonight."

"You're right there, Harley," Latham agreed. "Dear old Rex! Poor, brave old chap. It was—"

He ceased speaking and stared wildly at Harley. From the library below had come a piercing shriek. There came a second, a third! Latham dashed open the study door and he and Harley raced down into the library.

Phil Westbury was there alone. She was crouching on the floor over by the bookcases, her hands raised to her face, her wide open eyes staring wildly in the direction of the French windows, from which she had evidently retreated to the further limit of the room.

Latham ran across to her and raised her tenderly.

"My dear!" he said. "Whatever is the matter?"

"Oh!" She looked up at him, her eyes wide with fear, her face blanched. "The monk!"

"What do you mean, Miss Westbury?" asked Harley.

"He crossed!" she said as Latham led her to an armchair. "There! Outside the window!"

Harley turned and stared at the French windows. The storm had retreated temporarily and the moonlight shone outside, as was evident through the thin material of the curtain. The shadow of anyone crossing the terrace fairly near to the house would certainly have been visible.

"It was a horrible, crouching figure!" the girl went on, her voice shaking hysterically. "With a great hood drawn over its head! Oh, Harry!" She clutched at Latham. "Take me back again! I am frightened of this house!"

"Miss Westbury," said Harley soothingly, "don't unduly alarm yourself. You have not seen a ghost. I cannot explain at the moment, but I shall do so in good time. Be brave. You have nothing to fear."

From somewhere in the distance came a low rumble of thunder. Faintly, too, the notes of a foxtrot, played by the gramophone in the drawing room, reached them. Harley understood why Phil Westbury's screams had failed to attract the notice of the others.

"Oh," said the girl, who was fighting for composure, "was that thunder again."

"Yes," answered Harley. "They're getting it on the coast now."

Latham was holding the girl's hand and she looked up, smiling bravely.

"You must think me a dreadful coward, Mr. Harley."

"On the contrary, I love your courage," he assured her; "many women would have been prostrated."

"But," she pleaded, "it was not anything supernatural I saw? Please tell me it was not."

"It was not, Miss Westbury," Harley replied. "You may take my word for it."

She stood up, smiling more composedly.

"Then, I think I'll go and talk to Joyce a while," she said.

"Are you sure," asked Latham anxiously, "that you're all right?"

"Quite sure," replied the girl.

"Perhaps you would ask your brother to join us here, Miss Westbury," said Harley, opening the door.

Loudly now, from the gramophone in the drawing room, came the tones of a dance piece.

Jim came into the library.

"Cheerio!" he greeted them. "Want me to do something?"

"Yes," snapped Harley, "shut the door."

Jim scowled gloomily, but returned and closed the door, whereupon the sound of dance music became almost imperceptible.

"Westbury," said Harley.

"Yes?"

"Have you been sitting in that chair?"

He pointed to a deep rest chair upon the rug before the high, old-fashioned fireplace.

"No," Westbury answered.

"You, Latham?"

"No."

"Anybody else tonight, that you can remember?"

"Not that I can remember," returned Latham slowly, staring in a very puzzled fashion at Harley.

"Quite so," murmured the latter.

"Would you mind standing just there, Westbury?" He indicated a spot to the left of the study staircase. "And you, Latham, just there?"

Both men looked surprised, but recognizing that there was method in his madness, obeyed.

"Thanks," he murmured. "Now, from where you are, can you see anything of the image of Kali, Westbury?"

"What part of her image?"

"Any part."

"Not a bit; only the pedestal."

Harley moved farther away from the figure.

"Can you now, Latham?"

"No," was the reply.

Harley moved nearer again.

"Now?"

"Yes. I can see a little corner peeping out."

"Ah," said Harley, a note of satisfaction in his voice. "Might I trouble you to stand on the stair, Westbury, three steps up?"

Jim Westbury, hands deep in pockets, moved up the study stairs. "Is this a guessing story, or something?" he inquired.

But Harley ignored him and said, "Latham, please take my place, here."

Latham did so; and Harley, crossing the rest chair before the fireplace, seated himself in it.

"Can you see me from there, Westbury?" he demanded.

"Not an eyelash."

"You, Latham?"

"I can just see the top of your head."

"Good!" snapped Harley, standing up. He moved the chair about a yard to the right. "Now, suppose we join Van Dean and the ladies."

Latham laughed shortly.

"By all means," he said, "Anything to amuse you, Harley!"

As Westbury opened the door, the music of a one-step swept out to meet them, but as the three men went out and closed the door, there was silence again in the library.

Mohammed Khan entered, removed a coffee cup from the top of a bookcase, emptied several ashtrays and generally tidied the room. He was about to leave the library when the telephone bell rang. Mohammed Khan crossed and took up the instrument.

"Yes," he said, "it is. Will you please wait. I will bring him."

He put the receiver down and went out to the drawing room. A moment later, Van Dean came in and took up the instrument. He listened in growing consternation to the message and was just replacing the receiver when Harley returned.

"Anything wrong, Van Dean?" Harley asked.

"Wrong? Wrong?" echoed Van Dean distractedly. "Harley, your suspicions were all too true!"

"Tell me," said Harley.

"My old friend, Dr. Huang H'Si, of the Chinese Legation, has just phoned me."

"Well?"

Van Dean looked about him suspiciously.

"The Mandarin K is known to be in England!" he whispered.

"Hm," muttered Harley. "That's no news. He's here in Norfolk! What steps are they taking?"

"They have informed the Foreign Office."

"When?"

"Tonight."

"And then?"

"Dr. Huang H'Si," replied Van Dean, "thought it wise to advise me of the fact that—" He hesitated, all the old symptoms of high nervous tension reappearing in his sensitive face.

"Yes?" prompted Harley.

"The Mandarin K disappeared from London yesterday!"

"Quite so!" murmured the other grimly. And his glance was drawn almost magnetically to the big rest chair in front of the fireplace.

"Harley," said Van Dean hoarsely, "I try to keep a grip on my nerves, but I *know* the S. Group!" He rested his hand upon his bent back. *"This"*—and he clutched his breast over his heart—"and *these"*—touching the powerful spectacles which he wore—"are legacies of those fiends! Harley, of all of them—all of them I know by name—I would rather meet anyone than the Mandarin K!"

Paul Harley grasped his arm.

"I understand, man," he answered. "I understand. But we are at least forewarned. It will be our fault if we are taken by surprise. Quick, before we are interrupted: what do you know of the personal appearance of the Mandarin K? Did you ever see him?"

"Once, Harley," was the reply. "But he wore the cowl and robe of a *lama*. It was an effectual disguise."

Paul Harley started.

"Good God!" he muttered. "And you never saw him without the robe and the cowl of a priest of Lamaism?"

"Never. But I know many things about him. He is a linguist who speaks nearly every civilized language."

"I know all this," interrupted Harley. "Have I followed him half-around the world without learning to respect his acquirements? He is an excellent chemist. He nearly succeeded in poisoning me in Tientsin, and again in Hong Kong. He is a master of disguise. He sat beside me unsuspected in the Cairo Turf Club and tried to knife me when I came out!"

"What! He sat beside, you? Then you—"

"He certainly overheard all my conversation, of this I am sure." He paused. Again, the telephone bell had rung. "Who can this be?" he muttered.

"I can't imagine," returned Van Dean. "I'll go." He took up the receiver. "Yes," he said. "Yes, the line was engaged. Good! Hold on. For you, Harley. Innes, your secretary, speaking from Chancery Lane."

Harley took up the instrument,

"Is that you, Innes?" he asked. "Yes, yes! Ah, good! At last! What? Are you sure?"

Throughout the ensuing moments that he stood at the telephone, Burton van Dean watched him in almost agonized suspense, for he was a man come near to the end of his resources, a man who had suffered much, and bravely. Even had he not been so intent upon the telephone conversation, it is doubtful if he would have detected the fact that the door of the study had been slightly opened, as though someone within listened to the speaker at the telephone in the library.

"Good, Innes!" Harley was saying. "Is that all? Yes, I quite understand and I shall act accordingly. I learned another important fact tonight, but I cannot possibly tell it to you over the telephone. Stand by until three o'clock, Innes. I may want you to take certain action. Right. Goodbye."

He hung up the receiver and turned to the anxious man who had been hanging upon his words. The study door was closed again, silently.

"Let us go up to your study, Van Dean," said Harley, resting his hand upon the other's shoulder.

The two passed up the stairs to the study. On the landing, Harley halted for a moment.

"Van Dean," he said, "you and I are standing between what we call civilization and a horror five times blacker than the Great War. It's a very tiny shield, van Dean, just two lives, to protect all the white races!"

"God knows, it is!" muttered Van Dean.

"Brace up, Van Dean," said Harley, gripping him hard. "Tonight, the shield is going to be tested."

He opened the study door and turned up the light. They entered together. The room was empty.

VIII

Hidden Ears and Strange Sounds

A few moments later, Latham came into the library. To all appearances, it was empty, yet at the moment of entrance, he stood stock-still, looking around him and wondering why he could see no one. For some unaccountable reason, he had expected to find another in the room. Now, recognizing its emptiness, he wondered whom he had expected to find there and why he should experience surprise at finding no one.

He was conscious of growing uneasiness. The death of his dog had hit him harder than he had allowed to appear. It had served, too, to bring home to him the reality of the danger that overhung Burton van Dean. He wondered what secret the American possessed which could account for the extraordinary happenings disturbing the Abbey; and he wondered if Harley knew the explanation.

Following his brief pause, he crossed to the table, took a cigarette from a box and lighted it. He went over to the fireplace, seating himself upon the arm of the big rest chair and staring down at the empty hearth. Suddenly, the study door opened and Paul Harley came down, smoking a pipe.

"Hullo, old man!" he called on seeing Latham. "Thinking?"

"Yes," was the reply.

"What about?"

"Old Rex. I loved that hairy ruffian."

Harley clapped him on the shoulder and leaned on the mantel, facing him.

"The fortunes of war, Latham," he said. "I don't think the enemy got off quite scot free."

Latham looked up interestedly, noting the grim expression on the face of the speaker.

"What do you mean?"

"All in good time, Latham. Listen!" Harley looked about him suspiciously. He, too, was vaguely conscious of being watched whenever he found himself apparently alone in the library. "For some reason," he went on, "I have found myself thinking today, more than once, of the late Dr. Ulric Ernst."

"You have mentioned this before," said Laham, "but the connection escapes me. Why Ernst?"

"Because," replied Harley, "I am moderately certain that Ernst was the first victim of the Voice of Kali! Do you recall the circumstances of his death?"

Latham paused a moment before answering. He was listening to a distant rumbling sound; the storm was moving again in the direction of the Abbey.

"Frankly, I'm afraid I don't," he confessed. "I was in India at the time. He died in Cairo, if I remember rightly?"

Harley nodded.

"Yes. His health failed. He settled in Egypt and was on the point of giving to the world a new and deadly weapon of war, more deadly even than the Ernst torpedo. He died suddenly."

"Yes," mused Latham. "Ernst's Trajector; the papers were full of it. We were told it was going to supplant artillery and revolutionize warfare."

Silence fell for a moment.

"He died before giving any demonstration," said Harley.

Latham knocked the ash from his cigarette, slowly nodding his head.

"His secret died with him," he murmured. "Perhaps this is all for the best."

Harley took his pipe from between his teeth and stared down hard at the speaker.

"If he died of a Listening Death," he said, speaking deliberately, "and I am more than half-convinced that he did, then the S. Group murdered him! This being so, *did* his secret die with him?"

"Eh!" cried Latham. "You don't mean—"

"Can you imagine a war in which the enemy is armed with such a weapon?" interrupted Harley.

"The Ernst Trajector?"

"Certainly! If half we heard was true, this deadly thing makes trench warfare obsolete. It can strike through the earth! It can strike *through* the earth! It can strike through armor plating of battleships. It can strike through water and reach the hidden submarine!"

"You mean to suggest—"

Harley lowered his voice and his expression grew even more stern.

"I mean to suggest," he said, an icy note in his voice, his expression more stern, "that the S. Group may today be in possession of the secret of Ernst's Trajector!"

"Then God help us all!" muttered Latham.

"If I fail tonight, God help us all, indeed!"

"Tonight?"

"Tonight!" Harley repeated grimly. "You are Indian Army, old man, and I can tell you nothing about the unrest in the East that you don't know already. India is not to blame. India, as we know it, is loyal to the core. China is our friend. Japan showed her policy in the last war. Coming nearer home, Egypt, the older Egypt of Kitchener, is all for us. Yet there—"

He stopped, looking about him again in that oddly suspicious fashion.

"I know, Harley," Latham said softly.

"Do you? Ordinary European fanatics can be handled, but the horrible fanatics of mystical Asia—"

"The S. Group!" said Latham, almost in a whisper. "With its roots penetrating into all Asia's remotest confines!"

"You know?"

Latham nodded his head.

"Every man whose job of work takes him east of Suez knows."

Paul Harley relighted his pipe.

"The Foreign Office, here, gave me the task of tracing the men behind the movement," he went on. "Perhaps, in the midst of your regimental duties, you don't just realize what this organization means."

"I can hazard a guess!" Latham declared.

Harley touched the match end into the grate.

"It means the probable end of every white civilization!" he snapped. "First, that of our own country. But the turn of the others will come soon—a fight for life which may end one way or the other."

He stopped, staring hard at a framed photograph set in a recess of the over-mantel. He was not studying the photograph, however, but in it he could see reflected a tall lacquer cabinet that stood near the foot of the study stair. Suddenly, he went on again.

"The S. Group, which dares to plan the horrible things it does plan, revolves around one man."

"You know him?" asked Latham with suppressed excitement.

"He is known as the Mandarin K. Forget his nationality; he is an international genius. If I could trap that one man, that great man, I might retire from the service knowing that I had earned at least a few years of peace for this poor old, scarred world."

Again he stared intently at the photograph, unnoticed by Latham.

"You speak of tonight?" said Latham,

Harley, his glance fixed on the reflection of the cabinet by the foot of the stair, replied slowly.

"When I had almost despaired of a bag, a decoy duck took the water. Burton van Dean, America's greatest living Orientalist, blundered right into the headquarters of the S. Group."

"It's a miracle that he escaped with his life!" exclaimed Latham.

"A miracle, indeed," Harley agreed. "But here he is, in Norfolk; and here am I."

"Then the Mandarin K—"

Harley glanced aside from the framed photograph for a moment, staring hard at Latham. "The Mandarin K has followed him!" Suddenly, he raised his voice.

"Tonight," he added, "I am going to perform an experiment."

"What are you going to do?"

"You notice the shape of the chair upon the arm of which you are sitting at the present moment."

Latham glanced down at the deep rest chair in puzzled fashion.

"Yes," he replied. "It seems a very comfortable piece of furniture."

"I'm not thinking of its comfort," snapped Harley. He looked about him with an air of suspicion that seemed almost exaggerated. "But it is going to be my base of operations tonight! Placed as it is now, anyone seated in it will invisible from practically every other point of the library, only excepting the door leading into the conservatory, and the hearth rug, of course, where I am standing now."

"But what leads you to suppose that anything will happen tonight?" asked Latham.

"I am *sure* something will happen tonight!" snapped Harley in reply, his glance again seeking the framed photograph. "Come up to the study with me for a moment and I will explain my plan in greater detail."

There was something unnatural in Harley's method of speech, which Latham had not failed to notice; and, with a very puzzled expression upon his face, he left the library with the investigator. Side by side, they mounted the stairs to the study. When they had entered. Paul Harley closed the door carefully.

"Did you notice the position of that armchair, Latham?" he jerked abruptly. "The one you were sitting on?"

"Not particularly. Why?"

"Do you remember that I moved it earlier in the evening?"

"I remember that distinctly. Though what for, neither Westbury nor I could imagine."

"At any rate, you remember that I moved it. Well, someone has replaced it in its original position. Unless you moved it again. Did you?"

"No," said Latham blankly. "What's the significance?"

"Possibly none," was the reply; "but possibly a very deep one. Did you observe that I moved it once more before we left the library?"

"I am afraid I didn't." confessed Latham, laughing shortly. "I should never make a detective, Harley. One thing, however, I did notice."

"What was that?" asked the other eagerly.

"The way in which you raised your voice during the latter part of our conversation."

Harley nodded.

"I had a definite reason for doing so," he said. "You may have observed a very handsome old lacquer cabinet or cupboard that stands just at the foot of the stairs outside." He had lowered his voice how to a mere whisper. Latham, watching him intently, merely nodded in reply. "Well, someone was hiding in that cabinet, listening to every word I said!"

There followed a short silence. Then:

"Why in heaven's name didn't you trap him?" cried Latham.

Paul Harley raised his hand in protest.

"Softly, softly. If I had done that, what should I have learned? Assuming, for the sake of argument, that the eavesdropper had proved to be Wu Chang—"

"Do you suspect Wu Chang?"

"I have not said so," Harley answered. "I am merely endeavoring to illustrate my point. Assuming that the eavesdropper had been, shall we say, Parker, the gardener, would his presence in the cabinet have constituted definite evidence that he was a member of the S. Group? I can only see, as the result of making such a discovery, the dismissal of the culprit, and nothing gained."

"But, suppose," suggested Latham slowly, "that the eavesdropper had proved to be *not* a servant."

"Not a servant?" echoed Harley. "Mrs. Moody, for instance?"

Latham laughed, but there was very little merriment in his laugh.

"What's worrying me," he declared, "is the fact that there's some cold-blooded Eastern murderer concealed about the place. Remember, Harley, that there are women in the house. By the way, I am still unable to fathom your reasons for allowing the hidden enemy to overhear your plans for this evening."

"Simple enough," was the reply. "I *wanted* him, or her, to overhear them!"

"Good heavens, Harley! I can't understand."

"Listen!" Harley dropped into an armchair facing the other. "I have two tasks; or, rather, my task has two aspects. Let me explain what I mean. Some considerable time ago, Burton van Dean, having leased this house, applied to the local police for protection. I was not in England at the time, and the local authorities failed to recognize the importance of the case. Van Dean, who had installed all sorts of burglar alarms and other devices, stated that, in spite of these, someone had gained access on more than one occasion to the Abbey and had even gone so far as to ransack his private papers. A special constable was put on duty, but apparently this mysterious interference continued in spite of him. Thereupon, Van Dean went over the heads of the police and wrote to Scotland Yard.

"Wessex, of the Special Branch, a very promising officer, jumped to the truth of the matter. He came down and interviewed Van Dean, recognized that he had to deal with the S. Group, and had himself put personally in charge of the case. Sergeant Denby came down immediately and, cleverly working from a neighboring village, seems, poor fellow, to have penetrated fairly deeply into the mystery."

"But!" exclaimed Latham, "what was Wessex doing?"

"Wessex was also on the spot," said Harley with a smile; "but he had to deal with extraordinarily clever people and, at the time of my return to England, he had made comparatively little progress."

"Do you think they knew of his presence?"

"I don't," replied Harley, "but of this, of course, I cannot be sure. He was handicapped to a certain extent, as you will realize when you know the full facts. Accordingly, last Tuesday night—"

"That was the night the man died in the shrubbery!" interjected Latham excitedly.

Harley nodded.

"On that night, Wessex made arrangements for Denby to be admitted to the house."

"Admitted to the house!" echoed Latham. "How could he do

that? Did he obtain Van Dean's consent?"

"Not at all!" Harley assured him. "Van Dean was unaware of the care which was being taken of him. Oh, believe me, Latham, Scotland Yard is not effete, yet Detective Sergeant Denby was admitted to this very room last Tuesday night."

"But he was found in the shrubbery?"

"I know!" snapped Harley. "But he didn't *die* in the shrubbery. He died down there in the library. I am practically certain of it! All this is theory, however, I admit, but I am hoping to put it to the test tonight. The evidence of Wessex from this point onward is of no value, for the reason that, having arranged for Denby to come into the house, he was unable to remain, himself. The next piece of evidence, therefore, comes from Mrs. Moody, whose room is directly above the library. She was awakened by a strange sound."

"What kind of sound?"

"The very point that we have been unable to establish," was the reply. "In brief, Mrs. Moody is quite unable to describe this sound; she can only say that it was utterly unlike any sound that she had ever heard in her life before!"

"I don't follow. What does she mean?"

Harley shrugged his shoulders helplessly.

"I can only suppose," he said, "that she had heard the Voice of Kali!"

"The Voice of Kali? But what is the Voice of Kali? Surely no more than a figure of speech?"

"I don't think so," snapped Harley. "I think that it is a sound, but probably one that is difficult to describe. There is simply not another scrap of evidence to show what happened here on the night that Denby met his death. He was found by Parker in the early morning, lying in the shrubbery below the terrace."

"Yes," muttered Latham, "with that awful expression of listening upon his face. Was there any sign of a struggle, any footprints?"

"There could be no footprints!" cried Harley irritably. "The ground was baked hard by weeks of tropical heat."

"Was there any sign of a struggle?"

"No, nothing was disturbed, either in this room or the library."

"Yet you think his death took place in the library?"

"I am practically certain of it."

"Then how did he get into the shrubbery?"

"His body was dragged out through the French windows and dropped there."

"How can you possibly know that?"

"By a close examination, secretly conducted, on the library carpet, the steps and the terrace, I obtained evidence, slender, certainly, but evidence that went to confirm this theory. You see, the death of Denby brought *me* upon the scene; and the first step was to hush up the identity of the murdered man. Perhaps you will begin to realize the two aspects of the case. First, I have to apprehend the agent of the S. Group, to whom bolts, bars and barbed wire offer no obstacle; secondly, I have to solve the mystery of the Listening Death. It is some mysterious agency employed by these people to remove their enemies. I *must* know what it is!"

Latham shuddered involuntarily.

"Brrr!" he said. "Got the shivers! What does that mean? Someone walking over my grave, isn't it?"

"Yes," replied Harley absently, "or an enemy thinking about you."

"Did you really mean what you said to Phil a while ago," continued Latham, "that the nature of the cowled man was not an image of her imagination?"

"I did," said Harley. "I have learned from Van Dean that the Mandarin K uses the monkish robe and hood of a lama as a means of disguising himself. Probably other members of the group do likewise."

He became silent again, puffing reflectively lively at his pipe, and Latham watched him a while in silence.

"Harley," Latham said suddenly, "I recognize, of course, that, in the circumstances, no one must leave the Abbey tonight; but, naturally, I am anxious for the safety of Phil. We are dealing with people who know everybody's movements. You think, don't you, that the telegram that came to the Warren tonight was a forgery?"

"I do," replied Harley promptly. "They thought the presence of visitors here might interfere with their plans."

"Also," continued Latham, watching him closely, "you have a theory respecting the identity of this agent of the S. Group who gains access to the Abbey in spite of all Van Dean's devices."

"Why do you suggest this?" asked Harley.

"Suggest it!" cried the other. "Because I think it is true. And if you are hesitating to apprehend this awful criminal in our midst because you want to solve the mystery of the Listening Death, I feel called upon to remark that you are exposing women to a quite unnecessary risk!"

Harley stood up and glared down grimly at the speaker.

"Latham!" he snapped, "we have known one another for a long time. I have to deal with events as I find them. I could not foresee the position that would arise tonight. But, as I find it, so I must deal with it. This is not merely a question of apprehending an isolated criminal. If it were, I should not hesitate for a moment. You speak of exposing women to danger? Surely, you realize that if I fail in my campaign against this dreadful agency, it may mean the sacrifice not of two or three, but of millions of women to the rapacity of a great, ruthless, fanatical, colored tide, now stemmed and held back, but only awaiting *something,* something which I can dimly imagine, to be loosed upon the white races. Do you understand?"

Latham stood up and faced the speaker.

"Forgive me. I understand, Harley," he said quietly. "I spoke hastily, perhaps selfishly. You are right, of course. But, as to the nature of your real plan, I haven't the faintest glimmering."

"My plan," replied Harley, "is that which I allowed the eavesdropper in the cabinet to overhear. I am going to get everyone to bed and then return alone to the library, where I shall wait for the Voice of Kali!"

IX
Joyce Comes In

In the drawing room, some attempt had been made to disperse the gloom with music and dancing; but there was a hollowness in the merriment. That uncanny sense of danger that seemed to pervade the atmosphere round and about Burton van Dean had culminated in the mysterious death of the man in the Abbey shrubbery. The horror of it all and the ordeal of an unofficial inquiry had shaken everybody's nerves. Now, tonight, there was the story of the hooded man who had passed across the terrace in the moonlight.

"You know, dear," Mrs. Moody said to Phil Westbury, "much as I like Mr. Van Dean, I really don't think I shall be able to stand it much longer. I am beginning to believe that Jim is right when he says that Mr. Van Dean is haunted. I'm certain I shan't sleep a wink tonight."

"I wish we were back at the Warren," said the girl. "I can't help wondering and wondering about that strange telegram."

"Don't worry about it, dear," urged Mrs. Moody; "it may have come from the solicitor, after all."

"It came from London. But, Harry—that is, Captain Latham—is certain it was part of some plot."

Mrs. Moody laid down her knitting and took the girl's hands in her own.

"Phil, dear," she said coaxingly, "I have been wondering for a long time. Won't you tell me? Is it Captain Latham you care for?"

Phil Westbury blushed rosily; then the blush faded, leaving her very pale. She nodded her head and lowered her eyes in sudden confusion.

"Mother would never hear of it," she whispered. "What are we going to do?"

"Oh, my dear, my dear!" said Mrs. Moody, patting her hand encouragingly. "Why didn't you tell me before? Your mother would have listened to *me*. And is it all settled between you and Captain Latham?"

Again the girl nodded her head.

"Don't worry, dear," continued the old lady in her sweet, sympathetic way. "It will come all right."

"But his leave expires on Thursday," explained Phil almost tearfully. "We were going to tell mother tonight."

"Never mind, dear. Probably it will all turn out for the best."

And such was the influence of her restful personality that, for a while, Phil was soothed. She looked across at Joyce Gayford; but Joyce, ignoring the conversation of Jim, was watching the drawing room door for the return of Harley and Latham.

At that moment, it opened and Latham came in alone. Joyce immediately stood up and crossed to him.

"Captain Latham," she said, "I know you don't want to alarm mother and Phil, but you needn't worry about me. You are Mr. Harley's friend and you probably know the facts. What is the meaning of all this bogey business? Did Phil really see someone cross the terrace a while ago?"

Latham hesitated, glancing around the room and then back to the resolute face of the girl.

"Yes," he finally admitted. "Someone did cross the terrace."

"Dressed like a monk?"

"It sounds ridiculous, I know," replied Latham, "but, yes, I believe he was dressed in that way."

Jim Westbury had started the gramophone again, and Joyce had to raise her voice above the music of a foxtrot.

"I wanted to know," she explained, "because, about a week ago, I thought I saw a cowled man in the library one night."

"What!" exclaimed Latham. "And did you mention it to no one?"

"No," answered the girl composedly. "I thought I was dreaming. The place is supposed to be haunted by a monk, you know. But I have lived here for a good many years and have never seen the apparition."

"You have great courage. Miss Gayford," said Latham.

"No," she replied, "just common sense. But now I realize that I really did see someone. Tell me—" she glanced around to be sure that she was not overheard—"who is it?"

"I don't know," answered Latham. "Keep it from the others, but there's a stranger in the house."

She studied him for a moment with her clear eyes.

"Does Mr. Harley know?" she challenged.

"Yes," said Captain Latham, "I believe he does."

"Then why doesn't he act?"

"I'm afraid I can't tell you. He is a clever man who thoroughly understands his business. We must allow him to know best, I suppose."

He paused as Harley entered with Van Dean. Joyce, giving a quick glance at Latham, accepted a silent invitation from Jim Westbury to dance.

"Hullo," said Latham, "I wondered what had become of you."

"He came and knocked on my bedroom door, Latham," explained Van Dean, "and gave me the fright of my life.'"

"Sorry," said Harley, clapping his hand on Van Dean's shoulder; "but perhaps it was as well. You're growing morbid, man. Try to forget it, if only for an hour."

"What's the trouble?" asked Latham, glancing back toward the ladies.

"Van Dean is preparing a condensed statement," replied Harley, "a statement of certain matters known only to himself; facts he discovered in Tibet."

"But," Latham asked, "the book—"

"I'm a tired man," said Van Dean, "and tonight I feel that my race is run. It may be my book will never be completed. But there are things not yet put on paper which must be made known to our own peoples, even if I die tonight."

"Brace up, man!" snapped Harley brusquely. "You're not going to die tonight."

"Harley," was the reply, "I wish I had your spirit; but what I had, they broke. No, no! What I've begun, I'll finish. Another two or three pages, that's all. And then, anyway, I shall have done my bit. It'll be in my safe, addressed to you."

He turned to go.

"Make it as short as possible," said Harley significantly.

Van Dean nodded and went out.

Latham watched him to the door.

"It sounds a silly question," he said, "but do you think Van Dean is safe alone?"

"No," snapped. Harley, "I don't. That's why I banged on his door a while ago. Hang it all! I'll smoke a pipe with him while he writes."

He turned toward the door when Joyce, breaking away from Jim, ran toward him.

"What! Are you deserting us, too, Mr. Harley!" she cried. "We were just going to ask you to dance."

"Oh!" said Harley, pausing. "Might I suggest, without upsetting the party, that you have the gramophone taken into the library and continue the ball there?"

"But, whatever—" began Joyce. And then, reading urgency in the gray eyes which were watching her, "Oh, of course, yes. I suppose really there is more room in the library."

"Infinitely more suitable, I think,"said Harley. "Mr. Van Dean is finishing a piece of writing, and I am going to ask him to complete it in his study."

With his intuitive grasp of character, Paul Harley had recognized that Joyce Gayford was to be relied upon.

"May I leave these arrangements to you, Miss Gayford?" he concluded.

"Certainly," she said. "I quite agree with you."

He nodded to Latham and went out.

"Come on, Mumsie," cried Joyce, running across the room and ringing the bell. "We're all going into the library. We're going to take the gramophone in there."

"But," protested Mrs. Moody, "if Mr. Van Dean is working, and he always seems to be working, surely the noise will disturb him?"

A rumbling of thunder sounded rather nearer than before.

"At least," said Joyce, "it will be more cheerful than the storm."

"Yes," murmured Mrs. Moody, "I quite agree."

Mohammed Khan came in.

"Oh, Mohammed," said Joyce, "will you take the gramophone into the library?"

Mohammed Khan bowed and, under the supervision of Jim Westbury, conveyed the instrument and a number of selected records from the drawing room into the library. Mrs. Moody gathered up her work basket and followed; but Phil Westbury and Latham lingered behind.

"I suppose the idea of returning tonight, Harry," said the girl, "is perfectly hopeless?"

"Perfectly," he replied, putting his arm around her shoulders. "But don't worry; there's no danger at the Warren. There are queer things going on, Phil, and I'm sorry you are here. But—"

She looked up at him. "I don't mind, as you are here as well."

The gramophone was duly installed in the library to Jim Westbury's satisfaction; and, presently, Latham and Phil joined the party. There were ominous rumbles of thunder now, and the electrical disturbance of the atmosphere manifested itself curiously in the form of general nervousness. No one is wholly immune from the curious influence of a thunderstorm, and it seemed a jest of fate that this party, already wrought upon by a series of uncanny events, should be further tried by a natural phenomenon at no time pleasant.

Mohammed Khan had retired, and Jim, in his capacity of orchestra leader, was about to start the gramophone when Harley came in with Van Dean and crossed in the direction of the study stairs. Joyce looked up.

"Is there anything I can do, Mr. Van Dean?" she asked.

"Thanks, no," replied Van Dean. "I am just making a few notes. Your work, Miss Gayford—" and he forced a smile—"will begin tomorrow."

With which he nodded and went up the stairs to the study. Everyone noticed his extreme nervousness. Paul Harley allowed Van Dean to precede him; then, as he passed Latham, he whispered, "See that this room is *never empty,* until I return. And, by the way, look at the rest chair."

He went upstairs and disappeared into the study. The gramophone, started by Jim, proclaimed a popular melody. But Latham twisted his head sharply and looked in the direction of the fireplace. The big rest chair was once more in its usual position.

X
The Intruder

Jim Westbury and Joyce Gayford began to dance, as if impelled by some higher power. The shadow that overlay the Abbey temporarily was forgotten. For these two were dance fiends. Latham and Phil Westbury did not respond immediately, whereupon Jim bumped genially into Latham.

"Show a leg!" he cried.

He was dancing badly, as his partner had commented in her most acid fashion.

"What's wrong with you, Jim?" asked Latham.

"My shoe's come undone!" he called back.

"You seem to have engine trouble!" murmured Latham.

At that, Jim kicked his shoe off entirely, and, "That's that!" he exclaimed. And, ignoring his partner's frigid stare, he continued to dance.

Phil and Latham, standing up, were about to fall to the lure of the band record when Harley came out from the study, descended the stair and, crossing to the gramophone, raised the needle.

There came sudden silence. In the far distance sounded a rumbling of thunder. Then, short and sharp, the crack of a pistol shot.

"My God!" cried Latham. "What's that?"

Phil clung to him and Mrs. Moody clutched at Joyce, who had halted beside her chair.

"Harry," said Phil, in a hushed voice, "it was in the house!"

The agitated face of Burton van Dean now appeared at the

study door. There was a moment of tense silence, then a sound of hurrying footsteps, and into the library burst Wu Chang, a revolver in his hand!

In a trice, Harley had confronted the Chinaman. There came a rapid interchange of questions and answers in Chinese, unintelligible to everyone in the library except Van Dean.

"Let no one leave the room," said Harley sternly. And, followed by Wu Chang, he ran out.

"Oh, whatever has happened?" moaned Phil. "I'm frightened!"

"Wherever have they gone?" said Joyce, some of her self-possession deserting her.

"I'm going to see!" exclaimed Jim. "It's all very well, but—"

"No, no, don't go, Jim!" Mrs. Moody implored.

"No!" said his sister, clutching his arm. "I'm afraid. Stay here with us."

"But I mean to see," persisted Westbury.

So far had he proceeded when Paul Harley re-entered the library and closed the door behind him.

"I should like to reassure everybody, especially the ladies," he began, but his face was very stern. "You all heard the sound of a shot. It was fired by Wu Chang. I won't insult anyone's intelligence," he continued, "by endeavoring to hide the facts. Someone passed the window of Wu Chang's room. Wu Chang, whom I'm pleased to say I trust absolutely, challenged him; and being aware, as everyone in the house is aware, that there is a stranger amongst us, he, failing to get any reply, fired through the window."

"I didn't know," broke in the hoarse voice of Van Dean, "that Wu Chang had a revolver."

"Possibly not," returned Harley grimly. "But, in the circumstances, I cannot blame him. The point is that he missed his man."

"Someone in the grounds!" cried Jim Westbury. "I vote we arm ourselves and go out and hunt him!"

"On the contrary," replied Harley quietly, "I am in charge here, Westbury. We four men are going to investigate this matter thoroughly, once and for all."

"Oh, Mr. Harley!" Joyce interrupted. "Don't say you want us to go to our rooms, because—"

"Nevertheless," Harley answered, "through no fault of your own, you *are* going to be sent to bed!"

"Oh!" exclaimed Phil, "Stay with me, Joyce! I simply refuse to be left alone tonight!"

She looked despairingly at Latham.

"You will both stay with me, girls!" announced Mrs. Moody with an air of finality.

Latham glanced reassuringly at Phil Westbury and, although she had been about to speak again, she remained silent.

"With you, Mrs. Moody," said Harley, "I know they will be quite safe."

Van Dean, descending the stairs with the step of a weary man, now spoke.

"Miss Westbury," he said, "I haven't words to say how sorry I am for this."

"It's not your fault, Mr. Van Dean," the girl replied. "Please don't worry about it."

"But," cried Joyce, "can't we be of some use? It's awful to be locked up with things happening!"

"It's the passive part, Miss Gayford," Harley agreed, "and the harder, I admit; but you can help best by doing just as I ask."

"Oh, Lord!" exclaimed Jim Westbury. "Well, well. Bye-bye, Joyce! Good nighty, Aunt. Don't worry about mother, Phil. We've both had nights out before. That is, I mean to say—"

"Good night, Jim," interrupted Joyce. "Auntie won't expect you in a storm like this. Cheerio, everybody. If I hear a shindy, may I come down?"

"On no account!" snapped Harley.

As the ladies passed out of the library, Latham crossed and took Phil's hand.

"Good night," he said. "Don't be afraid. Just do as you're told." As the door closed, "Harley!" he said, lowering his voice, "is the Chinaman straight?"

"Yes!" replied Harley. "It's the other we have to count with—the one who was fired at."

"In Heaven's name, how did he get into the grounds of the Abbey?" Latham asked blankly.

"So much for my defenses, so much for my barbed wire and my alarms!" groaned Van Dean.

"It isn't credible, Harley!" declared Latham. "This S. Group is admittedly clever, dangerously clever, but they're only men, after all! Are the alarms set?"

"I tested them quite recently," replied Harley.

"Then only a spirit could have entered these grounds tonight without setting the bells ringing!"

"Yet," retorted Harley dryly, "we have the evidence of Miss Westbury, and now that of Wu Chang, that there is a stranger amongst us. Let's face the facts." He began to fill his pipe. "A member of the most dangerous fanatical organization in the world, the S. Group, is here in Norfolk, here in the grounds of the Abbey—in this house."

"I'd give all I possess," muttered Latham, "to have the women out of the place."

"It's impossible," said Harley. "Also, this man's purpose is undivided. He is here to remove Van Dean, or myself, or both of us! We have the doubtful honor to stand between this present civilization and a great uprising of other races. Some superstitions have a basis of truth. Now, throughout the Far East, the anger of the S. Group is associated with the Indian goddess, Kali. Am I right, Latham?"

"Absolutely," was the reply.

"The natives believe that the Listening Death is directed by the voice of Kali. Is that so, Van Dean?"

"It is," replied Van Dean in a low voice.

"Whatever produces the so-called Listening Death," went on Harley, "it is beyond doubt used by the S. Group. It was used recently here, as we know. Van Dean, I have explained to Latham about Denby."

"You haven't explained to me!" objected Jim Westbury.

"No; but we are counting on you, Westbury," Harley replied.

Burton van Dean dropped down upon a settee.

"I am past cool reflection," he confessed in a voice that shook pathetically. "Maybe that's understood and forgiven."

Paul Harley crossed and clapped him on the shoulder.

"We all understand," he assured him.

"A most dangerous fanatic," Van Dean continued, "a criminal genius—unique, maybe, in the whole world—is right here at my heels. I know it, I feel it. What is your plan, Harley?"

"I'm following inspiration rather than plan," was the reply. "Without attaching too much importance to the presence of an image of Kali in this room, I am convinced that this library is the center, the focus, of the enemy's activities. By the way, Van Dean, you are sure that this figure *did* come from your agent in Rangoon?"

"Harley!" exclaimed Van Dean. "Whatever do you mean? It was accompanied by a letter."

"Handwritten?"

"Typed. But the signature—"

"Hm!" muttered Harley. "I should like a glimpse of it. But tomorrow will do. And now I am going to post my guards. Westbury, you are armed, I know. Your post is in the dining room."

"What!" exclaimed Jim.

"Off you go. No lights, no smoking. If you hear a shot, be in the library under the speed record. Otherwise, wait for the word." Harley grimly pointed to the door.

"Right-o!" said Jim gloomily. "Count on me. But, honestly, I can't cope with it."

"Are all the servants in their rooms, Van Dean?" asked Harley as Jim went out.

"Yes," replied the other in a weak voice. "Mohammed Khan reported to me, you remember."

"And then retired?"

"Yes."

"Well, then, get along to your room—and lock your door!"

Van Dean stood up.

"A poor part," he said, "for *me!*"

"We all have our breaking point, Van Dean. You are perilously near yours. Remember! Don't open your door unless I come for you. Understand?"

Van Dean nodded wearily and walked out of the library. At the door, he turned.

"May the gods be with you tonight, Harley." he said.

XI

In the Library

"What now?" inquired Latham.

"Now," Harley replied, "my great experiment begins; and I have no time to lose in commencing. Therefore, Latham, will you be good enough to seat yourself in the rest chair before the fireplace."

"What?" said Latham, not comprehending.

"Just sit there for a moment and do as I direct. That's all."

"Right," the other agreed, impressed by the urgency of Harley's manner.

He crossed to the chair and sank down into its cushions.

"Now," continued Harley, "look around. You can see the image of Kali quite plainly, can you not?"

"Yes, quite plainly."

Harley grasped the heavy pedestal on which the strange figure rested and, moving it much nearer to the French windows, asked, "See it now?"

"Yes, I can still see it. But surely, Harley," he protested, "you have done all this before?"

"No," was the reply, "not this part."

He moved the figure yet farther.

"Can you see it now?"

"No."'

"What obstructs your view?"

"The lacquer cabinet at the foot of the stairs."

"Good," said Harley. "Operation number one completed. Now we will leave the library for a moment, first turning all the lights out."

"Right!" said Latham, smiling slightly. "This is all frightfully mysterious. But, no doubt you know what you're about."

Accordingly, the two men left the library, extinguishing the lights from the switch inside the door.

"The room which has been placed at your disposal for tonight," Harley inquired when they were in the corridor, "is right at the top of the house, is it not?"

"Yes, above Mrs. Moody's."

"Good. I will see you to your room."

With no further explanation to the puzzled Latham, Harley led the way upstairs and, on the top landing, halted, looking upward at a trap in the ceiling of the top corridor, which clearly gave access to the roof.

"Ah!" he muttered, whilst Latham watched him in silence. "There's probably a ladder somewhere for reaching that trap. I should have located it; it was careless of me."

"What about the cupboard at the end, there?" suggested Latham.

Harley nodded, went along to the cupboard, opened the door, and, sure enough, in addition to a quantity of spare linen, there was a short ladder.

"Excellent, Latham," he said, pulling it out. "We must not make too much noise. Now—" he placed the ladder against the wall under the trap—"the other two rooms on this corridor are at present unoccupied, I believe. Therefore, provided no one comes upstairs, we shall not be interrupted. You will mount guard during my absence.

"If anyone comes up—anyone, mind—it will be your job to invent some story to account for your presence and to induce the inquirer to return, without giving him, or her, an opportunity of seeing this ladder and the open trap. Do you understand?"

"Quite," said Latham, entering into the spirit of the thing. "Count upon me absolutely."

"Good!"

Harley nodded, mounted the ladder, and, without very much difficulty, raised the wooden trap.

"Look out," he said softly as he did so. "I'm afraid I can't avoid a shower bath, but there's no reason why you should not dodge it."

As he had anticipated, a stream of rainwater fell upon the carpet as the trap was raised; but, not heeding this, Harley climbed through and disappeared onto the roof. Latham peered upward, but could see no stars, whereby he concluded that the night was black. Ominous rumblings sounded in the distance; from some quality in the atmosphere it was easy to predict that, sooner or later, at some point not far from the Abbey, the electrical disturbance would culminate in a tremendous storm.

The object of Paul Harley's behavior, Latham was utterly unable to imagine. Neither his moving of the figure of Kali nor his present excursion upon the roof conveyed anything to Latham's mind. He could detect no association of ideas; but, recognizing that he did not know the root of the mystery, he wisely refrained from useless theorizing and, taking up his post at the head of the stairs, he patiently waited for Harley's return.

He had not long to wait. Harley was not gone more than two minutes. When he came back, however, and, lowering himself onto the top of the ladder, succeeded in replacing the trap and climbing down into the corridor, it was evident that the expedition had been successful. There was an almost fierce look in his gray eyes, but a grim smile upon his lips.

"Have you discovered something?" asked Latham.

"Yes."

"What?"

"An utterly mysterious thing," was the reply. "Its exact significance I can't grasp at present, but it confirms my theory. I have discovered another part of the murder machinery that has been installed here—of the machine of which poor Denby was the first victim. Tonight, I hope to unmask it all."

He returned the ladder to the cupboard.

"Now," he said, looking in dismay at the grime upon his hands, "we can proceed."

"Where do you go?" asked Latham blankly.

"Downstairs again."

"Good heavens! Do you really intend to return to the library alone?"

"Of course. Otherwise, my entire plan would fail."

"But, Harley," suggested Latham, laying his hand upon his arm, "let me come with you. You may need me."

Harley turned, looking into the other's face.

"I may need you, Latham, I admit," he replied, "but, unfortunately, I cannot avail myself of your offer, much as I should like to. It is imperative that I should be alone in the library tonight. Otherwise, the murder machine will not be set in motion, all my efforts will have been wasted."

"I don't understand," muttered Latham, "but now I am beginning to realize that some awful peril overhangs this house. It seems to center in the library; and the idea of your submitting yourself to it alone, is not a nice one to contemplate."

"I have my reasons," replied Harley quietly, "but many thanks, all the same. Now, will you be good enough to post yourself at the end of the corridor leading to Mrs. Moody's room, where the ladies are?"

"Is that all my job of work?" asked Latham blankly.

"It is. I count upon you."

They stared hard at one another for a moment in the dimly lighted passage, then Latham shrugged his shoulders.

"Right-o, Harley," he said. "It's your pigeon, I admit. If I hear ructions, I shall be into the library like a shot."

"Good enough," smiled Harley.

And then, going down the stairs, he crossed the lobby below. Latham, listening intently, just detected the opening of the library door. Then absolute silence fell, only broken by the ticking of a grandfather's clock in the hall and occasionally by the remote, ominous rumbling without.

Paul Harley, on entering the library, did not turn up the lights, but, taking an electric torch from his pocket, flashed its ray rapidly about the room. He examined the lacquer cabinet and the recess behind it. All the shadowy corners, he investigated. He opened the conservatory door and peered along the aisle between the palms; he reclosed the door; but did not lock it. Whereupon, he moved softly from point to point in the big room, peering into the wall cases and examining the fastenings of the French windows.

Then, creeping quietly to the door communicating with the lobby; he opened it once more and stood there, listening intently. He could hear no sound other than the ticking of the big clock; seemingly satisfied, he re-closed the door as quietly as he had opened it and stood in the library, endeavoring to become accustomed to the darkness.

He became aware of a sudden inward chill. The sixth sense was speaking to him urgently, telling him what his reason had already told him, that now, in the blackness of that room, he was about to come to close grips with the thing known and dreaded throughout the East as the Voice of Kali, the indescribable sound to which men listened—and died.

It was a situation that few could have handled with confidence; but courage is of many colors, and the training of Paul Harley had been an unusual one.

Almost silently, he crossed the long room from end to end. The big, deep armchair creaked slightly as he seated himself in it. Then the light of the electric torch shone out from the depths of the chair, touching the framed photograph in the recess of the overmantel. A moment it glittered there. To the accompaniment of a faint click, the ray disappeared. Utter darkness fell.

There were some moments of absolute silence. Then, heralded by several isolated drops, a perfect deluge of rain began to fall, bounding from the paved terrace upon the glass of the French windows, creating a sort of regular drumming sound which continued unremittently for a minute or more, then ceased as suddenly as it had begun.

A vivid flash of lightning weirdly illuminated the room. For an instant, every detail of the library was clearly visible, making the ensuing darkness seem greater than ever. Came a crash of thunder that vibrated through the house, which rolled and rolled, then died away in the distant echoes. Perfect silence reigned again, except for a faint and regular sound, so gentle as almost to be inaudible. It was a sound as of a person breathing somewhere in the library.

XII
The Sound

Up on the first landing, Latham waited in a state of indescribable suspense. Seated on the top stair, he watched for he knew not what, listening intently, yet not knowing for what he listened. Somewhere, a chord of memory awakened, and he endeavored to identify it. Presently, he was rewarded.

In spirit, he was carried back to a muddy trench not many miles from Ypres. Fantastic figures, hideously masked, surrounded him. He seemed to see again a little weather vane quivering in the breeze and to be waiting, waiting, waiting for a gas attack from the German lines. This suspense, this waiting for an intangible danger, was similar, he thought. He wondered how Westbury fared in the dining room; and the nature of Harley's dispositions puzzled him more and more.

He could see no point whatever in posting a man in the dining room, although the tactical importance of his own position was evident enough. Then, quite inevitably, his thoughts flew to Phil Westbury. He walked quietly along the corridor to the door of Mrs. Moody's private sitting room.

As he had anticipated, the women were wakeful. Mrs. Moody's soothing voice he detected, and the incisive tones of Joyce. Then, just for a moment, he heard the voice he had come to hear. Words he could not distinguish, nor did he wish to; but he was satisfied and he returned again to the stairhead, thinking that, of all the odd positions into which fate had ever thrust him, this one was the strangest of all.

Then came the rain, so suddenly as to startle him. He heard it beating on the roof above and rattling on the windows around. Vaguely, it irritated him, since such noise would prevent him hearing—what? He smiled at his own mental bewilderment. What did he expect to hear? The Voice of Kali? Yes, he, a cultivated Englishman who took pride in his common sense, found himself under the influence of a wave of Eastern superstition.

For his reason rebelled against this thing that Harley seemed to believe, but which surely belonged to the mysterious darkness of the Orient, out of which it had come.

"What is it?" he had asked. "Magic? Hypnotism?" And Harley

had answered, "Scientific murder!"

Stairs and corridor were wildly illuminated by a vivid flash of lightning. Followed a booming as of big guns over the house and the rattle and echo of thunder rolling about and about the building. He knew that the women would be alarmed and he longed to go to Mrs. Moody's room to reassure then, but he conquered the impulse and remained where he was.

The final reverberation died away. And then, in upon the new silence, intruded a sound. At the moment that he first detected it, for it began very softly, Latham found himself thinking of Mrs. Moody's evidence in regard to the night of Denby's death. It was "unlike any sound she had ever heard in her life."

Now he understood her inability to describe it, for this sound, if sound it could be called, which assailed him out of the silence was undoubtedly the same that she had heard on that occasion. It was the Voice of Kali!

Latham knew from the very first instant of its arising that he had never experienced an identical sensation in his life. This vibration that increased and increased with every passing moment seemed to numb his brain; so that, whilst it was more like a sound than anything else, it produced so singular an effect that, during its continuance, his senses seemed to become merged or confused. He could not say if the thing that held him rooted to the spot where he stood reached him through his sense of touch, taste, sight, smell or hearing. At its height, it was dreadful, almost insupportable.

Then, to awaken him from the stupor that this thing induced, came a dreadful, frenzied shriek—a choking deathly cry that rose in a wild crescendo and died away in a series of guttural moans.

The other horror—the Voice—the *thing*—he knew not how to define it—ceased at the same moment.

"Harley!" he whispered hoarsely, then cried the name aloud. *"Harley!"*

His scalp was tingling electrically. He was not master of himself and knew it. But, forcing his muscles to action, he staggered down the darkened stair and reached the lobby.

At the same moment, the dining room door burst open. There came the click of an electric switch. And there was Jim Westbury, revolver in hand, wild-eyed, running toward the library door. Westbury looked at Latham.

"Latham!" he cried. "You heard it?"

"My God! Of course, I heard it!"

They reached the door almost together, threw it open and leaped into the room.

"The switch!" gasped Westbury. "It's on your side." Then, "Harley! *Harley!"* he cried.

There were sounds of opening doors and hurrying footsteps. A blinding flash of lightning illuminated the room just as Latham found the switch and turned up the library lamps. Deafening thunder burst over the house; but Latham and Westbury, standing close together within the open doorway, looked wildly about the library.

The room was empty!

"The chair!" gasped Latham. "He's in the chair!"

In a frenzy of apprehension, he ran across the room, reached the deep rest chair and peered over the back of it.

It was empty!

"My God!" cried Westbury.

Latham turned in a flash. Westbury was staring at one of the wall cases, the glass door of which was swinging slowly open in response to the movement of a gilded Egyptian sarcophagus lid—one of the curiosities that Van Dean had imported.

Silently, the two men watched; and then, just before the ancient, painted thing, the gilded effigy of the woman whose mummy had lain beneath it, fell out into the room, it was seized from behind and replaced in position. Paul Harley stepped out and closed the door of the wall case.

"Forgive me," he said. "I did not mean to alarm you."

"Harley!" cried Westbury and Latham together.

"Thank God you're safe!" added the latter.

They all three turned as Burton van Dean, wrapped in a dressing gown, staggered into the library.

"Tell me! Tell me—" he began, then saw Harley and pulled up short.

"All right, Van Dean!" said Harley. "I'm safe."

Excited voices sounded from the lobby. The women were down.

"Stop them, somebody!" Harley snapped.

"Jim! Jim! What has happened?" came Joyce's voice.

"Please, go back," said Latham, stepping to the door. "Everyone is safe."

"Ladies," cried Harley, "I shall be glad if you will all return to Mrs. Moody's apartments and lock yourselves in!"

Behind the group huddled at the doorway, other voices could be heard.

"Order all the servants to their rooms," commanded Harley. "Latham! Lock the door."

Latham obeyed, leaving all that frightened party out in the lobby. The thunder sounded again, but this time more distantly.

"What in heaven's name does this mean?" implored Van Dean. "What has happened, Harley? I expected to find you—" and his voice shook—"dead!"

"So did someone else," said Harley shortly. "But brace yourself, Van Dean. There is more to come. If you don't feel capable of facing it, tell me frankly. I shall quite understand."

"I want to know the truth," whispered the American.

"So do I," said Latham. "That noise, that vibrating thing that seemed to pierce my brain! And then the shriek!"

Paul Harley looked sternly from face to face.

"Van Dean," he said, "what do you keep in this cabinet?"

He pointed to the tall lacquered cabinet that stood at the foot of the study stairs.

"Nothing," was the reply. "It is empty."

"Then, why is it kept locked?" demanded Harley.

"Because the door has been damaged at some time," replied Van Dean, "and the only way to keep it shut is to lock it. But, for heaven's sake, why do you ask, Harley?"

"I have a very good reason. Who has got the key of this cabinet?"

"I have."

"Where is it?"

"It's on the bunch with the others."

"Have you your keys with you?"

"No, they are in the table drawer in the study. You know where I keep them."

Harley nodded shortly and, turning away, walked up the study stair and into the study. A few moments later, he returned, carrying a bunch of keys. No one had spoken during his absence, but all three men had stood staring, as if petrified, at the lacquer cabinet at the stair-foot.

Excited voices could plainly be heard in the lobby outside the room, and, recognizing what their state of mind must be, Latham would have given much to have been enabled to speak words of comfort to soothe the mind of one at least among them. But such was the tense expectancy that held him that even that other claim faded beside it. He watched Harley descend the stairs and it seemed to him that he was unduly deliberate. But, finally, keys in hand, he reached the cabinet and faced the three men who were watching him.

"Much remains to be explained," he said. He held out the keys. "Which is the one, Van Dean?"

Van Dean, his fingers tremulous, selected a long, slender key from the bunch and returned them to Harley.

"Prepare yourselves," said the latter. "When I have unlocked this door, one of the minor mysteries will be solved."

He inserted the key in the lock. It operated and he turned it without difficulty. Then, his attitude tense, he slowly opened the door.

XIII
THE PHANTOM CYCLIST

A furtive figure passed the barred window of Wu Chang's quarters. The Chinese pipe was silent now, and the man who stole along the wet grass outside noticed that the light was out. In spite of the darkness, he hesitated for a moment ere darting from the outbuilding into the shadow of the trees. From there, however, three paces brought him to the kitchen garden. Evidently familiar with the path, he now broke into a run until he came to the door in the orchard wall. This he opened with a key, entered, and locked the door behind him. The orchard sloped down to the former moat, but the sky was so heavily overcast by thunderclouds that only one familiar with the ground could possibly have found the way. Presently, however, he came to the nettle-grown gully that marked the site of the former moat. In addition to the natural difficulties, the hollow was thickly set with barbed wire. Pausing at the edge of the gap, the man groped about in the undergrowth for a while and then came upon a stake stuck in the ground, to which was tied a piece of string.

He hauled upon this string, drawing it toward him, and presently, attached to the end of the string, came a rope. He hauled upon this in turn until it became fairly taut; then, tying it firmly about the stake, he swung out across the barbed wire below and worked his way along the rope until his feet rested upon the bank beside the road bounding the grounds of the Abbey.

Releasing his hold on the rope, he crawled through a gap in the hedge; and from the trunk of a tree which grew there, unknotted the rope and allowed it to fall back into the weed-grown moat, where, even in the daylight, it would be unlikely to be detected.

He looked along the dark and narrow lane which came out upon the highroad some twenty yards to the westward. For a while he stood there, watching, listening. But no sound reached his ears, save the *drip, drip, drip* of water from the leaves and the increasing rumble of thunder. He turned to the left, walking quickly away from the highroad and skirting the Abbey grounds. On the right were meadows and, presently, coming to a stile, the man crossed it, turning sharply to the right behind a thick-set hedge and reached a rough shed having a tarred roof and a door fastened with a padlock.

With a key that he carried, he unlocked the door and entered the shed. Closing the door behind him, he struck a match and lighted a candle that rested upon a ledge. There were a number of agricultural implements in the shed and also a motor bicycle; and it was to this that the man turned his attention. He quickly overhauled it, satisfied himself that everything was in order, and then, extinguishing the candle, wheeled the bicycle out of the shed onto the narrow footpath.

He reclasped the padlock and laboriously trundled the machine along the edge of the meadow, passed the stile and carried on for another thirty or forty yards until he came to a gate and, presently, with the bicycle, he was out in the lane. He rested a while, breathing heavily from his labors; then, lighting the headlamp, he succeeded, although not without difficulty, for the road was bad, in starting the bicycle.

Once mounted, he proceeded at a good speed along the lane, swung into a turning on the left, with part of the Abbey grounds now rising above him until the lane, ever bearing westward, finally brought him out upon the highroad. He followed this to within fifty yards of the Abbey lodge, then swung to the right and raced down a tree-arched narrow road at a speed that, on so dark a night, must have meant destruction to one not familiar with every foot of the route.

It was at this moment, as the racing cyclist, after recklessly dropping into the valley, had begun to whirl up the slope beyond, that Inspector Gorleston leaped out from the shadow of the hedge, about ten yards north of the Abbey lodge.

"Jones!" he cried. "Tewksbury!"

From a point south of the gate, a constable appeared, and a second from the gloom of a small coppice nearly facing the lodge.

"Get your machines out!" cried the inspector excitedly; "we've got him tonight! He's heading for the Warren. There is no turning before he gets to Yarmouth Road."

He ran back into the shadow of the hedge, the two constables imitating his movements. Presently, all three were mounted upon bicycles of the "push" type in use by the Force, and, Inspector Gorleston leading, were proceeding down the sloping lane on the track of a racing motorist.

But, considering the nature of the surface and having proper regard for his neck, the pace, as set by the inspector, was not comparable with that of the quarry.

As if the Fates had decided in favor of law and order, there came a temporary break in the storm clouds. Moving patches of light painted the road ahead and, taking advantage of the slope, the three riders increased their pace to such a degree that they were carried well up the acclivity and contrived to stick to their wheels for two hundred yards of the gradient before being compelled to dismount and push their bikes from thence onward to the brow of the hill.

Blackness closed in again and there came fitful flashes of distant lightning to the south. Now the ground was level and they rode along at a fair pace.

In the stillness, which was only broken by the distant rumbling of thunder, all could still faintly hear the pulsing of the motor far ahead of them.

"He's still on the road," said Gorleston. "We've a good chance this time."

His subordinates ventured no comment, but plodded along steadily in his wake.

This phantom cyclist had become a nightmare to the local police; intruding upon the monotony of their ordinary duty, he had so stimulated zeal that neither Jones nor Tewksbury resented this special duty. Indeed, recognizing that they were hot upon the heels of a mystery that had set fire to the local imagination, they had no regret for the comforts that they were foregoing, but, on the contrary, fell for the ardor of the chase. They were three very keen men who pursued the phantom cyclist that night, nor lightly to be discounted.

Meanwhile, the object of the chase, half a mile ahead of his pursuers, had slowed down as sighting some straggling outbuildings. A dog barked angrily in the distant farm to which the buildings belonged, but the phantom cyclist knew that he could afford to ignore this disturbance.

He dismounted and, evidently familiar with the ground, pushed his bicycle along a narrow path by the side of a barn, reached a weedy wilderness beyond and presently came to a disused cattle shed. There, he docked his bicycle and walked back again into the lane, having first extinguished the lamp.

At this time, the three pursuers were walking their bicycles up the slope, rather less than half a mile behind him.

He broke into a trot and carried on steadily past the cornfields until the lane ran through a straggling parkland. Here, he halted. He took a footpath to the right and, having followed this for fifty yards, plunged into undergrowth. Now the ground rose sharply and was studded irregularly with trees, but, beyond, a strangely forbidding object, uprose a ruined Norman tower. He was on the Warren property and a trespasser. But, undeterred by this fact, he pressed on, now moving cautiously, avoiding the breaking of any twigs and studying every step that he took.

More than once, he paused and listened. Lightning flashed fitfully away to the east and the thunder rumbled and re-echoed incessantly. But there was no sound to tell of human activity, either ahead of him or behind. He crept further forward cautiously, step by step, until at last there was no obstruction between him and the gaunt ruin.

He dropped down flat amongst the wet undergrowth, studying the building as well as he could see it in the dim light; by now, the wandering storm had obscured the sky all around.

Strangely forbidding, the ancient building uprose above the

trees. Rain dripped from the leaves and the night was filled with those curious sounds made by the earth inhaling rain.

Inspector Gorleston and his subordinates had come to the farm buildings and had dismounted.

XIV
The Listening Death

There was a hushed silence in the Abbey library as Paul Harley slowly opened the door of the lacquered cabinet. Then, as if impelled by a common impulse, the three who watched him recoiled.

"Merciful Heaven!" cried Van Dean.

But the others, save for a sharp inhalation, were silent.

Rigid in the cabinet, one hand resting upon the right and one upon the left side, was Mohammed Khan!

His face had an indescribably leaden hue. The head was tilted forward and to the left. His eyes were startlingly wide open and his whole expression was that of one who listened alertly to some important message.

Latham, stifling a great revulsion, stepped forward and touched the still figure.

"Dead!" he whispered.

"The Listening Death!" said Harley.

A cloud of horror, like a palpable thing, seemed to sweep out and envelop them all. Even Harley was not entirely untouched by it. He averted his face, closing the door of the cabinet and locking it.

"Latham," he said, "will you get out your car and bring it round to the front door? On your way, you might try to reassure the ladies. I leave it to you how much to tell and how much you withhold."

"Very well." Latham replied, and unlocked the library door and went out.

"Now, Westbury," Harley continued, "will you please telephone to the police. Give them the facts as briefly as possible. It will be close upon an hour before they arrive, giving ample time for me to complete my inquiries."

Jim Westbury appeared to be half-dazed. He listened to Harley with a sort of stupefied expression; then, as if the meaning of the words had suddenly come home to him, he walked out of the room without any comment whatever.

"And you, Van Dean," said Harley, "would be all the better for a stiff peg. I want to be alone here for ten minutes, uninterrupted. So, when you go out, I shall lock the door again. Will you give instructions that I am not to be disturbed? Then, when I have finished my inquiries here, there are a number of questions which I wish to ask you."

"Very well, Harley," was the reply.

But Van Dean glanced rapidly at the cabinet and rapidly away again. A question trembled upon his lips. He stifled it, however, and resting his hand on Paul Harley's shoulder for a moment, walked slowly from the library; his was a pathetic figure, that of a courageous man broken.

A quarter of an hour later, Harley came out into the lobby. Wu Chang, carrying a tray, was about to enter the drawing room.

"Wu Chang!" called Harley. "Tell Captain Latham to come."

The Chinaman nodded and went into the drawing room. A moment later, Latham came out.

"Want me, Harley?"

"Yes," was the reply. "I have something to show you."

They returned to the scene of the mysterious tragedy and once more Harley locked the door. Latham, looking quickly about him, made a discovery. The rest chair, the lacquer cabinet and the emblem of Kali were the three objects to which he particularly addressed his attention. And, on looking at the third, he exclaimed, "What's this?"

The front of the carven pedestal had been removed in some way! It was hollow, but the interior was entirely occupied by intricate-looking electrical devices! He stepped toward it, kneeling down and peering in.

"Come away from it, Latham," said Harley quietly.

Latham turned, startled.

"You're in the danger zone. Move to the other side."

"The danger zone?"

"Exactly!"

Latham backed hastily away from the pedestal.

"No need for me to inspect the correspondence from Van Dean's agent in Rangoon," said Harley dryly. "Either it was forged, or, if it was genuine, this thing was tampered with, either before it left Burma or between the time that it left the docks and reached Norfolk."

"But, Harley, what does it all mean? What is this thing? How does it operate? My God! I'll never forget—" he glanced hastily toward the cabinet—"the face of Mohammed Khan!"

"The Listening Death is not easily forgotten," Harley admitted. "But, as for the way this thing operates—well, it's mechanical genius. Unfortunately for himself, Mohammed Khan failed to realize that by moving this pedestal, I had placed his hiding place inside the danger zone. Incidentally, I was well out of it. I had marked that Egyptian coffin lid some time ago, and had provided myself with the key to the wall case."

"I am still in the dark," declared Latham blankly.

"In some respects, so am I," confessed Harley. "But there is much that I can explain. You see, as the room was originally arranged, a line drawn from the image of Kali across to the fireplace would pass through the rest chair, which habitually stands upon the hearth. I moved the image in such a way that this imaginary line from the pedestal to the fireplace would now pass through the lacquer cabinet."

"Yes," Latham nodded. "But what has the fireplace got to do with it?"

"A point that puzzled me for a long time, Latham. My researches were handicapped, you see, by the fact that I knew a spy of the S. Group to be in the house. But, tonight, I climbed onto the roof, if you recall."

"Yes. What for?"

"To examine the library chimney!" was the reply.

"The library chimney! And what did you find?"

"I found a piece of soft copper wire, with a tiny fitting attached to the end, protruding from the chimney. The other end of the wire I had already detected from here. It comes down to within three feet or so of the fireplace."

"But what is its purpose?"

"Its purpose, Latham, is to fix the direction of something—shall we say a wave—which proceeds from the mechanism in the pedestal of the Kali image."

At that, Latham stared almost affrightedly at the strange figure.

"What is this mechanism?"

"Well—in some respects it resembles a wireless receiving set; but there are certain differences. Do you begin to grasp the truth, Latham?"

Latham shook his head blankly.

"It is Ernst's Trajector!" snapped Harley. "Mohammed Khan was killed by Ernst's Trajector. It is some adaptation of wireless, a kind of wave that evidently has the property of penetrating all obstacles and destroying life instantly. In the case of human victims, it produces that ghastly, contorted expression which has become known as the Listening Death."

"Then," said Latham in a low voice, "the inventor, Ulric Ernst—"

"Was the first victim of his own invention! The S. Group were watching and waiting. How, we shall never know, but they used the Trajector to murder the inventor. Since then, they have employed it to remove their enemies. This thing"—he pointed to the image of Kali—"was introduced into the Abbey by the Mandarin K. Van Dean, all unsuspecting, gave the murder machine house room!"

"That horrible, indescribable sound," muttered Latham. "You heard it, Harley?"

Harley nodded. "I heard it. I believe we shall find that it is a new note—"

"A new note?"

"Yes, a sound which human ears have never before heard. Anyone upon whom it is concentrated, dies. There was no post-mortem in the case of Denby. I managed to prevent it. But, in the case of Mohammed Khan, I think we shall find that death was brought about by cerebral hemorrhage. It may interest you to know, Latham, that there is a length of cable running from the base of the pedestal of Kali to the lacquer cabinet."

"By which you mean . . . ?" said Latham.

"By which I mean that a concealed switch, reached through some hole in the ancient woodwork, controls the Trajector."

"What! It was worked from there?"

"It was. There is much irony in the fact that Mohammed Khan actually pressed the switch that caused his own death. It disconnects automatically when the pressure is removed."

"Van Dean trusted him implicitly!"

Harley nodded. "His credentials were forgeries. He was a spy of the S. Group, patiently watching, biding his time. He has a bad wound on his left arm, by the way."

He stared significantly at Latham as he spoke.

"What's the point?" asked the latter.

"The point is that it was caused by the teeth of your dog! Oh! There's no doubt of it. Mohammed Khan was the man who penetrated into Van Dean's study this evening. Mohammed Khan, in all probability, murdered Detective Sergeant Denby."

"But," cried Latham, "he died outside, in the shrubbery!"

"He didn't, Latham," snapped Harley. "*This* is the death chamber. I moved that chair three times tonight; and three times it was moved back again into focus. Denby was lured into this room, into that chair; and there, in that chair, he died! His body was dragged out into the shrubbery by Mohammed Khan!"

"Mohammed Khan, of course, held duplicate keys?"

"Yes. They are on him now. He had pierced the woodwork so that he could lock the cabinet from the inside. No doubt you understand now why Van Dean's orders for the removal of that murder machine were never carried out?"

"Mohammed Khan intercepted them?"

"Exactly. He wore some sort of cowled garment when engaged upon any work which would have been difficult to explain, had he been detected in it."

"Trusting to be taken for an apparition if anyone met him?"

"That is my idea," agreed Harley.

They were silent for a moment, listening to threatening peals of the storm that seemed to be approaching again.

"The object of it all is what I can't fathom," declared Latham.

"Simple enough," said Harley. "I was the object! I will explain later. There is still much to do."

"I quite agree, Harley. The heart of the mystery appears to me to be not here in the Abbey at all. I mean to say, if this thing is worked by wireless, where is the transmitter?"

Harley stared at him silently for a moment.

"I am not sure," he replied, "but I think I know where the transmitter is. If your car is ready, we will start now."

He paused. There came a loud knocking on the door. Crossing, he threw it open.

Westbury was standing there, practically all the members of the household grouped behind him.

"Good heavens, Harley!" he cried. "What's the meaning of this? Parker, the gardener, has disappeared!"

XV

One Who Passed By

Some ten minutes after the departure of Harley and Latham, the rest of the party, seated in the drawing room and endeavoring to forget the horror which was locked up in the library, were startled by the tones of a distant, deep-toned bell.

"Oh, murder!" cried Jim Westbury. "What's that?"

"It's the bell of the lodge!" said Joyce in a hushed voice. Then, "Why, of course. It is probably the local police and the doctor. Mr. Harley must have relocked the gate."

There was a momentary pause.

"Can you let me have the keys, Van Dean?" said Westbury, standing up. "I'll go down and unlock it."

"Oh, Jim," muttered Mrs. Moody, "you ought not to go alone!"

"We will go together," said Van Dean, rising.

"No, *I'll* go with him," Joyce volunteered.

"Oh, no, you will not, dear!" pronounced Mrs. Moody.

"Really," Joyce declared, "I don't know how you can think of going out of this room!"

There came a knock at the door and Wu Chang came in.

"Wu Chang can go," said Van Dean. "*My* presence is small use," he added pathetically.

"Wu Chang won't!" cried Westbury stoutly. "*I'm* going! All right, Wu Chang," he cried, and went out of the room.

In the lobby, as Westbury unfastened the front door, Bates, the chauffeur, joined him.

"If you're going down to the lodge, sir," he said, "I think I'll come with you, if I may."

Secretly welcoming the man's company, Jim replied, with an effort at nonchalance, "Right-o, Bates. Are you armed?"

"No, sir. Are you?"

"Yes, rather! I've got a revolver in my pocket."

Presently, as the party waited in the drawing room, listening intently and in a high state of tension, a shrill electric bell began to ring, apparently in the library.

"Good heavens!" cried Phil, "what is it?" She clung to Mrs. Moody.

"It's the alarm," said Van Dean. "I re-set it after Harley went. It will go on ringing all night unless I stop it now."

"Oh, good gracious!" said Joyce, who had sprung to her feet. "Of course! How foolish we are. I will stop it, Mr. Van Dean; sit down."

"But, my dear," exclaimed Phil, "you are surely not going into the *library!*"

"It's the shortest way into the study, where the bell is ringing," was the reply. "Therefore, why not? My dear, a dead man can't hurt one. It was when he was alive that we should have been afraid of him!"

She walked quickly and resolutely from the drawing room and was heard crossing the lobby and opening the library door. There was an interval of half a minute and then the bell ceased. Joyce returned, a little pale, but quite composed.

"You're wonderful, Joyce," said Phil. "I couldn't have entered that room if my salvation had depended upon it."

"Neither could I, dear," returned Mrs. Moody.

And now voices could be heard from the drive.

"Good gracious!" exclaimed Joyce, going out into the lobby. "Surely, there is a woman amongst them!"

"A woman!" cried Phil. "How can that be?"

"I don't know, but I'm sure I heard a woman's voice."

Quick footsteps became audible crossing the lobby and Jim Westbury appeared, full of excitement.

"What do you think?" he cried. "Mother's here!"

"What!" said Phil, standing up very suddenly.

"The telegram was a fake! The solicitor never turned up! Mother was in a panic and sent Willis down to the police. So, on their way here, they called; and she insisted on being brought along. So like her!"

Phil had grown very pale until Mrs. Moody, taking her arm affectionately, said, "Leave it all to me, dear. I know exactly what you're thinking. But I understand your mother perfectly; so don't be afraid."

Now, into the lobby came the superintendent from Middle Boro', with a sergeant and the police surgeon, the latter escorting Mrs. Westbury, fur-wrapped and very agitated. She was a handsome woman of much stronger personality than her daughter.

"Oh, my dear!" exclaimed Mrs. Moody. "This has been such a terrible night!"

A deafening peal of thunder crashed and reverberated around the house.

Meanwhile, Harley and Latham were speeding down that sloping lane along which Inspector Gorleston and his subordinates had preceded them not so very long before. Conversation was spasmodic.

"Do you think this nameless mandarin is operating the thing personally?" asked Latham.

"I am inclined to think he is," Harley cried back. "Van Dean had news tonight from a reliable source that the Mandarin K, who was known to be in London, had left yesterday."

"Why was he not arrested, if he was known to be in London?"

"My dear fellow!" Harley laughed unmirthfully. "If you knew how many clever men all over the world have tried to capture the Mandarin K, you would be more sympathetic toward Scotland Yard!"

He spoke with a suppressed excitement that communicated itself to his companion.

"You have hopes of apprehending him tonight?" suggested the latter.

"Yes, but I am not really sanguine. There are so many things I don't understand."

"You say that all this murder plot is directed against you and not against Van Dean?"

"I did say so, yes. Let me explain. They evidently conceived the idea of using Van Dean as a decoy. That was why they let him go when he blundered so far into their secrets in Tibet. That was why he returned alive. Having watched him settle here in Norfolk, they proceeded to manifest themselves in such a way that he could not well fail to apply to the police for protection. Their persecution increased to a point where Scotland Yard necessarily intervened. By the arrival of Wessex on the scene, they knew that the truth was out and that sooner or later I, too, should be on the spot. Their installation of the murder machine was not meant for Van Dean—they could have dealt with him twenty times over—but for me!"

"But what about the death of Denby?" cried Latham.

"Poor Denby had learned too much," was the reply. "At all costs, it became necessary to deal with him. I can only suppose that he had partially solved the mystery of the Ernst Trajector; but only partially, or he would not have met his end in that way. Tonight, Latham, I received a message from Innes, my secretary, in London. The authorities have been at work along certain lines night and day since I left. Their inquiries resulted this evening in the discovery that Mohammed Khan was an impostor, a very clever one. The credentials that he presented to the agency were quite in order. He had actually been a butler in the service of an Indian officer, now retired.

"It needed a lot of tracing out, Latham, but at last the men at work upon the job discovered that, prior to his entering the household of the colonel, he had been, beyond all doubt, associated with a known member of the S. Group! I might have acted at once, but I waited."

"I don't understand why, Harley!" cried Latham.

"I will tell you. I knew that, in some way, the S. Group had learned of these inquiries, and I expected desperate danger to prompt desperate measures. Accordingly, I waited in order to solve the mystery of the Listening Death. Hullo! What's this?"

They had arrived at the farm buildings adjoining the road. Here, leaning against a wall, were three bicycles. They pulled up and jumped out.

"This is extraordinary!" said Latham. "Because, so far as I remember, there is a footpath just beyond here which leads when it is light enough to follow it, to the Warren!"

"Ah," said Harley, examining the bicycles, "does it lead anywhere else?"

"Nowhere in particular. It skirts the mound on which the ruined tower stands."

"I thought so!" cried Harley. "I thought so!"

The night was now black as pitch, save for flickers of lightning on the further slope, where the Abbey stood. There was an incessant rumbling of thunder.

"I place myself in your hands, Latham. The owners of these bicycles have undoubtedly gone along that path. Let us do the same."

"I am at your service," replied Latham shortly. "Have you any idea what this means?"

"Yes, a faint one," muttered Harley. "The local police are here before us, that's what it means!"

"The local police?"

"Yes, and I only hope they have not bungled badly."

"But what can have led them here?"

"I think I know that also, but, as I may be wrong, I won't mention my theory at the moment. Do we turn to the right here?"

"Yes, through the trees. By Jove!"

Latham paused and looked back. There had been a tremendous flash of lightning over by the Abbey, followed by deafening peals of thunder.

"They are getting it over there."

He turned and pressed on, followed by Harley, picking their way in the new darkness amongst the tree trunks.

"The most significant thing that has happened tonight since the death of Mohammed Khan," said Latham, "is the disappearance of Parker. Does that fit into your theory of the affair?"

"It does,'" replied Harley shortly. "Are we near the tower now?"

"Yes. If it were light, we could see it."

"Then don't talk any more. We must proceed cautiously now. Make as little noise as possible."

In silence, they trekked on until Latham paused and grasped Harley's arm.

"I think we are nearly at the foot of the place now," he whispered. "Do you want to go in?"

"No. Hush! Be quite still for a moment."

His sixth sense had become suddenly alert. He experienced so acutely the odd inner depression that he knew, although his reason could give no explanation, that a deadly peril lurked very near to him in the surrounding darkness. Nerves at high tension, he stood, listening.

Suddenly, Latham pressed his arm and, bending close to his ear, whispered, "Someone moving near us!"

Harley grasped his shoulder in reply, but did not speak. There was no sound to tell of that presence which both of them had detected in their different manners. But that that someone, or something, approached them out of the darkness, neither doubted.

"Drop down slightly," said Harley. And down they both went into the undergrowth at the moment that the night was again whitely illuminated by lightning. Right above them loomed the ruined tower, but no living thing could be seen in that momentary illumination.

The storm had settled now over the farther slope, but when the thunder came, it echoed hollowly and weirdly in the shell of the old ruin. Then silence fell once more, an awe-inspiring silence.

A sense of some near presence was experienced by both. Then, from the shell of the building ahead, came a sudden cry of "Hold him!"

"Out of the way!" cried another angry voice.

"Quick! He is going through the window!"

Excited shouts and sounds of stumbling and falling followed.

Latham leaped to his feet.

"What now?" he demanded.

Harley sprang forward.

"Into the tower!" he cried. "But we are too late! We are too late! *He* passed us out there in the darkness!"

XVI
The Tower

In the library of the Abbey, the gruesome police inquiry was being conducted. The body of Mohammed Khan lay upon a settee. The police surgeon, rising from his knees, his examination concluded,shook his head in puzzled fashion.

"There is this wound on the arm, superintendent," he said, "which seems to have been inflicted by the teeth of some animal. No other marks of violence whatever."

"Then what should you say was the cause of death, doctor?"

"Well," the surgeon replied slowly, "it sounds a queer thing to say, but he looks remarkably as if he'd been struck by lightning!"

"Struck by lightning?"

"To be sure, I have only seen one man in my life who had died in that way. Over at Moss's farm, two years ago, you remember?"

The superintendent nodded.

"Well, the body presented much the same appearance," said the doctor.

"Of course, we can't do much," complained the superintendent, "until the Scotland Yard man who has the case in hand appears on the scene. He should be here now."

"What Scotland Yard man?" inquired Jim Westbury, who had remained in the library and undergone a lengthy interrogation.

"Inspector Wessex. Perhaps you didn't know he was here?"

"He's not here!" declared Jim. "He hasn't been here. There have been no Scotland Yard men in the house!"

The superintendent smiled.

"He may not have been in the house," he replied, "but he has been on the case."

"Then, where is he?"

The superintendent continued to smile.

"That's just what I want to know," he said. "We haven't been dealt with quite fairly. We've been kept in the dark all along; and now, without knowing the facts which led up to this man's death, how can we be expected to do anything?"

He turned to his assistant, who was curiously examining the mechanism in the pedestal in the image of Kali, which had been moved into the center of the room. "Any ideas?" he asked him.

"Can't say I have, sir. Looks rather like a receiving set."

"It's not a receiving set," declared Jim Westbury. "It's the thing that caused this man's death!"

The superintendent shrugged his shoulders, looking helplessly at the doctor.

"Do you see any connection, doctor?" he asked.

"Not the slightest," was the reply. "Except—" The medical man's expression suddenly changed. "Well, I don't know!" he added. "There might be, there might be—"

A vivid flash of lightning illuminated the room and the building seemed to shake in sympathy with the reverberations of the thunder that followed.

"The storm seems to be centering right over us," commented the superintendent; "that last flash was very near the house."

"Very near!" mused the doctor, looking vaguely at the electrical mechanism in the pedestal and all about the room, as if he questioned something.

Finally, he stared again at the strangely drawn face of the dead man who lay stretched on the settee. A second blaze of lightning came and cries of alarm were heard in the drawing room.

"That," said the superintendent, "was a still nearer one!"

Amid the deafening crash of thunder, the four men in the library looked at one another. And in all their eyes was a question.

As the last hollow echo died away, "The sound that you heard at the time of this man's death, Mr. Westbury," said the doctor, "could you describe it?"

"I never heard anything like it before," Westbury declared. "It left my scalp all tingling."

"You mean that literally?"

"Quite literally," was the reply. "As though—as though—" He fumbled for words.

"Did you ever have an electric massage?" interjected the doctor abruptly.

"Never!" Jim Westbury replied blankly.

"Oh! So that isn't going to help us. But—" and a strange expression crossed his face—"do you mind, superintendent, if we all leave this room now? At any rate"—he paused significantly—"until the storm has abated."

"I don't mind," replied the superintendent. "I can do nothing further until Inspector Wessex turns up."

"Good!" said the doctor. "Then we will go, if you don't mind!"

Each man experienced an unaccountable sense of relief on passing from the library into the lobby. The last to leave was the superintendent, who closed the door behind him.

"My God!" cried Westbury. "That's got the house!"

A third fork of lightning had leaped down upon the Abbey. There was a strange, quivering sound. The atmosphere seemed to vibrate. Every light went out. A vivid blue radiance prevailed in the lobby for several moments. There came a vicious sparking from the library that they had just left, then a dull explosion; then darkness fell. And, with an ear-splitting roar, the very heavens seemed to open above them!

"Just in time!" said the doctor grimly.

Out of the drawing room burst a panic-stricken party. But the doctor had thrown open the library door.

"Who has a torch?" he cried sharply. "The lights have failed!"

"Here you are!" said Jim Westbury. "My God, what's happened?"

Vaguely, the light of the torch illuminated the big room they had so recently quitted. Pungent fumes filled it.

The image of Kali lay upon the floor, amid the smoking ashes of its pedestal.

Three minutes prior to this, Harley and Latham had groped their way in through the ruined doorway of the ruined tower two miles away from the Abbey. A desperate fight was raging there, somewhere above them.

"Is there a stairway?" cried Harley.

The light of his electric lamp suddenly illuminated the ruinous place in which they stood.

"Yes! Right ahead of you!"

There, sure enough, were the remains of a spiral stair leading to a fragmentary floor above them. Harley went stumbling up, Latham close behind him. Lightning was splitting the blackness on the further slope and thunder was booming wildly away over the Abbey.

Onto a partially ruined landing, they made their way.

"Hands up!" said a loud voice.

Two lanterns moved in the darkness. And, stretched on the floor, still struggling and uttering threats, was a man who wore handcuffs! Immediately in front of Harley, revolver in hand, stood Inspector Gorleston!

"Mr. Harley!" cried the prisoner from the floor, "he's escaped! Explain to this imbecile who I am!"

"Lower your revolver, Inspector Gorleston," said Harley sternly. "You may not know me, but my name is Paul Harley, and this is Captain Latham. We are both guests at the Abbey. Your prisoner is Detective Inspector Wessex of Scotland Yard!"

"I don't believe it!" cried Gorleston.

"Will you look at my notebook!" cried Wessex. "That will tell you everything. By God, you'll pay for this!"

The inspector was shaken.

"But this man is Parker, who has been posing as a gardener at the Abbey!" he protested. "He's been dashing around the countryside on a motor bicycle at night. And—"

"Release him!" snapped Harley. "At once! You should not have interfered. You had definite orders to stand aside."

He stamped his foot angrily upon the ground. "Too late, Latham!" he said bitterly. "We are too late!" He turned to the inspector as Wessex, released, got up.

"Clear this building!" he ordered. "I want everybody out of it."

"But," objected Gorleston—

"Listen!" Inspector Wessex crossed and confronted him. "Mr. Paul Harley's in charge of this case. He's acting for the government. You have done enough mischief for one night. Just obey orders!"

Accordingly, a strange party, they stumbled down the ruined stairs and out of the tower and stepped out on the slope. "Was anyone here when you arrived, Wessex?" asked Harley.

"I am almost certain there was, Mr. Harley," was the reply. "I watched for a long time, and then I crept into the place and up the stair to the point where you found me. There is some way to a higher platform and I was trying to find it when those—" He shrugged his shoulders angrily.

"Gorleston followed you?"

"Evidently," returned Wessex.

"It may not be too late," began Harley.

And then there came a dreadful interruption.

A vivid flash of lightning gleamed on the distant Abbey slope. Everyone was conscious of an uncomfortable, tingling sensation. There came a deafening crash from somewhere high in the ruined tower. A great spurt of blue flame leaped up, far over their heads. There was a rending, tremulous roar. The very ground heaved beneath their feet.

"Run! Run for your lives!" cried Harley.

He turned, and to the accompaniment of booming thunder, they raced headlong down the slope, stumbling sometimes, but always recovering and running away—away from the tower, which, having survived many centuries, now was tottering!

As they all threw themselves exhaustedly down at the base of the little hill, the old tower fell with a shuddering crash, in smoking ruins.

"Good God!" gasped Latham. "But the lightning was two miles away—it could not have struck—"

"It struck the Abbey!" replied Harley, horror in his tone. "It struck the copper wire in the library chimney! And by some reflex action, some law we don't understand, all that electrical force passed from the *receiver* in the pedestal of Kali to the *Ernst transmitter* at the top of this tower!"

"Merciful heaven!" moaned Latham. "I pray there was no one in the library!"

"To which," said Paul Harley grimly, "I add a prayer that the fiend who planned this thing was still in the tower when it fell!"

"We may never know for sure, Mr. Harley," came the awe-stricken tones of Wessex.

"I shall know!" was the answer. *"He* has failed. But if he has escaped, my task is all before me!"

THE HOUSE OF THE GOLDEN JOSS

I

A Strange Disappearance

"Stop when we pass the next lamp and give me a light for my pipe."

"Why?"

"No! Don't look round," warned my companion. "I think someone is following us. And it is always advisable to be on guard in this neighborhood."

We had nearly reached the house in Wade Street, Limehouse, which my friend used as a base for East End operations. The night was dark but clear, and I thought that presently, when dawn came, it would bring a cold, bright morning. There was no moon, and as we passed the lamp and paused, we stood in almost total darkness.

Facing in the direction of the Board School, I struck a match. It revealed my ruffianly-looking companion—in whom his nearest friends must have failed to recognize Mr. Paul Harley of Chancery Lane.

He was glancing furtively back along the street, and when, a moment later, we moved on, I, too, had detected the presence of a figure stumbling towards us.

"Don't stop at the door," whispered Harley, for our follower was only a few yards away.

Accordingly, we passed the house in which Harley had rooms and had proceeded some fifteen paces farther when the man who was following us stumbled in between Harley and myself, clutching an arm of either.

"Mates!" said the man huskily. "Mates, if you know where I can get a drink, take me there!"

Paul Harley laughed shortly. I had determined after one glance at the man that he was merely a drunken fireman, newly recovered from a prolonged debauch.

"Where 'ave yer been, old son?" growled Harley in that wonderful dialect of his which I had so often and so vainly sought to cultivate. "You look as though you'd 'ad one too many already."

"I ain't," declared the fireman, who appeared to be in a semi-dazed condition. "I ain't 'ad one since ten o'clock last night. It's dope wot's got me, not rum."

"Dope!" said Harley sharply. "Been 'avin' a pipe, eh?"

"If you've got a corpse-reviver anywhere," continued the man in that curious, husky voice, "'ave pity on me, mate. I seen a thing tonight wot give me the jim-jams."

"All right, old son," said my friend good-humoredly, "about turn! I've got a drop in the bottle, but me an' my mate sails tomorrow, an' it's the last."

"'Eaven bless yer!" growled the fireman; and we retraced our steps.

As we approached the street lamp and its light shone upon the haggard face of the man walking between us, Harley stopped, and:

"Wot's up with yer eye?" he inquired.

He suddenly tilted the man's head upward and peered closely into one of his eyes.

"Nothin' up with it, is there?" said the other.

"Only a lump o' mud," growled Harley, and, with a very dirty handkerchief, he pretended to remove the imaginary stain.

His examination of the man's eyes had evidently satisfied him that our acquaintance had really been smoking opium.

We paused immediately outside the house for which we had been bound, and, as I had the key, I opened the door and the three of us stepped into a little dark room. Harley closed the door and we stumbled upstairs to a low first-floor apartment facing the street. There was nothing in its appointments, as revealed in the light of an oil lamp burning on the solitary table, to distinguish it from a thousand other such apartments which may be leased for a few shillings a week in the neighborhood. That adjoining might have told a different story, for it more closely resembled an actor's dressing room than a seaman's lodging; but the door was kept scrupulously locked.

"Sit down, old son," said my friend heartily, pushing forward an old armchair. "Fetch out the grog, Jim; there's about enough for three."

I walked to a cupboard as the fireman sank limply down in the chair and took out a bottle and three glasses. When the man, who, as I could now see quite plainly, was suffering from the after-effects of opium, had eagerly gulped the stiff drink which I handed to him, he looked round.

"You've saved my life, mates," he declared. "I've 'ad a 'orrible nightmare, I 'ave—a nightmare. See?"

"Where have you been?" inquired Harley, taking a drink from his own glass and then beginning to reload his pipe; "at Chinese Charlie's or at Number Fourteen?"

"Neither of 'em!" cried the fireman, some evidence of animation appearing in his face. "I been at Kwen Lung's."

"In Pennyfields?"

"That's 'im, the old bloke with the big joss. I allers goes to see Ma Lorenzo when I'm in Port o' London. I've seen 'er for the last time, mates."

He banged a big and dirty hand upon the table.

"Last night, I see murder done, an' only that I know they wouldn't believe me, I'd walk across to Limehouse P'lice Station presently and put the splits on 'em, I would."

"Sure you wasn't dreamin'?" Harley inquired facetiously.

"Dreamin'!" cried the man. "Dreams don't leave no blood be'ind, do they?"

"Blood!" I exclaimed.

"That's what I said—blood! When I woke up this mornin', there was blood all on that grinnin' joss—the blood wot 'ad dripped from 'er shoulders when she fell."

"Eh!" said Harley. "Blood on whose shoulders? Wot the dickens are you talkin' about, old son?"

"'Ere"—the fireman turned in his chair and grasped Harley by the arm—"listen to me, and I'll tell you somethin', I will. I'm goin' in the *Seahawk* in the morning, see? But if you want to know somethin', I'll tell yer. Drunk or sober, I always bars the p'lice, but if you like to tell 'em, I'll put you on somethin' worth tellin'. Sure the bottle's empty, mates?"

I caught Harley's glance and divided the remainder of the whisky evenly between the three glasses.

"Good 'ealth," said the fireman, and disposed of his share at a draught. "That's bucked me up wonderful."

He lay back in his chair, and, from a little tobacco-box, began to fill a short clay pipe.

"Look 'ere, mates, I'm soberin' up, like, after the smoke, an' I can see, I can see plain' as nobody'll ever believe me. Nobody ever does, worse luck, but 'ere goes. Pass the matches."

He lighted his pipe and looked about in a vaguely aggressive way:

"Last night," he resumed, "after I was chucked out of the dock gates, I made up my mind to go and smoke a pipe with old Ma Lorenzo. Round I goes to Pennyfields, and she don't seem glad to see me. There's nobody there; only me. Not like the old days, when you 'ad to book your seat in advance."

He laughed grimly.

"She didn't want to let me in at first, said they was watched, that if a Chink 'ad an old pipe wot 'ad b'longed to 'is grandfather, it was good enough to get 'im fined fifty quid. Anyway, me bein' an old friend, she spread a mat for me and filled me a pipe. I asked after old Kwen Lung, but, of course, 'e was out gamblin', as usual; so, after old Ma Lorenzo 'ad made me comfortable an' gone out, I 'ad the place to myself, and, presently, I dozed off."

He paused and looked about him defiantly.

"I dunno 'ow long I slept," he continued, "but, some time in the night, I kind of 'alf woke up."

At that, he twisted violently in his chair and glared across at Harley:

"You been a pal to me," he said; "but tell me I was dreamin' again and I'll smash yer grimy face!"

He glared for a while, then, addressing his narrative more particularly to me, he resumed:

"It was a scream wot woke me—a woman's scream. I didn't sit up; I couldn't. I never felt like it before. It was the same as bein' buried alive, I should think. I could see an' I could 'ear, but I couldn't move one wretched muscle in my body. Foller me? An' wot did I see, mates, an' wot did I 'ear? I'm goin' to tell yer. I see old Kwen Lung's daughter—"

"I didn't know 'e 'ad one," murmured Harley.

"Then you don't know much!" shouted the fireman. "I knew years ago, but 'e kept 'er stowed away somewhere up above, an' last night was the first time I ever seen 'er. It was 'er shriek wot 'ad reached me, reached me through the smoke. I don't take much stock in Chink gals in general, but this one's mother was no Chink, I'll swear. She was just as pretty as a bloomin' ivory doll, an' as little an' as white . . . an' that old swine, Kwen Lung, 'ad tore the dress off of 'er shoulders with a great whip!"

Harley was leaning forward now, intent upon the man's story, and, although I could not get rid of the idea that our friend was relating the events of a particularly unpleasant opium dream, nevertheless, I was fascinated by the strange story and by the stranger manner of its telling.

"I saw the blood drip from 'er bare shoulders, mates," the man continued huskily, and with his big, dirty hands, he strove to illustrate his words. "An' that old yellow fien' lashed an' lashed until the poor gal was past screamin'. She just sunk down on the floor all of a 'eap, moanin' an' moanin'. Lawks! I can 'ear 'er moanin' now!

"Meanwhile, 'ere's me, with murder in me 'eart, lyin' there watchin', an' I can't speak, no! I can't even curse the yellow rat, an' I can't move—not a 'and, not a boot! Just as she fell there, right up against the joss, an' 'er blood trickled down on 'is gilded feet, old Ma Lorenzo comes staggerin' in. I remember all this as clear as print, mates, remember it plain, but wot 'appened next ain't so good an' clear. Somethin' seemed to bust in me 'ead. Only, just before I went off, the winder—there's only one in the room—was smashed to smithereens, an' somebody came in through it."

"Are you sure?" said Harley eagerly. "Are you sure?"

That he was intensely absorbed in the story, he revealed by a piece of bad artistry, very rare in him. He temporarily forgot his dialect. Our marine friend, however, was too much taken up with his own story to notice this slip, and:

"Dead sure!" he shouted.

He suddenly twisted round in his chair.

"Tell me I was dreamin', mate," he invited, "and if *you* ain't dreamin', in 'arf a tick, it won't be because I 'aven't put yer to sleep!"

"I ain't arguin', old son," said Harley soothingly. "Get on with the yarn."

"Ho!" said the fireman, mollified, "so long as you ain't. Well, then, it's all blotted out after that. Somebody come in at the winder, but 'oo it was or wot it was, I can't tell yer, not for fifty quid. When I woke up, which is about 'arf an hour before you see me, I'm all alone—see? There's no sign of Kwen Lung, nor the gal, nor old Ma Lorenzo, nor nobody. I sez to myself wot you keep on sayin'. I sez, 'You're dreamin', Bill.'"

"But I don't think you was," declared Harley. "Straight, I don't."

"I know I wasn't!" roared the fireman, and banged the table lustily. "I see 'er blood on the joss an' on the floor where she lay."

"This morning?" I interjected.

"This mornin', in the light of the little oil lamp where old Ma Lorenzo 'ad roasted the pills! It's all still an' quiet, an' I feel more dead than alive. I'm goin' to give 'er a hail, see? When I sez to myself, 'Bill,' I sez, 'put out to sea; you're amongst Kaffirs, Bill.' It occurred to me as old Kwen Lung might wonder 'ow much I knew. So I beat it. But, when I got in the open air, I felt I'd never make my lodgin's without a tonic. That's 'ow I come to meet you, mates.

"Listen. I'm away in the old *Seahawk* in the mornin', but I'll tell you somethin'. That yellow devil killed his daughter last night! Beat 'er to death. I see it plain. The sweetest, prettiest bit of ivory as Gawd ever put breath into. If 'er body ain't in the river, it's in the 'ouse. Drunk or sober, I never could stand the splits, but, mates"—he stood up, and, grasping me by the arm, he drew me across the room, where he also seized Harley in his muscular grip—"mates," he went on earnestly, "she was the sweetest, prettiest little gal as a man ever clapped eyes on. One of yer, walk into Limehouse Station an' put the coppers wise. I'd sleep easier at sea if I knew old Kwen Lung 'ad gone west on a rope's end."

II
An Opium Den

For fully ten minutes after the fireman had departed, Paul Harley sat staring abstractedly in front of him, his cold pipe between his teeth; and, knowing his mood, I intruded no word upon this reverie, until:

"Come on, Knox," he said, standing up suddenly. "I think this matter calls for speedy action."

"What! Do you think the man's story was true?"

"I think nothing, I am going to look at Kwen Lung's joss."

Without another word, he led the way downstairs and out into the deserted street. The first gray half-tones of dawn were creeping into the sky, so that the outlines of Limehouse loomed like dim silhouettes about us. There was abundant evidence in the form of noises strange and discordant that many workers were busy on dock and riverside, but the streets through which our course lay were almost empty. Sometimes, a furtive shadow would move out of some black gully and fade into a dimly-seen doorway in a manner peculiarly unpleasant and Asiatic. But we met no palpable pedestrian throughout the journey.

Before the door of a house in Pennyfields, which closely resembled that which we had left in Wade Street in that it was flatly uninteresting, dirty and commonplace, we paused. There was no sign of life about the place and no lights showed at any of the windows, which appeared as dim cavities—eyeless sockets in the gray face of the building as dawn proclaimed the birth of a new day.

Harley seized the knocker and knocked sharply. There was no response, and he repeated the summons, but, again, without effect. Thereupon, with a muttered exclamation, he grasped the knocker a third time and executed a veritable tattoo upon the door. When this had proceeded for about half a minute or more:

"All right, all right!" came a shaky voice from within. "I'm coming."

Harley released the knocker, and, turning to me:

"Ma Lorenzo," he whispered. "Don't make any mistakes."

Indeed, even as he warned me, heralded by a creaking of bolts and the rattling of a chain, the door was opened by a fat, shapeless, half-caste woman of indefinable age, in whose dark eyes now sunken in bloated cheeks, in whose full, though drooping lips, and even in the whole overlaid contour of face and figure, it was possible to recognize the traces of former beauty. This was Ma Lorenzo, who for many years had lived at that address with old Kwen Lung, of whom strange stories were told in Chinatown.

As Bill Jones, A.B., my friend, Paul Harley, was well known to Ma Lorenzo, as he was well known to many others in that strange colony which clusters round the London Docks. I sometimes enjoyed the privilege of accompanying my friend on some tour of investigation through the weird resorts which abound in that neighborhood, and indeed, we had been returning from one of these Baghdad nights when our present adventure had been thrust upon us.

Assuming a wild and boisterous manner, which he had at command:

"'Urry up, Ma!" said Harley, entering without ceremony. "I want to introduce my pal, Jim, 'ere, to old Kwen Lung and make it all right for him before I sail."

Ma Lorenzo, who was half Portuguese, replied in her peculiar accent: "This is no time to come waking me up out of bed!"

But Harley, brushing past her, was already inside the stuffy little room, and I hastened to follow.

"Kwen Lung!" shouted my friend loudly. "Where are you? Brought a friend to see you."

"Kwen Lung no hab," came the complaining tones of Ma Lorenzo from behind us.

It was curious to note how long association with the Chinese had resulted in her catching the infection of that pidgin English, which is a sort of esperanto in all Asiatic quarters.

"Eh!" cried my friend, pushing open a door on the right of the passage and stumbling down three worn steps into a very evil-smelling room. "Where is he?"

"Go play *pak-a-pu*. Not come back."

Ma Lorenzo, having relocked the street door, had rejoined us, and as I followed my friend down into the dim and uninviting apartment, she stood at the top of the steps, hands on hips, regarding us.

In her pose there lurked the memory of a once-slender figure, and, looking at her and then round the foul room in which sickly opium fumes still lingered, I thought of this woman's life and wondered. The insidious yellow lure is something that few white men understand, but of which such women as this—and every Chinatown holds many—could tell strange and tragic stories.

The place, which was quite palpably an opium den, must have disappointed anyone familiar with the more ornate houses of Chinese vice in San Francisco and elsewhere. The bare floor was not particularly clean, and the few decorations that the room boasted were garishly European for the most part. A deep divan, evidently used sometimes as a bed, occupied one side of the room, and just to the left of the steps reposed the only typically Oriental object in the place.

It was a strange thing to see in so sordid a setting—a great, gilded joss, more than life-size, squatting, hideous, upon a massive pedestal; a figure fit for some native temple, but strangely out of place in that dirty little Limehouse abode.

I had never before visited Kwen Lung, but the fame of his golden joss had reached me, and I knew that he had received many offers for it, all of which he had rejected. It was whispered that Kwen Lung was rich, that he was a great man among the Chinese, and even that some kind of religious ceremony periodically took place in his house. Now, as I stood staring at the famous idol, I saw something that made me stare harder than ever.

The place was lighted by a hanging lamp from which depended bits of colored paper and several gilded silk tassels; but, dim as the light was, it could not conceal those tell-tale stains.

There was blood on the feet of the golden idol!

All this I detected at a glance, but, ere I had time to speak:

"You can't tell me that tale, Ma!" cried Harley. "I believe 'e was smokin' in 'ere when we knocked."

The woman shrugged her fat shoulders.

"No hab," she repeated. "You two johnnies clear out. Let me sleep."

But, as I turned to her, beneath the nonchalant manner I could detect a great uneasiness; and in her dark eyes there was fear. That Harley also had seen the bloodstains, I was well aware, and I did not doubt that, furthermore, he had noted the fact that the only mat which the room boasted had been placed before the joss, doubtless to hide other stains upon the boards.

As we stood so, I presently became aware of a current of air passing across the room in the direction of the open door. It came from a window before which a tawdry red curtain had been draped. Either the window behind the curtain was wide open, which is alien to Chinese habits, or it was shattered. Whilst I was wondering if Harley intended to investigate further:

"Come on, Jim!" he cried boisterously, and clapped me on the shoulder; "the old fox don't want to be disturbed."

He turned to the woman:

"Tell him when he wakes up, Ma," he said, "that if ever my pal, Jim, wants a pipe, he's to 'ave one. Savvy? Jim's square."

"Savvy," replied the woman, and she was wholly unable to conceal her relief. "You clear out now, and I tell Kwen Lung when he come in."

"Right-o, Ma!" said Harley. "Say, I'll be 'ome again in a month."

Grasping me by the arm, he lurched up the steps and the two of us presently found ourselves out in the street again. In the growing light, the squalor of the district was more evident than ever, but the comparative freshness of the air was welcome after the reek of that room in which the golden idol sat leering, with blood at his feet.

"You saw, Harley?" I exclaimed excitedly. "You saw the stains, and I'm certain the window was broken!"

Harley nodded shortly.

"Back to Wade Street!" he said. "I allow myself fifteen minutes to shed Bill Jones, able seaman, and to become Paul Harley of Chancery Lane."

"What steps shall you take?" I asked.

"First step, search Kwen Lung's house from cellar to roof. Second step: entirely dependent upon result of first. The Chinese are subtle, Knox. If Kwen Lung has killed his daughter, it may require all the resources of Scotland Yard to prove it."

"But—"

"There is no 'but' about it. Chinatown is the one district of London which possesses the property of swallowing people up."

III
Captain Dan

Half an hour later, as I sat in the inner room before the great dressing table, laboriously removing my disguise—for I was utterly incapable of metamorphosing myself, like Harley, in fifteen minutes—I heard a rapping at the outer door. I glanced nervously at my face in the mirror.

Comparatively little of "Jim" had yet been removed, for, since time was precious to my friend, I had acted as his dresser before setting to work to remove my own makeup. There were two entrances to the establishment, by one of which Paul Harley invariably entered and invariably went out, and from the other by which "Bill Jones" was sometimes seen to emerge, but never Paul Harley. That my friend had made good his retirement, I knew, but, nevertheless, if I had to open the door of the outer room, it must be as "Jim."

Thinking it impolitic not to do so, since the one who knocked might be aware that he had come in but not gone out again, I hastily readjusted that side of my mustache that I had partially removed, replaced my cap and muffler, and, carefully locking the door of the dressing room, crossed the outer apartment and opened the door.

It was Harley's custom never to enter or leave these rooms

except under the mantle of friendly night, but, at so early an hour, I confess I had not expected a visitor. Wondering whom I should find there, I opened the door.

Standing on the landing was a fellow-lodger who permanently occupied the two top rooms of the house. Paul Harley had taken the trouble to investigate the man's past, for Captain Dan, the name by which he was known in the saloons and worse resorts which he frequented, was palpably a broken-down gentleman; a piece of flotsam caught in the yellow stream. Opium had been his downfall. How he lived, I never knew, but Harley believed he had some small but settled income, sufficient to enable him to kill himself in comfort with the black pills.

As he stood there before me in the early morning light, I was aware of some subtle change in his appearance. It was fully six months since I had seen him last, but, in some vague way, he looked younger. Haggard he was, with an ugly cut showing on his temple, but not so lined as I remembered him. Some former man seemed to be struggling through the opium-scarred surface. His eyes were brighter, and I noted with surprise that he wore decent clothes and was cleanly shaved.

"Good morning, Jim," he said. "You remember me, don't you?"

As he spoke, I observed, too, that his manner had altered. He who had consorted with the sweepings of the doss houses now addressed me as a courteous gentleman addresses an inferior—not haughtily or patronizingly, but with a note of conspicuous superiority and self-respect wholly unfamiliar. Almost, it threw me off my guard, but remembering in the nick of time that I was still "Jim":

"Of course, I remember you, Cap'n," I said. "Step inside."

"Thanks," he replied, and followed me into the little room.

I placed for him the armchair which our friend the fireman had so recently occupied, but:

"I won't sit down," he said.

And now I observed that he was evidently in a condition of repressed excitement. Perhaps he saw the curiosity in my glance, for he suddenly rested both his hands on my shoulders, and:

"Yes, I have given up the dope, Jim," he said; "done with it forever. There's not a soul in this neighborhood I can trust; yet, if ever a man wanted a pal, I want one today. Now, you're square, my lad. I always knew that, in spite of the dope; and if I ask you to do a little thing that means a lot to me, I think you will do it. Am I right?"

"If it can be done, I'll do it," said I.

"Then listen. I'm leaving England in the *Patna* for Singapore. She sails at noon tomorrow and passengers go on board at ten o'clock. I've got my ticket, papers in order, but—" he paused impressively, grasping my shoulder hard—"I must get on board *tonight.*"

I stared him in the face.

"Why?" I asked.

He returned my look with one searching and eager; then:

"If I show you the reason," said he, "and trust you with all my papers, will you go down to the dock—it's no great distance—and ask to see Marryat, the chief officer? Perhaps you've sailed with him?"

"No," I replied guardedly. "I was never on the *Patna.*"

"Never mind. When you give him a letter, which I shall write, he will make the necessary arrangements for me to occupy my stateroom tonight. I knew him well," he explained, "in—the old days. Will you do it, Jim?"

"I'll do it with pleasure," I answered.

"Shake!" said Captain Dan.

We shook hands heartily.

"Now, I'll show you the reason," he added. "Come upstairs."

Turning, he led the way upstairs to his own room, and, wondering greatly, I followed him in. Never having been in Captain Dan's apartments, I cannot say if they, like their occupant, had changed for the better. But I found myself in a room surprisingly clean and with a note of culture in its appointments that was even more surprising.

On a couch by the window, wrapped in a fur rug, lay the prettiest half-caste girl I had ever seen, east or west. Her skin was like cream rose petals and her abundant hair was of wonderful, lustrous black. Perhaps it was her smooth, warm color that suggested the idea, but, as her cheeks flushed at sight of Captain Dan and the long, dark eyes lighted up in welcome, I thought of a delicate painting on ivory, and I wondered more and more what it could all mean.

"I have brought Jim to see you," said Captain Dan. "No, don't trouble to move, dear."

But, even before he had spoken, I had seen the girl wince with pain as she had endeavored to sit up to greet us. She lay on her side in a rather constrained attitude, but, although her sudden movement had brought tears to her eyes, she smiled bravely and extended a tiny ivory hand to me.

"This is my wife, Jim!" said Captain Dan.

I could find no words at all, but merely stood there, looking very awkward and feeling almost awed by the indescribable expression of trust in the eyes of the little Eurasian, as, with her tiny fingers hidden in her husband's clasp, she lay looking up at him.

"Now you know, Jim," said he, "why we must get aboard the *Patna* tonight. My wife is really too ill to travel; in fact, I shall have to carry her down to the cab, and such a proceeding in daylight would attract an enormous crowd in this neighborhood!"

"Give me the letters and the papers," I answered. "I will start now."

His wife disengaged her hand and extended it to me.

"Thank you," she said in a queer little silver-bell voice. "You are good. I shall always love you."

IV
The Gilded Idol

It must have been about eleven o'clock that night when Paul Harley rang me up. Since we had parted in the early morning, I had had no word from him, and I was all anxiety to tell him of the quaint little romance which, unknown to us, had found a setting in the room above.

In accordance with my promise, I had seen the chief officer of the *Patna;* and, from the start of surprise which he gave on opening Captain Dan's letter, I judged that Mr. Marryat and the man who for so long had sunk to the lowest rung of the ladder had been close friends in those "old days." At any rate, he had proceeded to make the necessary arrangements without a moment's delay, and the couple were to go on board the *Patna* at nine o'clock.

It was with a sense of having done at least one good deed that I finally quitted our Limehouse base and returned to my rooms. Now, at eleven o'clock at night, came a message.

"Can you come round to Chancery Lane at once?" said Harley. "I want you to run down to Pennyfields with me."

"Some development in the Kwen Lung business?"

"Hardly a development, but I'm not satisfied, Knox. I hate to be beaten."

Twenty minutes later, I was sitting in Harley's study, watching him restlessly promenading up and down before the fire.

"The police searched Kwen Lung's place from foundation to tiles," he said. "I was there, myself. Old Kwen Lung conveniently kept out of the way—still playing *pak-a-pu,* no doubt. But Ma Lorenzo was in evidence. She blandly declared that Kwen Lung never had a daughter! And, in the absence of our friend, the fireman, who sailed in the *Seahawk*—and whose evidence, by the way, is legally valueless—what could we do? They could find nobody in the neighborhood prepared to state that Kwen Lung had a daughter or that Kwen Lung had no daughter. There are all sorts of fables about the old fox, but the facts about him are harder to get at."

"But," I exclaimed, "the bloodstains on the joss!"

"Ma Lorenzo stumbled and fell there on the previous night, striking her skull against the foot of the figure."

"What nonsense!" I cried. "We should have seen the wound last night."

"We might have done," said Harley musingly. "I don't know when she inflicted it on herself, but I *did* see it this morning."

"What!"

"Oh, the gash is there all right, partly covered by her hair."

He stood still, staring at me oddly.

"One meets with cases of singular devotion in unexpected quarters sometimes," he said.

"You mean that the woman inflicted the wound upon herself in order—"

"To save old Kwen Lung—exactly! It's marvelous."

"Good heavens!" I exclaimed. "And the window?"

"Oh, it was broken right enough—by two drunken sailors fighting in the court outside. Sash and everything, smashed to splinters."

He began irritably to pace the carpet again:

"It must have been a devil of a fight!" he added savagely.

"Meanwhile," said I, "where is old Kwen Lung hiding?"

"But more particularly," cried Harley, "where has he hidden the poor victim? Come along, Knox! I'm going down there for a final look round."

"Of course, the premises are being watched?"

"Of course—and also, of course, I shall be the laughing stock of Scotland Yard if nothing results."

It was close on midnight when, once more, I found myself in Pennyfields. Carried away by Harley's irritable excitement, I had quite forgotten the romance of Captain Dan; and when, having exchanged greetings with the detective upon duty hard by the house of Kwen Lung, we presently found ourselves in the presence of Ma Lorenzo, I scarcely knew for a moment if I were "Jim" or my proper self.

"Is Kwen Lung in?" asked Harley sternly.

The woman shook her head.

"No," she replied. "He sometimes stop away a whole week."

"Does he?" jerked Harley. "Come in, Knox; we'll take another look round."

A moment later, I found myself again in the room of the golden joss. The red curtain had been removed from before the shattered window, but, otherwise, the place looked exactly as it had looked before. The atmosphere was much less stale, however, but there was something repellent about that great, gilded idol smiling eternally from his pedestal beside the door.

I stared into the leering face, and it was the face of one who knew and who might have said, “Yes! This and other things equally strange have I beheld in many lands, as well as England! Much I could tell. Many things grim and terrible, and some few joyous; for, behold! I smile but am silent.”

For a while, Harley stared abstractedly at the bloodstains on the pedestal of the joss and upon the floor, beneath from which the matting had been pulled back. Suddenly, he turned to Ma Lorenzo:

“Where have you hidden the body?” he demanded.

Watching her, I thought I saw the woman flinch, but there was enough of the Oriental in her composition to save her from self-betrayal. She shook her head slowly, watching Harley through half-closed eyes.

“Nobody hab,” she replied. And I thought, for once, that her lapse into pidgin had been deliberate and not accidental.

When, finally, we quitted the house of the missing Kwen Lung, and when Harley, having curtly acknowledged “Good night” from the detective on duty, we came out into Limehouse Causeway.

“You have not overlooked the possibility, Harley,” I said, “that this woman’s explanation may be true, and that the fireman of the *Seahawk* may have been entertaining us with an account of a weird dream?”

“No!” snapped Harley. “Neither will Scotland Yard overlook it.”

He was in a particularly impossible mood, for he so rarely made mistakes that to be detected in one invariably brought out those petulant traits of character which may have been due in some measure to long residence in the East. Recognizing that he would rather be alone, I parted from him at the corner of Chancery Lane and returned to my own chambers.

For some odd reason, but possibly because the fact had occurred to me just as I was retiring, I remembered the next morning that I had not told Harley about the romantic wedding of Captain Dan. As I had left my friend in very ill-humor, I thought that this would be a good excuse for an early call, and, just before eleven o’clock, I walked into his office. Brace, his invaluable secretary, showed me into the study at the back.

“Hallo, Knox,” said Harley, looking up from a little silver Buddha which he was examining, “have you come for news of the Kwen Lung case?”

“No,” I replied. “Is there any?”

Harley shook his head.

“It seems like fate,” he declared, “that this thing should have been sent to me this morning.” He indicated the silver Buddha. “A present from a friend who knows my weakness for Chinese ornaments,” he explained grimly. “It reminds me of that golden joss of Kwen Lung’s!”

I took up the little image and examined it with interest. It was most beautifully fashioned in the patient Oriental way, and there was a little hinged door in the back that fitted so perfectly that, when closed, it was quite impossible to detect its presence.

"I suppose you didn't find a jewel inside?" I said lightly.

"No," he replied. "There was nothing inside."

But, even as he uttered the words, his whole expression changed, and so suddenly as to startle me. He sprang up from the table.

"Have you an hour to spare, Knox?" he cried excitedly.

"I can spare an hour, but what for?"

"For Kwen Lung!"

Four minutes later, we were speeding in the direction of Limehouse, and not a word of explanation to account for this sudden journey could I extract from my friend. Therefore, I beguiled the time by telling him of my adventure with Captain Dan.

"I have been almost perfectly blind, Knox," he said, "but not quite so perfectly blind as you!"

I stared at him in amazement, but he merely laughed and offered no explanation of his words.

Presently, then, I found myself yet again in the familiar room of the golden joss. Ma Lorenzo, in whom some hidden anxiety seemed to have increased since I had last seen her, stood at the top of the stairs, watching us. Upon what idea my friend was operating and what he intended to do, I could not imagine; but, without a word to the woman, he crossed the room, and, grasping the great golden idol with both hands, he dragged it forward!

As he did so, there was a stifled shriek, and Ma Lorenzo, stumbling down the steps, threw herself on her knees before Harley!

"No, no!" she moaned, "not until I tell you. I tell you everything first!"

"To begin with, tell me how to open this thing," he said sternly.

The woman rose unsteadily and, walking slowly round the joss, manipulated some hidden fastening, whereupon the entire back of the thing opened like a door! From what was within, she shudderingly averted her face, but Harley, stepping back against the wall, peered into the cavity.

"Heavens!" he muttered. "Come and look, Knox."

Prepared by his manner for some gruesome spectacle, I obeyed, and from that which I saw, I recoiled in horror.

"Harley," I whispered, "Harley! Who is it?"

The spectacle had truly sickened me. Crouched within the narrow space enclosed by the figure of the idol was the body of an old and wrinkled Chinaman! His knees were drawn up to his chin, and his head so compressed upon them that little of his features could be seen.

"It is Kwen Lung," murmured Ma Lorenzo, standing with clasped hands and wild eyes over by the window. "And I am glad he is dead!"

Such a note of hatred came into her voice as I had never heard.

"He is vile, a demon, a mocking, cruel demon! Long, long years ago, I would have killed him, but always I was afraid. I tell you everything, everything. This is how he comes to be dead. The little one"—again her voice changed, and a note of almost grotesque tenderness came into it—"the lotus flower that is his own daughter, flesh of his flesh, he keeps a prisoner as the women of China are kept up there—up above." She raised one fat finger aloft. "He does not know that someone comes to see her—someone who used to come to smoke, but who gave it up because he had looked into the dear one's eyes. He does not know that she goes with me to see her man. Ah! We *think* he does not know! I—I arrange it all. A week ago, they were married. On Tuesday night, when Kwen Lung die, I plan for her to steal away forever, forever."

Tears now were running down the woman's fat cheeks, and her voice quivered emotionally.

"For me, it is the end, but for her, it is the beginning of life. All right! I don't matter a damn! She is young and beautiful. Ah, God, so beautiful! A drunken pig comes here and finds his way in, so I give him the smoke, and, presently, he sleeps, but it makes delay.

"At last, the sailor pig sleeps and I call softly to my dear little one that the time has come. I have gone out into the street, locking the door behind me, to see if her man is waiting, and I hear her shrieks—her shrieks! I hurry back. My hands tremble so much that I can scarcely unlock the door. At last I enter, and I see and I know that yellow devil has learned all and has been playing with us like cat and mouse! He is lashing her with a great whip—that tiny, sweet flower!"

She choked in her utterance, and, turning to the gilded joss that contained the dead Chinaman, she shook her clenched hands at it, and the expression on her face I can never forget.

"As I shrieked curses at him, crash goes the window, and I see her husband spring into the room! The tender one had fallen there, at the feet of the joss, and Kwen Lung, his teeth gleaming—like a rat, like a devil—turns to meet him. So he is when her man strike him once. Just once, here." She rested her hand upon her heart. "And he falls—and he coughs. He lie still. For him, it is finished. Ah!"

She threw up her hands.

"That is all. I tell you no more."

"One thing more," said Harley sternly; "the *name* of the man who killed Kwen Lung?"

At that, Ma Lorenzo slowly raised her head and folded her arms across her bosom. There was something one could never forget in her expression.

"Not if you burn me alive!" she answered in a low voice. "No one ever knows that—from *me.*"

Then my friend did a singular thing. Walking over to the gilded joss, he reclosed the opening and, not without a great effort, pushed the great idol back.

"There are times, Knox," he said, staring at me oddly, "when I'm glad that I am not an official agent."

Whilst I watched him, dumbfounded, he walked across to the woman and touched her on the shoulder.

"Get ready as soon as you like," said he tersely. "I'll have the man removed who is watching the house and you can reckon on forty-eight hours to make yourself scarce."

With never another word, he seized me by the arm and hurried me out of the place. Ten paces along the street, a shabby-looking fellow was standing, leaning against a pillar. Harley stopped, and:

"Even the greatest men make mistakes sometimes, Hewitt," he remarked. "I'm throwing up the case; probably, Inspector Wessex will do the same. Good morning."

On towards the Causeway he led me, for not a word was I capable of uttering; and, just before we reached that artery of Chinatown, from downriver came the deep, sustained note of a steamer's siren, the warning of some big liner leaving dock

"That will be the *Patna,"* said Harley. "She sails at twelve o'clock, I think you said!"

THE WHITE HAT

"Hullo, Brace," said Paul Harley as his secretary entered. "Someone is making a devil of a row outside."

"This is the offender, Mr. Harley," said Brace, and handed my friend a visiting card.

Glancing at the card, Harley read aloud: "Major J.E.P. Ragstaff, Cavalry Club, London."

Meanwhile, a loud, harsh voice that would have been audible in a full gale was roaring in the lobby. "Nonsense!" I could hear the major shouting. "Balderdash! There's more fuss than if I had asked for an interview with the Prime Minister!"

Brace's smile developed into a laugh, in which Harley joined.

"Admit the major," he said.

Into the study, where Harley and I had been seated, quietly smoking, there presently strode a very choleric gentleman. He wore a horsy check suit and white spats, and his tie closely resembled a stock. In his hand, he carried a heavy malacca cane, gloves and one of those tall, light-gray hats commonly termed white. He was below medium height, slim and wiry; his gait and the shape of his legs, his build, all proclaimed the dragoon. His complexion was purple, and the large white teeth visible beneath a bristling gray mustache added to the natural ferocity of his appearance. Standing just within the doorway, "Mr. Paul Harley?" he shouted. It was apparently an inquiry, but it sounded like a reprimand.

My friend, standing before the fireplace, his hands in his pockets and his pipe in his mouth, nodded brusquely. "I am Paul Harley," he said. "Won't you sit down?"

Major Ragstaff, glancing angrily at Brace as the latter left the study, tossed his stick and gloves on a settee and, drawing up a chair, seated himself stiffly upon it as though he were in a saddle. He stared straight at Harley. "You are not the sort of person I expected, sir," he declared. "May I ask if it is your custom to keep clients dancin' outside on the mat and all that—on the blasted mat, sir?"

Harley suppressed a smile and I hastily reached for my cigarette case, which I had placed upon the mantel shelf.

"I am always, naturally, pleased to see clients, Major Ragstaff," said Harley, "but a certain amount of routine is necessary even in civilian life. You had not advised me of your visit and it is contrary to my custom to discuss business after five o'clock."

As Harley spoke, the major glared at him continuously. "I've seen you in India!" he roared; *"damme!* I've seen you in India—and, yes! In Turkey! Ha! I've got you now, sir!" He sprang to his feet. "You're the Harley who was in Constantinople in 1912."

"Quite true."

"Then I've come to the wrong shop."

"That remains to be seen, major."

"But I was told you were a private detective, and all that."

"So I am," said Harley quietly. "In 1912, the Foreign Office was my client. I am now at the service of anyone who cares to employ me."

The major seemed to be temporarily stricken speechless by the discovery that a man who had acted for the British government should be capable of stooping to the work of a private inquiry agent. Staring all about the room with a sort of naive wonderment, he drew out a big silk handkerchief and loudly blew his nose, all the time eying Harley questioningly. Replacing his handkerchief, he directed his regard upon me.

"This is my friend, Mr. Knox," said Harley; "you may state your case before him without hesitation, unless—"

I rose to depart.

"Sit down, Mr. Knox! Sit down, sir!" shouted the major. "I have no skeletons in the cupboard. I simply want something explained which I am too thick-headed—too damned thick-headed, sir—to explain myself."

He resumed his seat and, taking out his wallet, extracted from it a small newspaper cutting that he offered to Harley.

"Read that, Mr. Harley," he directed. "Read it aloud."

Harley obeyed and read as follows:

"Before Mr. Smith at Marlborough Street Police Court, John Edward Bampton was charged with assaulting a well-known clubman in Bond Street on Wednesday evening. It was proved by the constable who made the arrest that robbery had not been the motive of the assault, and Bampton confessed that he bore no grudge against the assailed man; indeed, that he had never seen him before. He pleaded intoxication, and the police surgeon testified that, although not actually intoxicated, his breath had smelled strongly of liquor at the time of his arrest. Bampton's employers testified to a hitherto blameless character, and as the charge was not pressed, the man was dismissed with a caution."

Having read the paragraph, Harley glanced at the major with a puzzled expression.

"The point of this quite escapes me," he confessed.

"Is that so?" said Major Ragstaff. "Is that so, sir? Perhaps you will be good enough to read *this.*"

From his wallet, he took a second newspaper cutting, smaller than the first and gummed to a sheet of club notepaper. Harley took it and read as follows:

"Mr. De Lana, a well-known member of the Stock Exchange, who met with a serious accident recently, is still in a precarious condition."

The puzzled look on Harley's face grew more acute, and the major watched him with an expression that I can only describe as one of fierce enjoyment. "You're thinkin' I'm a damned old fool, ain't you?" he shouted suddenly.

"Scarcely that," said Harley, smiling slightly, "but the significance of these paragraphs is not apparent, I must confess. The man Bampton would not appear to be an interesting character, and since no great damage has been done, his drunken frolic hardly comes within my sphere. Of Mr. De Lana of the Stock Exchange, I never heard, unless he happens to be a member of the firm of De Lana & Day?"

"He's not a member of that firm, sir," shouted the major. "He *was,* up to six o'clock this evenin'."

"What do you mean, exactly?" inquired Harley, and the tone of his voice suggested that he was beginning to entertain doubts of the major's sanity or sobriety.

"He's dead!" declared the major. "Dead as the Begum of Bangalore! He died at six o'clock. I've just spoken to his widow on the telephone."

I suppose I must have been staring very hard at the speaker and, certainly, Harley was doing so, for he suddenly directed his fierce gaze toward me. "You're completely stumped, sir, and so's your friend!" shouted Major Ragstaff.

"I confess it," replied Harley quietly; "and, since my time is of some little value, I would suggest, without disrespect, that you explain the connection, if any, between yourself, the drunken Bampton and Mr. De Lana of the Stock Exchange, who died, you inform us, at six o'clock this evening as the result, presumably, of injuries received in an accident."

"That's what I'm here for!" cried Major Ragstaff. "In the first place, then, I am the party, although I saw to it that my name was kept out of print, whom the drunken lunatic assaulted."

Harley, pipe in hand, stared at the speaker perplexedly.

"Understand me," continued the major, "I am the person—I, Jack Ragstaff—he assaulted. I was walking down from my quarters in Maddox Street, on my way to dine at the club, same as I do every night o' my life, when this flamin' idiot sprang upon me, grabbed my hat"—he took up his white hat to illustrate what had occurred—"not this one, but one like it—pitched it on the ground and jumped on it!"

Harley was quite unable to conceal his smile as the excited old soldier dropped his conspicuous headgear on the floor and indulged in a vigorous pantomime designed to illustrate his statement.

"Most extraordinary," said Harley. "What did you do?"

"What did I do?" roared the major. "I gave him a crack on the head with my cane, and I said things to him which couldn't be repeated in court. I punched him, and likewise hoofed him, but the hat was completely done in. Damn crowd collected, hearin' me swearin' and bellowin'. Police and all that; names and addresses and all that balderdash. Man lugged away to guardroom and me turnin' up at the club with no hat. Damn ridiculous spectacle at my time o' life."

"Quite so," said Harley soothingly; "I appreciate your annoyance, but I am utterly at a loss to understand why you have come here and what all this has to do with Mr. De Lana of the Stock Exchange."

"He fell out of the window!" shouted the major.

"Fell out of a window?"

"Out of a window, sir, a second-floor window, ten yards up a side street! Pitched on his skull—marvel he wasn't killed outright!"

A faint expression of interest began to creep into Harley's glance. "I understand you to mean, Major Ragstaff," he said deliberately, "that, while your struggle with the drunken man was in progress, Mr. De Lana fell out of a neighboring window into the street?"

"Right!" shouted the major. "Right, sir!"

"Do you know this Mr. De Lana?"

"Never heard of him in my life until the accident occurred. Seems to me the poor devil leaned out to see the fun and overbalanced. Felt responsible, only natural, and made inquiries. He died at six o'clock this evenin', sir."

"H'm," said Harley reflectively. "I still fail to see where I come in. From what window did he fall?"

"Window above a sort of tea shop, called Café Dame—silly name. Place on a corner. Don't know name of side street."

"H'm. You don't think he was pushed out, for instance?"

"Certainly not!" shouted the major. "He just fell out, but the point is, he's dead!"

"My dear sir," said Harley patiently, "I don't dispute that point; but what on earth do you want of me?"

"I don't know what I want!" roared the major, beginning to walk up and down the room, "but I know I ain't satisfied, not easy in my mind, sir. I wake up of a night, hearin' the poor devil's yell as he crashed on the pavement. That's all wrong. I've heard hundreds of death yells, but"—he took up his malacca cane and beat it loudly on the table—"I haven't woke up of a night dreamin' I heard 'em again."

"In a word, you suspect foul play?"

"I don't suspect anything!" cried the other excitedly, "but some-one mentioned your name to me at the club—said you could see through concrete and all that—and here I am. There's something wrong, radically wrong. Find out what it is and send the bill to me. Then, perhaps, I'll be able to sleep in peace."

He paused and, again taking out the large silk handkerchief, blew his nose loudly. Harley glanced at me in rather an odd way. "There will be no bill, Major Ragstaff," he said; "but if I can see any possible line of inquiry, I will pursue it and report the result to you. . . ."

"What do you make of it, Harley?" I asked.

Paul Harley returned a work of reference to its shelf and stood staring absently across the study. "Our late visitor's history does not help us much," he replied. "A somewhat distinguished army career, and so forth, and his only daughter, Sibyl Margaret, married the fifth Marquis of Ireton. She is, therefore, the noted society beauty, the Marchioness of Ireton. Does this suggest anything to your mind?"

"Nothing whatever," I said blankly.

"Nor to mine," murmured Harley.

The telephone bell rang.

"Hullo!" called Harley. "Yes. That you, Wessex? Have you got the address? Good. No, I shall remember it. Many thanks. Goodbye."

He turned to me. "I suggest, Knox," he said, "that we make our call and then proceed to dinner, as arranged."

Since I was always glad of an opportunity of studying my friend's methods, I immediately agreed, and before long, leaving the lights of the two big hotels behind, our cab was gliding down the long slope that leads to Waterloo Station. Thence, through crowded, slummish highroads, we made our way via Lambeth to that dismal thoroughfare, Westminster Bridge Road, with its forbidding, often windowless houses and its peculiar air of desolation.

The house for which we were bound was situated at no great distance from Kennington Park and, telling the cabman to wait, Harley and I walked up a narrow, paved path, mounted a flight of steps and rang the bell beside a somewhat time-worn door, above which was an old-fashioned fanlight dimly illuminated from within.

A considerable interval elapsed before the door was opened by a marvelously untidy servant girl who had apparently been interrupted in the act of blackleading her face. Partly opening the door, she stared at us agape, pushing back wisps of hair from her eyes, and with every movement daubing more of some mysterious black substance upon her countenance.

"Is Mr. Bampton in?" asked Harley.

"Yus, just come in. I'm cookin' his supper."

"Tell him that two friends of his have called on rather important business."

"All right," said the black-faced one. "What name is it?"

"No name. Just say two friends of his."

Treating us to a long, vacant stare and leaving us standing on the step, the maid (in whose hand I perceived a greasy fork) shuffled along the passage and began to mount the stairs. An unmistakable odor of frying sausages now reached my nostrils. Harley glanced at me quizzically, but said nothing until the Cinderella came stumbling downstairs again.

"Go up," she directed. "Second floor, front. Shut the door, one of yer."

She disappeared into gloomy depths below as Harley and I, closing the door behind us, proceeded to avail ourselves of the invitation. There was very little light upon the staircase, but we managed to find our way to a poorly furnished bedroom where a small table was spread for a meal. Beside the table, in a chintz-covered armchair, a thick-set young man was seated, smoking a cigarette, a copy of the *Daily Telegraph* upon his knee.

He was a very typical lower middle-class, nothing-in-particular young man, but there was a certain truculence indicated by his square jaw, and that sort of self-possession which sometimes accompanies physical strength was evidenced in his manner as, tossing the paper aside, he stood up.

"Good evening, Mr. Bampton," said Harley genially. "I take it"—pointing to the newspaper—"that you are looking for a new job?"

Bampton stared with a suspicion of anger in his eyes; then, meeting the amused glance of my friend, he broke into a smile very pleasing and humorous. He was a fresh-colored young fellow with hair inclined to redness, and, smiling, he looked very boyish, indeed.

"I have no idea who you are," he said, speaking with a faint north-country accent, "but you evidently know who I am and what has happened to me."

"Got the boot?" asked Harley confidentially.

Bampton, tossing the end of his cigarette into the grate, nodded grimly. "You haven't told me your name," he said, "but I think I can tell you your business." He ceased smiling. "Now, look here, I don't want any more publicity. If you think you are going to make a funny newspaper story out of me, change your mind as quick as you like. I'll never get another job in London as it is. If you drag me any farther into the limelight, I'll never get another job in England."

"My dear fellow," replied Harley soothingly, at the same time extending his cigarette case, "you misapprehend the object of my call. I am not a reporter."

"What!" said Bampton, pausing in the act of taking a cigarette—"then what the devil are you?"

"My name is Paul Harley, and I am a criminal investigator."

He spoke the words deliberately, his eyes fixed upon the other's face; but, although Bampton was palpably startled, there was no trace of fear in his straightforward glance. He took a cigarette from the case. "Thanks, Mr. Harley," he said. "I cannot imagine what business has brought you here."

"I have come to ask you two questions," Harley answered. "Number one: Who paid you to smash Major Ragstaff's white hat? Number two: How much did he pay you?"

To these questions, I listened in amazement, and my amazement was evidently shared by Bampton. He had been in the act of lighting his cigarette, but he allowed the match to burn down nearly to his fingers and then dropped it with a muttered exclamation in the fire. "I don't know how you found out," he said, "but you evidently know the truth. Provided you assure me that you are not out to make a silly-season newspaper story, I'll tell you all I know."

Harley laid his card on the table. "Unless the ends of justice demand it," he said, "I give you my word that anything you care to say will go no farther. You may speak freely before my friend, Mr. Knox. Simply tell me in as few words as possible what led you to court arrest in that manner."

"Right," replied Bampton, "I will."

He half closed his eyes, reflectively. "I was having tea in the Lyons Café, to which I always go, last Monday afternoon about four o'clock, when a man sat down facing me and got into conversation."

"Describe him."

"He was a man rather above medium height. I should say about my own build; dark, going gray. He had a neat mustache and a short beard, and the look of a man who had traveled a lot. His skin was very tanned, almost as deeply as yours, Mr. Harley. Not at all the sort of chap that goes in there as a rule. After a while, he made an extraordinary proposal. At first, I thought he was joking; then, when I grasped the idea that he was serious, I concluded he was mad. He asked me how much a year I earned, and I told him Peters & Peters paid me £150. He said: 'I'll give you a year's salary to knock a man's hat off!'"

As Bampton spoke the words, he glanced at us with twinkling eyes, but, although for my own part, I was merely amused, Harley's expression had grown very stern. "Of course, I laughed," continued

Bampton, "but when the man drew out a fat wallet and counted ten five-pound notes on the table, I began to think seriously about his proposal. Even supposing he was cracked, it was absolutely money for nothing.

"'Of course,' he said, 'you'll lose your job, and you may be arrested, but you'll say that you had been out with a few friends and were a little excited, also that you never could stand white hats. Stick to that story, and the balance of a hundred pounds will reach you on the following morning.'

"I asked him for further particulars, and I asked him why he had picked me for the job. He replied that he had been looking for some time for the right man; a man who was strong enough physically to accomplish the thing, and someone"—Bampton's eyes twinkled again—"with a bit of dash in him, but, at the same time, a man who could be relied upon to stick to his guns and not to give the game away.

"You asked me to be brief and I'll try to be. The man in the white hat was described to me, and the exact time and place of the meeting. I just had to grab his white hat, smash it and face the music. I agreed. I don't deny that I had a couple of stiff drinks before I set out, but the memory of that fifty pounds locked up here in my room, and the further hundred promised, bucked me up. It was impossible to mistake my man; I could see him coming toward me as I waited just outside a sort of little restaurant called the Café Dame. As arranged, I bumped into him, grabbed his hat and jumped on it."

He paused, raising his hand to his head reminiscently.

"My man was a bit of a scrapper," he continued. "I've never heard such language in my life, and the way he laid about me with his cane is something I am not likely to forget in a hurry. A crowd gathered, naturally, and I was pinched. That didn't matter much. I got off lightly; and although I've been dismissed by Peters & Peters, twenty crisp fivers are locked in my trunk, there, with the ten which I received in the city."

Harley checked him. "May I see the envelope in which this money arrived?" he asked.

"Sorry," replied Bampton, "but I burned it. I thought it was playing the game to do so. It wouldn't have helped you much, though," he added; "it was an ordinary, common envelope, posted in the city, address typewritten, and not a line enclosed."

"Registered?"

"No."

Bampton stood looking at us with a curious expression on his face.

"There's one point," he said, "on which my conscience isn't easy. You know about that poor devil who fell out of a window? Well, it would never have happened if I hadn't kicked up a row in the street. There's no doubt he was leaning out to see what the disturbance was about when the accident occurred."

"Did you actually see him fall?" asked Harley.

"No. He fell from a window several yards behind me in the side street, but I heard him cry out, and as I was lugged off by the police, I heard the bell of the ambulance which came to fetch him."

He paused again and stood rubbing his head ruefully.

"H'm," said Harley; "was there anything particularly remarkable about this man in the Lyons Café?"

Bampton reflected silently for some moments. "Nothing much," he confessed. "He was evidently a gentleman, wore a blue topcoat, a dark tweed suit and what looked like a regimental tie, but I didn't know the colors. He was very tanned, as I have said, even to the backs of his hands—and, oh, yes, there was one point: he had a gold-covered tooth."

"Which tooth?"

"I can't remember, except that it was on the left side, and I always noticed it when he smiled."

"Did he wear any ring or pin which you would recognize?"

"No."

"Was there anything queer in his speech or voice?"

"No. He spoke like thousands of other Englishmen."

Harley nodded briskly and buttoned up his overcoat. "Thanks, Mr. Bampton," he said; "we will detain you no longer."

As we descended the stairs, where the smell of frying sausages had given place to that of something burning—probably the sausages—Harley said:

"I was half inclined to think that Major Ragstaff's ideas were traceable to a former touch of the sun. I begin to believe that he has put us on the track of a pretty unusual crime. I am sorry to delay dinner, Knox, but I propose to call at the Café Dame."

On entering the doorway of the Café Dame, we found ourselves in a narrow passage. In front of us was a carpeted stair and to the right a glass-paneled door communicating with a discreetly lighted little dining room that seemed to be well patronized. Opening the door, Harley beckoned to a waiter. "I wish to see the proprietor," he said.

"Mr. Meyer is engaged at the moment, sir," he answered.

"Where is he?"

"In his office, upstairs, sir. He will be down in a moment."

The waiter hurried away and Harley stood glancing up the stairs, as if in doubt what to do.

"I can't imagine how such a place can pay," he muttered. "The rent must be enormous in this district."

But, even before he ceased speaking, I became aware of an excited conversation that was taking place in some apartment, above.

"It's scandalous!" I heard in a woman's shrill voice. "You have no right to keep it! It's not your property, and I'm here to demand that you give it up."

A man's voice replied in voluble broken English, but I could only distinguish a word here and there. I saw that Harley was interested, for, catching my questioning glance, he raised his finger to his lips enjoining me to be silent.

"Oh, that's the game, is it?" continued the female voice. "Of course, you know it's blackmail?"

A flow of unintelligible words answered this speech.

"I shall come back with someone," cried the woman, "who will *make* you give it up!"

"Knox," whispered Harley in my ear, "when that woman comes down, follow her! I'm afraid you will bungle the business, and I would not ask you to attempt it if big things were not at stake. Come back here; I shall wait."

As a matter of fact, his sudden request had positively astounded me, but, before I had time for any reply, a door suddenly banged open above and a respectable-looking woman, who might have been some kind of upper servant, came quickly down the stairs. Without seeming to notice our presence, she rushed past us and went out into the street.

"Off you go, Knox!" said Harley.

Seeing myself committed to an unpleasant business, I slipped out of the doorway and saw the woman five or six yards away, hurrying in the direction of Piccadilly. I had no difficulty in following her, for she was evidently unsuspicious of my presence, and when, presently, she mounted a westward-bound bus, I did likewise. Though she found a seat inside, I went on top and occupied a place on the near side, where I could observe anyone leaving the vehicle.

At Hyde Park Corner, I saw the woman descending, and when, presently, she walked up Hamilton Place, I was not far behind her. At the door of an imposing mansion, she stopped, and in response to a ring of the bell, the door was opened by a footman and the woman hurried in. Evidently, she was an inmate of the establishment; and conceiving that my duty was done when I had noted the number of the house, I retraced my steps to the corner and, hailing a taxicab, returned to the Café Dame.

I inquired of the same waiter whom Harley had accosted whether my friend was there.

"I think a gentleman is upstairs with Mr. Meyer," said the man.

"In his office?"

"Yes, sir."

I mounted the stairs and, before a half-open door, paused. Harley's voice was audible within, so I knocked and entered. I discovered Harley standing by an American desk. Beside him, in a revolving chair that, with the desk, constituted the principal furniture of a tiny office, sat a man in a dress suit which had palpably not been made for him. He had a sullen and suspiciously Teutonic cast of countenance and he was engaged in a voluble but hardly intelligible speech as I entered.

"Ha, Knox!" said Harley, glancing over his shoulder, "did you manage?"

"Yes," I replied.

Harley nodded shortly and turned again to the man in the chair.

"I am sorry to give you so much trouble, Mr. Meyer," he said, "but I should like my friend here to see the room above."

At this moment, my attention was attracted by a singular object that lay upon the desk in a litter of bills and accounts. This was a piece of rusty iron bar, somewhat less than three feet in length, that once had been painted green.

"You are looking at this tragic fragment, Knox," said Harley, taking up the bar. "Of course"—he shrugged his shoulders—"it explains the whole unfortunate occurrence. You see, there was a flaw in the metal at this end, here"—he indicated the spot—"and the other end had evidently worn loose in its socket."

"But I don't understand."

"It will all be made clear at the inquest, no doubt. A most unfortunate thing for you, Mr. Meyer."

"Most unfortunate," declared the proprietor of the restaurant, extending his thick hands pathetically. "Most ruinous to my business."

"We will go upstairs now," said Harley. "You will kindly lead the way, Mr. Meyer, and the whole thing will be quite clear to you, Knox."

As the proprietor walked out of the office and upstairs to the second floor, Harley whispered in my ear: "Where did she go?"

"No. 45 Hamilton Place," I replied in an undertone.

"Good God!" muttered my friend and clutched my arm so tightly that I winced. "Good God! This crime was the work of a genius!"

Opening a door on the second landing, Mr. Meyer admitted us to a small supper room. Its furniture consisted of a round dining table, several chairs, a couch and very little else. I observed, however, that the furniture, carpet and a few other appointments were of a character much more elegant than those of the public room, below. A window that overlooked the street was open, so that the plush curtains which had been drawn aside moved slightly in the draft.

"The window of the tragedy, Knox," explained Harley. He crossed the room.

"If you will stand here, beside me, you will see the gap in the railing caused by the breaking away of the fragment which now lies on Mr. Meyer's desk. Some few yards to the left, in the street below, is where the assault took place of which we have heard, and the unfortunate Mr. De Lana, who was dining here *alone*—an eccentric custom of his—naturally ran to the window upon hearing the disturbance, leaned out, supporting his weight upon the railing. The rail collapsed and—we know the rest."

"It will ruin me!" groaned Meyer. "It will give bad repute to my establishment."

"I fear it will," agreed Harley sympathetically, "unless we can manage to clear up one or two little difficulties which I have observed. For instance"—he tapped the proprietor on the shoulder confidentially—"have you any idea, any hazy idea, of the identity of the woman who was dining here with Mr. De Lana on Wednesday night?"

The effect of this simple inquiry upon the proprietor was phenomenal. His fat, yellow face assumed a sort of leaden hue, and his already prominent eyes protruded abnormally. He licked his lips.

"I tell you—already I tell you," he muttered, "that Mr. De Lana, he engage this room every Wednesday and sometimes also Friday, and dine here by himself."

"And I tell you," said Harley sweetly, "that you are an inspired liar. You smuggled her out by the side entrance after the accident."

"The side entrance?" muttered Meyer. "The side entrance?"

"Exactly; the side entrance. There is something else which I must ask you to tell me. Who had engaged this room on Tuesday night, the night before the accident?"

The proprietor's expression remained uncomprehending. "A gentleman," he said. "I never see him before."

"Another solitary diner?" suggested Harley.

"Yes, he is alone all the evening, waiting for a friend who does not come."

"Ah!" mused Harley—"alone all the evening, was he? And his friend disappointed him. May I suggest that he was a dark man? Gray at the temples, having a dark beard and mustache and a very tanned face?"

"Yes! Yes!" cried Meyer, and his astonishment was patently unfeigned. "It is a friend of yours?"

"A friend of mine, yes," said Harley absently, but his expression was very grim. "What time did he finally leave?"

"He waited until after eleven o'clock. The dinner is spoiled. He pays, but does not complain."

"No," said Harley musingly, "he had nothing to complain about. One more question, my friend. When the lady escaped hurriedly on Wednesday night, what was it that she left behind and what price are you trying to extort from her for returning it?"

At that, the man collapsed entirely.

"Ach, Gott!" he cried, and raised his hand to his clammy forehead. "You will ruin me. I am a ruined man. I don't try to extort anything. I run an honest business—"

"And a profitable one," added Harley. "Even at Bond Street rentals, I assume that this house is a golden enterprise."

"Ah!" groaned Meyer. "I am ruined, so what does it matter? I tell you everything. I know Mr. De Lana, who engages my room regularly, but I don't know who the lady is who meets him here. No! I swear it! But always it is the same lady. When he falls, I am downstairs in my office and I hear him cry out. The lady comes running from the room and begs of me to get her away without being seen and to keep all mention of her out of the matter."

"What did she pay you?" asked Harley.

"Pay me?" muttered Meyer, pulling up shortly in the midst of his statement.

"Pay you. Exactly. Don't argue; answer."

"She promised one hundred pounds," he confessed hoarsely.

"But you surely did not accept a mere promise? Out with it. What did she give you?"

"A ring," came the confession at last.

"A ring. I see. I will take it with me, if you don't mind. And now, finally, what was it that she left behind?"

"Ach Gott!" moaned the man, dropping into a chair and resting his arms upon the table. "It is all a great panic, you see. I hurry her out by the back stair from this landing and she forgets her bag."

"Her bag? Good."

"Then I clear away the remains of dinner, so I can say Mr. De Lana is dining alone. It is as much my interest as the lady's."

"Of course! I quite understand. I will trouble you no more, Mr. Meyer, except to step into your office and to relieve you of that incriminating evidence, the lady's bag and her ring."

"Do you understand, Knox?" said Harley as the cab bore us toward Hamilton Place. "Do you grasp the details of this scheme?"

"On the contrary," I replied, "I am absolutely at sea."

Nevertheless, I had forgotten that I was hungry in the excitement that now claimed me. For, although the thread upon which these seemingly disconnected things hung was invisible to me, I recognized that Bampton, the city clerk, the bearded stranger who had made so singular a proposition to him, the white-hatted major, the dead stockbroker and the mysterious woman whose presence in the case the clear sight of Harley had promptly detected, all were linked together by some subtle chain. I was convinced, too, that my friend held at least one end of that chain in his grasp.

"In order to prepare your mind for the interview which I hope to obtain this evening," continued Harley, "let me clear up one or two points which may seem obscure. In the first place, you recognize that anyone leaning out of that window on the second floor would almost automatically rest his weight upon the iron bar which was placed there for that very purpose, since the ledge is unusually low?"

"Quite," I replied, "and it also follows that if the bar gave way, anyone thus leaning on it would be pitched into the street."

"Correct."

"But, my dear fellow," said I, "how could such an accident have been foreseen?"

"You speak of an accident. This was no accident! One end of the bar had been filed completely through, although the file marks had been carefully concealed with rust and dirt; and the other end had been wrenched out from its socket and then replaced in such a way that anyone leaning upon the bar could not fail to be precipitated into the street!"

"Good heavens! Then you mean—"

"I mean, Knox, that the man who occupied the supper room on the night before the tragedy—the dark man, tanned and bearded—spent his time in filing through that bar—in short, in preparing a death trap!"

I was almost dumbfounded. "But, Harley," I said, "assuming that he knew his victim would be the next occupant of the room, how could he know—?"

I stopped. Suddenly, as if a curtain had been raised, the details of what I now perceived to be a fiendishly cunning murder were revealed to me.

"According to his own account, Knox," said Harley, "Major Ragstaff regularly passed along that street with military punctuality at the same hour every night. You may take it for granted that the murderer was well aware of this. As a matter of fact, I happen to *know* that he was. We must also take it for granted that the murderer knew of these little dinners for two which took place in the private room above the Café Dame every Wednesday—and sometimes on Friday. Around the figure of the methodical major—with his conspicuous white hat as a sort of focus—was built up one of the most ingenious schemes of murder with which I have ever come in contact. The victim literally killed himself."

"But, Harley, the victim might have ignored the disturbance."

"That is where I first detected the touch of genius, Knox. He recognized the voice of one of the combatants—or his companion did. Here we are."

The cab drew up before the house in Hamilton Place. We alighted and Harley pressed the bell. The same footman whom I had seen admit the woman opened the door.

"Is Lady Ireton at home?" asked Harley.

As he uttered the name, I literally held my breath. We had come to the house of Major Ragstaff's daughter, the Marchioness of Ireton, one of society's most celebrated and beautiful hostesses—the wife of a peer famed alike as sportsman, soldier and scholar.

"I believe she is dining at home, sir," said the man. "Shall I inquire?"

"Be good enough to do so," replied Harley, and gave him a card. "Inform her that I wish to return to her a handbag which she lost a few days ago."

The man ushered us into an anteroom off the lofty and rather gloomy hall, and closed the door.

"Harley," I said in a stage whisper, "am I to believe—"

"Can you doubt it?" returned Harley with a grim smile.

A few moments later, we were shown into a charmingly intimate little boudoir in which Lady Ireton was waiting to receive us. She was a strikingly handsome brunette, but, tonight, her face, which normally I think possessed rich coloring, was almost pallid, and there was a hunted look in her dark eyes which made me wish to be anywhere rather than where I found myself.

"I fail to understand your message, sir," she said, and I admired the imperious courage with which she faced him. "You say you have recovered a handbag which I had lost?"

Harley bowed and, from the pocket of his greatcoat, took out a silken tasseled bag. "The one which you left in the Café Dame, Lady Ireton," he replied. "Here, also, I have"—from another pocket he drew out a diamond ring—"something which was extorted from you by the fellow, Meyer."

Without touching her recovered property, Lady Ireton stood beside the chair from which she had arisen, her gaze fixed as if hypnotically upon the speaker.

"My friend, Mr. Knox, is aware of all the circumstances," continued the latter, "but he is as anxious as I am to terminate this painful interview. I surmise that what occurred on Wednesday night was this—correct me if I am wrong: While dining with Mr. DeLana, you heard sounds of a quarrel in the street below. May I suggest that you recognized one of the voices?"

Lady Ireton, still staring straight before her at Harley, inclined her head in assent. "I heard my father's voice," she said hoarsely.

"Quite so," he continued. "I am aware that Major Ragstaff is your father." He turned to me: "Do you recognize the touch of genius at last?"

Then, again addressing Lady Ireton:

"You naturally suggested to your companion that he should look out of the window in order to learn what was taking place. The next thing you knew was that he had fallen into the street?"

Lady Ireton shuddered and raised her hands to her face. "It is retribution," she whispered. "I have brought this on myself. But *he* does not deserve—" Her voice faded into silence.

"You refer to your husband, Lord Ireton?" said Harley.

Lady Ireton nodded and, again recovering power of speech: "It was to have been our last meeting," she said, looking up at Harley. She shuddered, and her eyes blazed into sudden fierceness. Then, clenching her hands, she looked aside. "Oh, the shame of this hour!" she whispered.

And I would have given much to have been spared the spectacle of this proud woman's humiliation. But Paul Harley was scientifically remorseless. I could detect no pity in his glance.

"I would give my life willingly to spare my husband the knowledge of what has happened," said Lady Ireton in a low, monotonous voice. "Three times I sent my maid to Meyer to recover my bag, but he demanded a price which even *I* could not pay. Now, it is all discovered, and Harry will know."

"That, I fear, is unavoidable, Lady Ireton," declared Harley. "May I ask where Lord Ireton is at present?"

"He is in Africa. After big game."

"H'm," said Harley, "in Africa, and after big game? I can offer you one consolation, Lady Ireton. In his own interests, Meyer will stick to his first assertion that Mr. De Lana was dining alone."

A strange, horribly pathetic look came into the woman's haunted eyes. "You—you—are not acting for—?" she began.

"I am acting for no one," replied Harley tersely. "Upon my friend's discretion, you may rely as upon my own."

"Then why should *he* ever know?" she whispered.

"Why, indeed," murmured Harley, "since he is in Africa?"

As we descended the stair to the hall, my friend paused and pointed to a life-sized oil painting by London's most fashionable portrait painter. It was that of a man in the uniform of a Guards officer, a dark man, slightly gray at the temples, his face very tanned, as if by exposure to the sun.

"Having had no occasion for disguise when the portrait was painted," said Harley, "Lord Ireton appears here without the beard, and, as he is not represented smiling, one cannot see the gold tooth!"

"But, Harley—it was murder!"

"Not within the meaning of the law, Knox. Lord Ireton is officially in Africa—and he went actually after 'big game.' The counsel is not born who could secure a conviction. We are somewhat late, but shall have less difficulty in finding a table at Princes'."

THE MAN WITH THE SHAVEN SKULL

I
A Strange Disappearance

"Pull that light lower," ordered Inspector Wessex. "There you are, Mr. Harley; what do you make of it?"

Paul Harley and I bent gingerly over the ghastly exhibit to which the C.I.D. official had drawn our attention, and to view which we had journeyed from Chancery Lane to Wapping.

This was the body of a man dressed solely in ragged shirt and trousers. But the remarkable feature of his appearance lay in the fact that every scrap of hair—from chin, lip, eyebrows and skull—had been *shaved off!*

There was another facial disfigurement, peculiarly and horribly Eastern, which my pen may not describe.

"Impossible to identify!" murmured Harley. "Yes, you were right, inspector; this is a victim of Oriental deviltry. Look here, too!"

He indicated three small wounds, one situated on the left shoulder and the others on the forearm of the dead man.

"The divisional surgeon cannot account for them," replied Wessex. "They are quite superficial, and he thinks they may be due to the fact that the body got entangled with something in the river."

"They are due to the fact that the man had a birthmark on his shoulder and something—probably a name or some device—tattooed on his arm," said Harley quietly. "Some few years ago, I met with a similar case in the neighborhood of Stambûl. A woman," he added significantly.

Detective-Inspector Wessex listened to my companion with respect, for, apart from his established reputation as a private inquiry-agent that had made his name familiar in nearly every capital of the civilized world, Paul Harley's work in Constantinople during the six months preceding war with Turkey had merited higher reward than it had ever received. Had his recommendations been adopted, the course of history must have been materially changed.

"You think it's a Chinatown case, then, Mr. Harley?"

"Possibly," was the guarded answer.

Paul Harley nodded to the constable in charge, and the ghastly figure was promptly covered up again. My friend stood staring vacantly at Wessex, and, presently:

"The chief actor, I think, will prove to be not Chinese," he said, turned and walked out.

"If there's any development," remarked Wessex as the three of us entered Harley's car, which stood at the door, "I will, of course, report to you, Mr. Harley. But, in the absence of any clue or mark of identification, I fear the verdict will be, 'Body of a man unknown,' etc., which has marked the finish of a good many in this cheerful quarter of London."

"Quite so," said Harley absently. "It presents extraordinary features, though, and may not end as you suppose. However—where do you want me to drop you, Wessex, at the Yard?"

"Oh no," answered Wessex. "I made a special visit to Wapping just to get your opinion on the shaven man. I'm really going down to Deepbrow, to look into that new disappearance case; the daughter of the gamekeeper. You'll have read of it?"

"I have," said Harley shortly.

Indeed, readers of the daily press were growing tired of seeing on the contents bills: "Another girl missing." The circumstance (which might have been no more than coincidence) that three girls had disappeared within the last eight weeks, leaving no trace behind, had stimulated the professional scribes to link the cases, although no visible link had been found, and to enliven a somewhat dull journalistic season with theories about "a new Mormon menace."

The vanishing of this fourth girl had inspired them to some startling headlines, and the case had interested me personally for the reason that I was acquainted with Sir Howard Hepwell, one of whose gamekeepers was the stepfather of the missing Molly Clayton. Moreover, it was hinted that she had gone away in the company of Captain Ronald Vane, at that time a guest of Sir Howard's at the manor.

In fact, Sir Howard had phoned to ask me if I could induce Harley to run down, but my friend had expressed himself as disinterested in a common case of elopement. Now, as Wessex spoke, I glanced aside at Harley, wondering if the fact that so celebrated a member of the C.I.D. as Detective-Inspector Wessex had been put in charge would induce him to change his mind.

We were traversing a particularly noisy and unsavory section of the Commercial Road, and although I could see that Wessex was anxious to impart particulars of the case to Harley, so loud was the din that I recognized the impossibility of conversing, and, therefore:

"Have you time to call at my rooms, Wessex?" I asked.

"Well," he replied, "I have three-quarters of an hour."

"You can do it in the car," said Harley suddenly. "I have been asked to look into this case myself, and before I definitely decline, I should like to hear your version of the matter."

Accordingly, we three presently gathered in my chambers, and Wessex, with one eye on the clock, outlined the few facts at that time in his possession respecting the missing girl.

Two days before the news of the disappearance had been published, broadcast under such headings as I have already indicated, a significant scene had been enacted in the gamekeeper's cottage.

Molly Clayton, a girl whose remarkable beauty had made her a central figure in numerous scandalous stories, for such is the charity of rural neighbors, was detected by her stepfather, about eight in the evening, slipping out of the cottage.

"Where be ye goin', hussy?" he demanded, grasping her promptly by the arm.

"For a walk!" she replied defiantly.

"A walk wi' that fine soger from t' manor!" roared Bramber furiously. "You'll be sorry yet, you barefaced gadabout! Must I tell you again that t' man's a villain?"

The girl wrenched her arm from Bramber's grasp and blazed defiance from her beautiful eyes.

"He knows how to respect a woman—what *you* don't!" she retorted hotly.

"So I don't respect you, my angel?" shouted her stepfather. "Then you know what you can do! The door's open and there's few'll miss you!"

Snatching her hat, the girl, very white, made to go out. Whereat the gamekeeper, a brutal man with small love for Molly, and maddened by her taking him at his word, seized her suddenly by her abundant fair hair and hauled her back into the room.

A violent scene followed, at the end of which Molly fainted and Bramber came out and locked the door.

When he came back about half-past nine, the girl was missing. She did not reappear that night, and the police were advised in the morning. Their most significant discovery was this:

Captain Ronald Vane, on the night of Molly's disappearance, had left the manor house after dining alone with his host, Sir Howard Hepwell, saying that he proposed to take a stroll as far as the Deep Wood.

He never returned!

From the moment that gamekeeper Bramber left his cottage,

and the moment when Sir Howard Hepwell parted from his guest after dinner, the world to which these two people, Molly Clayton and Captain Vane, were known, knew them no more!

I was about to say that they were never seen again. But to me has fallen the task of relating how and where Paul Harley and I met with Captain Vane and Molly Clayton.

At the end of the inspector's account:

"H'm," said Harley, glancing under his thick brows in my direction, "could you spare the time, Knox?"

"To go to Deepbrow?" I asked with interest.

"Yes; we have ten minutes to catch the train."

"I'll come," said I. "Sir Howard will be delighted to see you, Harley."

II
The Clue of the Photographs

"What do you make of it, inspector?" asked my friend.

Detective-Inspector Wessex smiled and scratched his chin.

"There was no need for me to come down!" he replied. "And certainly no need for *you,* Mr. Harley!"

Harley bowed, smiling, at the implied compliment.

"It's a common or garden elopement!" continued the detective. "Vane's reputation is absolutely rotten and the girl was clearly infatuated. He must have cared a good bit, too. He'll be cashiered, as sure as a gun!"

Leaving Sir Howard at the manor, we had joined Inspector Wessex at a spot where the baronet's preserves bordered a narrow lane. Here, the ground was soft, and the detective drew Harley's attention to a number of footprints by a stile.

"I've got evidence that he was seen here with the girl on other occasions. Now, Mr. Harley, I'll ask you to look over these footprints."

Harley dropped to his knees and made a brief but close examination of the ground round about. One particularly clear imprint of a pointed toe he noticed especially; and Wessex, diving into the pocket of his light overcoat, produced a patent-leather shoe, such as is used for evening wear.

"He had a spare pair in his bag," he explained nonchalantly, "and his man did not prove incorruptible!"

Harley took the shoe and placed it in the impression. It fitted perfectly!

"This is Molly Clayton, I take it?" he said, indicating the prints of a woman's foot.

"Yes," assented Wessex. "You'll notice that they stood for some little time and then walked off, very close together."

Harley nodded absently.

"We lose them along here," continued Wessex, leading up the lane; "but at the corner, by the big haystack, they join up with the tracks of a motor-car! I ask for nothing clearer! There was rain that afternoon, but there's been none since."

"What does the captain's man think?"

"The same as I do! He's not surprised at any madness on Vane's part, with a pretty woman in the case!"

"The girl left nothing behind—no note?"

"Nothing."

"Traced the car?"

"No. It must have been hired or borrowed from a long distance off."

Where the tracks of the tires were visible, we stopped, and Harley made a careful examination of the marks.

"Seems to have had a struggle with her," he said dryly.

"Very likely!" agreed Wessex without interest.

Harley crawled about on the ground for some time, to the great detriment of his Harris tweeds, but finally arose, a curious expression on his face—which, however, the detective evidently failed to observe.

We returned to the manor house, where Sir Howard was awaiting us, his good-humored red face more red than usual; and in the library, with its sporting prints and its works for the most part dealing with riding, hunting, racing and golf (except for a sprinkling of Nat Gould's novels and some examples of the older workmanship of Whyte-Melville), we were presently comfortably ensconced. On a side table were placed a generous supply of liquid refreshments, cigars and cigarettes; so that we made ourselves quite comfortable, and Sir Howard restrained his indignation until each had a glass before him and all were smoking.

"Now," he began, "what have you got to report, gentlemen? You, inspector," he pointed with his cigar toward Wessex, "have seen Vane's man and all of you have been down to look at these damned tracks. I only want to hear one thing; that you expect to trace the disgraceful couple. I'll see to it"—his voice rose almost to a shout—"that Vane is kicked out of the service, and as to that shameless brat of Bramber's, I wish her no worse than the blackguard's company!"

"One moment, Sir Howard, one moment," said Harley quietly; "there are always two sides to a case."

"What do you mean, Mr. Harley? There's only one side that interests me—the outrage inflicted upon my hospitality by this dirty guest of mine. For the girl, I don't give twopence; she was bound to come to a bad end."

"Well," said Harley, "before we pronounce the final verdict upon either of them, I should like to interview Bramber. Perhaps," he added, turning to Wessex, "it would be as well if Mr. Knox and I went alone. The presence of an official detective sometimes awes this class of witness."

"Quite right, quite right!" agreed Sir Howard, waving his cigar vigorously. "Go and see Bramber, Mr. Harley; tell him that no blame attaches to himself whatever; also, tell him with my compliments that his stepdaughter is—"

"Quite so, quite so," interrupted Harley, endeavoring to hide a smile. "I understand your feelings, Sir Howard, but again I ask you to reserve your verdict until all the facts are before us."

As a result, Harley and I presently set out for the gamekeeper's cottage, and as the man had been warned that we should visit him, he was on the porch, smoking his pipe. A big, dark, ugly fellow he proved to be, of a very forbidding cast of countenance. Having introduced ourselves:

"I always knowed she'd come to a bad end!" declared gamekeeper Bramber, almost echoing Sir Howard's words. "One o' these gentlemen o' hers was sure to be t' finish of her!"

"She had other admirers—before Captain Vane?"

"Aye! The hussy! There was a black-faced villain not six months since! He got t' vain cat to go to London an' have her photograph done in a dress any decent woman would 'a' blushed to look at! Like one o' these Venuses up at t' manor! Good riddance! She took after her mother!"

The violent old ruffian was awkward to examine, but Harley persevered.

"This previous admirer caused her to be photographed in that way, did he? Have you a copy?"

"No!" blazed Bramber. "What I found, I burnt! He ran off, like I told her he would—an' her cryin' her eyes out! But the pretty soger dried her tears quick enough!"

"Do you know this man's name?"

"No. A foreigner, he was."

"Where were the photographs done—in London, you say?"

"Aye."

"Do you know by what photographer?"

"I don't! An' I don't care! Piccadilly, they had on 'em, which was good enough for me."

"Have you her picture?"

"No!"

"Did she receive a letter on the day of her disappearance?"

"Maybe."

"Good day!" said Harley. "And let me add that the atmosphere of her home was hardly conducive to ideal conduct!"

Leaving Bramber to digest this rebuke, we came out of the cottage. Dusk was falling now, and by the time that we regained the manor, the place was lighted up. Inspector Wessex was waiting for us in the library, and:

"Well?" he said, smiling slightly as we entered.

"Nothing much," replied Harley dryly, "except that I don't wonder at the girl's leaving such a home."

"What's that! What!" roared a big voice, and Sir Howard came into the room. "I tell you, Bramber only had one fault as a stepfather; he wasn't heavy-handed enough. A bad lot, sir, a bad lot!"

"Well, sir," said Inspector Wessex, looking from one to another, "personally, beyond the usual inquiries at railway stations, etc., I cannot see that we can do much here. Don't you agree with me, Mr. Harley?"

Harley nodded.

"Quite," he replied. "There is a late train to town, which I think we could catch if we started at once."

"Eh?" roared Sir Howard; "you're not going back tonight? Your rooms are ready for you, damn it!"

"I quite appreciate the kindness, Sir Howard," replied Harley; "but I have urgent business to attend to in London. Believe me, my departure is unavoidable."

The blue eyes of the baronet gleamed with the simple cunning of his kind.

"You've got something up your sleeve," he roared. "I know you have, I know you have!"

Inspector Wessex looked at me significantly, but I could only shrug my shoulders in reply; for, in these moods, Harley was as inscrutable as the Sphinx.

However, he had his way, and Sir Howard hurriedly putting a car in commission, we raced for the local station and just succeeded in picking up the express at Claybury.

Wessex was rather silent throughout the journey, often glancing in my friend's direction, but Harley made no further reference to the case beyond outlining the interview with Bramber, until, as we were parting at the London terminus, Wessex to report to Scotland Yard and I to go to Harley's rooms:

"How long do you think it will take you to find that photographer, Wessex?" he asked. "Piccadilly is a sufficient clue."

"Well," replied the inspector, "nothing can be done tonight, of course, but I should think by mid-day tomorrow, the matter should be settled."

"Right," said Harley shortly. "May I ask you to report the result to me, Wessex?"

"I will report without fail."

III
Ali of Cairo

It was not until the evening of the following day that Harley rang me up, and:

"I want you to come round at once," he said urgently. "The Deepbrow case is developing along lines which, I confess, I had anticipated, but which are dramatic nevertheless."

Knowing that Harley did not lightly make such an assertion, I put aside the work upon which I was engaged and hurried around to Chancery Lane. I found my friend, pipe in mouth, walking up and down his smoke-laden study in a state which I knew to betoken suppressed excitement, and:

"Did Wessex find your photographer?" I asked on entering.

"Yes," he replied. "A first-class man, as I had anticipated. As I had further anticipated, he did a number of copies of the picture for the foreign gentleman—about fifty, in fact!"

"Fifty!"

"Yes! Does the significance of that fact strike you?" asked Harley, a queer smile stealing across his tanned, clean-shaven face.

"It is an extraordinary thing for even an ardent admirer to have so many reproductions done of the same picture!"

"It is! I will show you now what I found trodden into one of the footprints where the struggle took place beside the car."

Harley produced a piece of thick silk twine.

"What is it?"

"It is a link, Knox—a link to seek which I really went down to Deepbrow." He stared at me quizzically, but my answering look must have been a blank one. "It is part of the tassel of one of those red cloth caps commonly called, in England, a fez!"

He continued to stare at me and I to stare at the piece of silk; then:

"What is the next move?" I demanded. "Your new clue rather bewilders me."

"The next move," he said, "is to retire to the adjoining room and make ourselves look as much like a couple of Oriental commercial travelers as our correctly British appearance will allow!"

"What?" I cried.

"That's it!" laughed Harley. "I have a perpetual tan, and I think

I can give you a temporary one which I keep in a bottle for the purpose."

Twenty minutes later, then, having quitted Harley's chambers by a back way opening into one of those old-world courts which abound in this part of the metropolis, two quietly attired Eastern gentlemen got into a cab at the corner of Chancery Lane and proceeded in the direction of Limehouse.

There are haunts in many parts of London whose very existence is unsuspected by all but the few; haunts unvisited by the tourist and even unknown to the copy-hunting pressman. Into a quiet thoroughfare not three minutes' walk from the busy life of West India Dock Road, Harley led the way. Before a door sandwiched in between the entrance to a Greek tobacconist's establishment and a boarded shopfront, he paused and turned to me.

"Whatever you see or hear," he cautioned, "express no surprise. Above all, show no curiosity."

He rang the bell beside the door, and almost immediately it was opened by a Negress, grossly and repellently ugly.

Harley pattered something in what sounded like Arabic, whereat the Negress displayed the utmost servility, ushering us into an ill-lighted passage with every evidence of respect. Following this passage to its termination, an inner door was opened and a burst of discordant music greeted us, together with a wave of tobacco smoke. We entered.

Despite my friend's particular injunctions to the contrary, I gave a start of amazement.

We stood in the doorway of a fairly large apartment having a divan round three of its sides. This divan was occupied by ten or a dozen men of mixed nationalities—Arabs, Greeks, lascars and others. They smoked cigarettes for the most part and sipped *mokha* from little cups. A girl was performing a wriggling dance upon the square carpet occupying the center of the floor, accompanied by a Nubian boy who twanged upon a guitar, and by most of the assembled company, who clapped their hands to the music or droned a low, tuneless dirge.

Shortly after our entrance, the performance terminated and the girl retired through a curtained doorway at the farther end of the room. Our presence being now observed, suspicious glances were cast in our direction, and a very aged man, who sat smoking a *narghile* near the door by which the girl had made her exit, gravely waved towards us the amber mouthpiece which he held in his hand.

Harley walked straight across to him, I close at his heels. The light of a lamp that hung close by fell fully upon my friend's face; and, rising from his seat, the old man greeted him with the dignified and graceful salutation of the East. At his request, we seated ourselves beside him, and, while we all three smoked excellent Turkish cigarettes, Harley and he conversed in a low tone. Suddenly, at some remark of my friend's, our strange host rose to his feet, an angry frown contracting his heavy eyebrows.

Silence fell upon the company.

In a loud and peremptory voice, he called out something in Arabic.

Instantly, I detected a fellow near the entrance door, whom I had not hitherto observed, slipping furtively into the shadow, with a view, as I thought, to secret departure. He seemed to be deformed in some way and had the most evil, pock-marked face I had ever beheld in my life. Angrily, the majestic old man recalled him. Whereupon, with a sort of animal snarl quite indescribable, the fellow plucked out a knife! Two men who had been on the point of seizing him fell back, and:

"Hold him!" shouted Harley, springing forward. "Hold him! It's Ali of Cairo!"

But Harley was too late. Turning, the strange and formidable-looking Oriental ran like the wind! Ere hand could be raised to stay him, he was through the doorway!

"That settles it," said Harley grimly, as once more I found myself in a cab beside him. "I was right; but he'll forestall us!"

"*Who* will forestall us?" I asked in bewilderment.

"The biggest villain in Europe, Asia or Africa!" cried my companion. "I have wasted precious time today. I might have known." He drummed irritably upon his knees. "The place we have just left is a sort of club, you understand, Knox, and Hákîm is the proprietor or host as well as being an old gentleman of importance and authority in the Moslem world. I told him of my suspicions—which step I should have taken earlier—and they were instantly confirmed. My man was there—recognized me—and bolted! He'll forestall us."

"But, my dear fellow," I said patiently—"who is this man, and what has he to do with the Deepbrow case?"

"He is the blackest scoundrel breathing!" answered Harley bitterly. "As to what he has to do with the case—why did he bolt? At any rate, I know where to find him now—and we *may* not be too late after all."

"But who and what is this man?"

"He is Ali of Cairo! As to *what* he is—you will soon learn."

IV
The House By the River

On quitting the singular Oriental club, Harley had first raced off to a public telephone, where he had spoken for some time—as I now divined—to Scotland Yard. For, when we presently arrived at the headquarters of the Metropolitan Police, I was surprised to find Inspector Wessex awaiting us. Leaning out of the cab window:

"Yes?" called Harley excitedly. "Was I right?"

"You were, Mr. Harley," answered Wessex, who seemed to be no less excited than my companion. "I got the man's reply an hour ago."

"I knew it!" said Harley shortly. "Get in, Wessex; we haven't a minute to waste."

The inspector joined us in the cab, having first given instructions to the chauffeur. As we set out once more:

"You have had very little time to make the necessary arrangements," continued my friend.

"Time enough," replied Wessex. "They will not be expecting us."

"I'm not so sure of it. One of the biggest villains in the civilized world recognized me three minutes before I called you up, and then made good his escape. However, there is at least a fighting chance."

Little more was said from that moment until the end of the drive, both my companions seeming to be consumed by an intense eagerness to reach our destination. At last the cab drew up in a deserted street. I had rather lost my bearings, but I knew that we were once more somewhere in the Chinatown area, and:

"Follow us until we get into the house," Harley said to Inspector Wessex, "and wait out of sight. If you hear me blow this whistle, bring up the men you have posted—as quick as you like! But make it your particular business to see that *no one gets out!*"

Into a pitch-dark yard we turned, and I felt a shudder of apprehension upon observing that it was the entrance to a wharf. Dully gleaming in the moonlight, the Thames, that grave of many a ghastly secret, flowed beneath us. Emerging from the shadow of the archway, we paused before a door in the wall on our left.

At that moment, something gleamed through the air, whizzed past my ear and fell with a metallic jingle on the stones!

Instinctively, we both looked up.

At an unlighted window on the first floor, I caught a fleeting glimpse of a dark face.

"You were right!" I said. "Ali of Cairo has forestalled us!"

Harley stooped and picked up a knife with a broad and very

curious blade. He slipped it into his pocket nonchalantly.

"All evidence!" he said. "Keep in the shadow and bend down. I am going to stand on your shoulders and get into that window!"

Wondering at his daring, I nevertheless obeyed; and Harley succeeded, although not without difficulty, in achieving his purpose. A moment after, he had disappeared in the blackness of the room above.

"Stand clear, Knox!" I heard.

Two of the cushion seats sometimes called "poof-ottomans" were thrown down, and:

"Up you come!" called Harley. "I'll grasp your hands if you can reach."

It proved no easy task, but I finally managed to scramble up beside my friend—to find myself in a dark and stuffy little room.

"This way!" said Harley rapidly—"upstairs."

He led the way without more ado, but it was with serious misgivings that I stumbled up a darkened stair in the rear of my greatly daring friend.

A pistol cracked in the darkness—and my fez was no longer on my head!

Harley's repeater answered and we stumbled through a heavily curtained door into a heated room, the air of which was laden with some Eastern perfume. In the dim light from a silken-shaded lantern, a figure showed momentarily, darting across the place before us.

Again Harley's pistol spoke, but, as it seemed, ineffectively.

I had little enough opportunity to survey my surroundings; yet, even in those brief, breathless moments, I saw enough of the place wherein we stood to make me doubt the evidence of my senses! Outside, I knew, lay a dingy wharf amid a maze of mean streets; here was an opulently furnished apartment with a strong Oriental note in the decorations!

Snatching an electric torch from his pocket, Harley leaped through a doorway draped with rich Persian tapestry, and I came close on his heels. Outside was darkness. A strong draft met us; and, passing along a carpeted corridor, we never halted until we came to a room filled with the weirdest odds and ends, apparently collected from every quarter of the globe.

Crack!

A bullet flattened itself on the wall behind us!

"Good job he can't shoot straight!" rapped Harley.

The ray of the torch suddenly picked out the head and shoulders of a man who was descending through a trap in the floor! Ere we had time to shoot, he was gone! I saw his brown fingers relax their hold—and a bundle that he had evidently hoped to take with him was left lying upon the floor.

Together, we ran to the trap and looked down.

Slowly moving tidal water flowed darkly beneath us! For twenty breathless seconds, we watched—but nothing showed upon the surface.

"I hope his swimming is no better than his shooting," I said.

"It can avail him little," replied Harley grimly; "a river-police boat is waiting for anyone who tries to escape from that side of the house. We are by no means alone in this affair, Knox. But, firstly, what have we here!" He took up the bundle that the fugitive had deserted.

"Something incriminating when Ali of Cairo dared not stay to face it out! He would never have deserted this place in the ordinary way. That fellow who was such a bad shot was left behind when the news of our approach reached here, to make a desperate attempt to remove some piece of evidence! I'll swear to it. But we were too soon for him!"

All the time, he was busily removing the pieces of sacking and scraps of Oriental stuff with which the bundle was fastened; and, finally, he drew out a dress suit, together with the linen, collar, shoes and underwear—a complete outfit, in fact—and on top of the whole was a soft gray felt hat!

Eagerly, Harley searched the garments for some name of a maker by which their owner might be identified. Presently, inside the lining of the breast pocket, where such a mark is usually found, he discovered the label of a well-known West End firm.

"The police can confirm it, Knox!" he said, looking up, his face slightly flushed with triumph; "but I, personally, have no doubt!"

"You may have no doubt, Harley," I retorted, "but I am full of doubt! What is the significance of this discovery to which you seem to attach so much importance?"

"At the moment," replied my friend, "never mind; I still have hopes—although they have grown somewhat slender—of making a much more important discovery."

"Why not permit the police to aid in the search?"

"The police are more useful in their present occupation," he replied. "We are dealing with the most cunning knave produced by East or West, and I don't mean to let him slip through my fingers if he is in this house! Nevertheless, Knox, I am submitting you to rather an appalling risk, I know; for our man is desperate, and if he is still in the place will prove as dangerous as a cornered rat."

"But the man who dropped through the trap?"

"The man who dropped through the trap," said Harley, "was not Ali of Cairo—and it is Ali of Cairo for whom I am looking!"

"The hunchback we saw tonight?"

Harley nodded, and, having listened intently for a few moments, proceeded again to search the singular apartments of the abode.

In each was evidence of Oriental occupancy; indeed, some of the rooms possessed a sort of *Arabian Nights* atmosphere. But no living creature was to be seen or heard anywhere. It was while the two of us, having examined every inch of wall, I should think, in the building, were standing staring rather blankly at each other in the room with the lighted lantern that I saw Harley's expression change.

"Why," he muttered, "is this one room illuminated—and all the others in darkness?"

Even then, the significance of this circumstance was not apparent to me. But Harley stared critically at an electric switch that was placed on the immediate right of the door and then up at the silk-shaded lantern which lighted the room. Crossing, he raised and lowered the switch rapidly, but the lamp continued to burn uninterruptedly!

"Ah!" he said—"a good trick!"

Grasping the wooden block to which the switch was attached, he turned it bodily—and I saw that it was a masked knob; for, in the next moment, he had pulled open the narrow section of wall—which proved to be nothing less than a cunningly fitted door!

A small, dimly lighted apartment was revealed, the Oriental note still predominant in its appointments, which, however, were few, and which I scarcely paused to note. For, lying upon a mattress in this place was a pretty, fair-haired girl!

She lay on her side, having one white arm thrown out and resting limply on the floor, and she seemed to be in a semi-conscious condition, for, although her fine eyes were widely opened, they had a glassy, witless look, and she was evidently unaware of our presence.

"Look at her pupils," rapped Harley. "They have drugged her with *bhang!* Poor, pretty fool!"

"Good God!" I cried. "Who is this, Harley?"

"Molly Clayton!" he answered. "Thank heaven we have saved one victim from Ali of Cairo."

V

The Harem Agency

Owing to the instrumentality of Paul Harley, the public never learned that the awful riverside murder, called by the press, in reference to the victim's shaven skull, "the barber atrocity," had any relation to the Deepbrow case. It was physically impossible to identify the victim, and Harley had his own reasons for concealing the truth. The house on the wharf, with its choice Oriental furniture, was seized by the police; but, strange to relate, no arrest was made in connection with this most gruesome outrage. The man who dropped through the trap had been wounded by one of Harley's shots, and he sank for the last time under the very eyes of the crew of the police cutter.

It was at a late hour on the night of this concluding tragedy that I learned the amazing truth underlying the case. Wessex was still at work in the East End upon the hundred and one formalities that attached to his office, and Harley and I sat in the study of my friend's chambers in Chancery Lane.

"You see," Harley was explaining, "I got my first clue down at Deepbrow. The tracks leading to the motor-car. They showed—to anyone not hampered by a preconceived opinion—that the girl and Vane had not gone on together (since the man's footprints proved him to have been *running),* but that *she* had gone first and that *he* had run after her! Arguments: (a) he heard the approach of the car; or (b) he heard her call for help. In fact, it almost immediately became evident to me that someone else had met her at the end of the lane; probably someone who expected her, and whom she was going to meet when she *accidentally* encountered Vane! The captain was not attired for an elopement, and, more significant still, he said he should stroll to the Deep Wood, and that was where he did stroll to; for it borders the road at this point!

"I had privately ascertained from the postman that Molly Clayton actually received a letter on that morning! This resolved my last doubt. She was not going to meet Vane on the night of her disappearance."

"Then whom?"

"The old love! He who some months earlier had had over fifty seductive pictures of this undoubtedly pretty girl prepared for a purpose of his own!"

"Vane interfered?"

"When the girl saw that they meant to take her away, she no doubt made a fuss! He ran to the rescue! They had not reckoned on his being there, but these are clever villains, who leave no clues—except for one who has met them on their own ground!"

"On their own ground! What do you mean, Harley? Who are these people?"

"Well—where do you suppose those fifty photographs went?"

"I cannot conjecture!"

"Then I will tell you. The turmoil in the East has put wealth and power into unscrupulous hands. But, even before the war, there were marts, Knox—open marts—at which a Negro girl might be purchased for some £30, and a Circassian for anything from £250 to £500! Ah! You stare! But, I assure you, it was so. Here is the point, though: there were, and still are, private dealers! Those photographs were circulated among the *nouveaux riches* of the East! They were employed in the same way that any other merchant employs a catalogue. They reached the hands of many an opulent and abandoned 'profiteer' of Damascus, Stambûl—where you will. Molly's picture would be one of many. Remember that hundreds of pretty girls disappear from their homes—taking the whole of the world—every year. Clearly, English beauty is popular at the moment! And," he added bitterly, "the arch-villain has escaped!"

"Ali of Cairo!" I cried. "Then Ali of Cairo—"

"Is the biggest *slave-dealer* in the East!"

"Good God! Harley—at last I understand!"

"I was slow enough to understand it myself, Knox. But, once the theory presented itself, I asked Wessex to get into immediate touch with the valet he had already interviewed at Deepbrow. It was the result of his inquiry to which he referred when we met him at Scotland Yard tonight. Captain Vane had a large mole *on his shoulder* and a girl's name, together with a small device, tattooed *on his forearm*—a freak of his Sandhurst days—"

"Then, the man with the shaven skull—"

"Is Captain Ronald Vane! May he rest in peace. But *I* never shall until the crookback dealer in humanity has met his just deserts."

THE BLACK MANDARIN

I
Hebron's Mail

With increasing irritation, I listened to the sound of someone belaboring the knocker of the top set, immediately above me. Dimly, I could hear, too, the purring of a bell. I did not know Michael Hebron, my new neighbor; I had not seen him since he had entered into occupation of the chambers, but that he was from home at the moment seemed evident.

Therefore, throwing open my door, I stepped out upon the landing, looked up. "Hullo, there!" I cried. "Mr. Hebron is out. Can I help you?"

The pill-box cap of a district messenger appeared over the rail of the stair-head.

"A letter for Mr. Hebron, sir," the boy called down. "Will you sign for it?"

"Certainly," I answered. "He shall have it immediately he returns."

At that, the messenger came down and I signed the green slip that he handed to me, taking charge of a square envelope made of unusually thick, amber-colored paper. Bestowing silent maledictions upon the absent man, whose affairs not only disturbed my work, but also called upon me to pay his tips, I dismissed the boy and went back to my study, carrying the envelope.

I tossed it on the table and returned to my uncompleted article. The clock told me that a messenger would ere long be clamoring at my own door for copy; and, biting hard upon my pipe, I concentrated on the task that must be finished by eleven o'clock though the heavens fell.

Surely enough, I had yet a hundred words or so to write when my bell rang. The sequence of my argument running in my head to a kind of rhythm, I stood up, walked to the outer door, opened it.

"Wait in the lobby," I said, turned, and walked back.

Three minutes of feverish scribbling brought my work to a close. I pinned the sheets together and went out to hand them to the messenger. At the door of the room, I pulled up short.

Seated in the lobby chair was my friend, Paul Harley.

"Well, Knox," he said, looking up at me with his quizzical smile, "I have waited."

"Harley!" I cried. "Was it you I opened to?"

"Careless of you, Knox," he returned, shaking his head. "Slipshod—not worthy of the merest boob. Just think, I might have been the Prince of Wales, or, on the other hand, I might have been the most bloodthirsty ruffian in Europe. Yet, without a glance, you mutter: 'Wait in the lobby'—involving, in the first case, royal displeasure; in the second, certainly, robbery, possibly murder."

"My dear fellow," I said, laughing, "excuse my preoccupation. I was expecting a boy from—ah, here he is!"

The bell rang and I opened the door to find the messenger from the newspaper. I handed him the copy, which he placed in his satchel and departed.

Then, turning, "That's that!" I exclaimed. "What do you say to a whisky and soda, Harley? You look overtired."

"Overtired!" he echoed. "I am dead beat, Knox."

We entered the study and Paul Harley dropped wearily into the armchair beside my writing table. Pallor it were impossible to detect because of his bronzed skin, but I thought that some of the old, eager vitality was lacking tonight, and I wondered upon what obscure problem of the underworld he was expending his dynamic energy. The grayness at his temples was becoming increasingly noticeable; but, for all his present weariness, I knew that Paul Harley of Chancery Lane yet retained his unique position—that of the man in whom Home Office and Foreign Office reposed their entire confidence.

Crossing to a little side table, I poured out a stiff peg. My hand on the lever of the siphon, I turned. "Say when," I invited.

Harley did not reply. He had not heard me. Instead, he held the amber-colored envelope left by the district messenger immediately under his nose, and he was smelling vigorously.

"Harley," I said, "what are—you doing?"

He lowered the envelope and glanced up at me from under his heavy brows. His face was transfigured. Languor was gone. He was revivified. "Smelling," he answered. "Knox"—he stood up—"have you smelled this letter?"

"Certainly not! Why should I?"

"But you should," he assured me, and extended the amber envelope. "Oblige me, Knox, by doing so."

I took the letter and sniffled suspiciously. I suspected some trick. However, I discovered it to be delicately perfumed. I stared uncomprehendingly at my friend. "Evidently," I said, "my neighbor is a man of gallantry."

"I am not interested in the state of Mr. Michael Hebron's heart," replied Harley. "I am merely interested in the quality of the perfume. Is it familiar to you?"

"Not at all. But perfumes are outside my province, Harley."

"Possibly. But you would recognize attar of roses, and the many floral bouquets also, no doubt—the preparations of the popular French firms?"

"You flatter me. I doubt it. But what is the point?"

"The point is that this envelope is perfumed with none of these."

"Indeed. What, then?"

"Just this, Knox." Harley laid the letter on my blotting pad and pointed his finger at me forensically. "There is an aristocracy of perfumes, as there is an aristocracy of wines and cigars. In prewar days, if you had told me that you had tasted a particular wine of a particular vintage, I could have informed you with which of the grand dukes you had dined. Certain rare and choice brands of cigars in the same way were peculiar to certain ducal houses. This perfume"—he lowered the pointed finger and rested it upon the amber envelope—"is used by only one connoisseur, to my knowledge, in Europe!"

"But, Harley—can you be sure of this?"

"Humanly, yes. In your own experience, Knox, you have seen how a peculiar blend of tobacco can afford a clue to a wanted man. I have studied tobacco exhaustively. Is it not evident that perfume plays the same part where a woman is concerned? In these commercial days, I know of only three perfumes that cannot be obtained in the public market. This"—he pressed his hand upon the letter—"happens to be one of them!"

"Meaning?" said I.

"Meaning that Fate guided my steps to your door, Knox!"—he rested his hand on my shoulder—"I have been at work in Chinatown for days and nights looking for the clue that lies here on your table!"

"In Chinatown!" I exclaimed. "But what on earth can this letter to Mr. Michael Hebron have to do with Chinatown?"

"That, we have to learn," replied Harley. He removed his topcoat and laid it, with his hat, upon a chair. "About half and half, Knox"—nodding in the direction of the siphon. "I need a stimulant."

Abstractedly, for the tenor of all this passed my comprehension, I prepared two drinks, setting one before my friend, who was now seated at the table, studying my neighbor's letter intently.

"What do you know about this man, Hebron?" he asked abruptly, holding the envelope against the shade of the lamp.

"Nothing," I replied, dropping into the armchair vacated by Harley. "He has lived in the top set for a month or more. I have never seen him, and I don't know his business."

"Then how do you come to be in possession of his private correspondence?"

I briefly explained, filling my pipe the while.

"Good," muttered Harley. "It is Kismet. If I may borrow your tobacco jar, Knox, I will fill my own pipe. While I am so engaged, perhaps you will be good enough to put a kettle on and to bring me a loaf—a new loaf, if you have one."

"Put a kettle on and bring you a loaf!" I said incredulously. "My dear fellow, if you have had no dinner, I can manage something better than skilly!"

"Thanks, Knox," he replied, studying the back of the envelope. "But it is food for the mind that I am seeking at the moment. A very complicated seal," he muttered. "But we must do our best."

"Harley!" I said sharply, standing up, "some part of your design begins to dawn upon me. For what purpose you require a loaf, I cannot imagine; but am I to understand that you calmly propose to steam open a letter left in my care?"

He turned about, facing me. His clean-shaven face wore its grimmest expression.

"Knox," said he, meeting my half angry, half incredulous stare, "did you ever know me to stoop to a dirty trick?"

"Never," I returned without hesitation.

"Very well. This"—he indicated the amber-colored envelope—"is no love letter. It is sealed, as you can see, but the seal is one I have never met with before. It is also scented—and the scent tells me that it comes from the most dangerous woman in London—in Europe—perhaps in the world. Your neighbor, Michael Hebron, if not an accomplice of this woman, is one of her victims. Therefore, we are going either to prove his guilt or to save him—"

"But, Harley—" I interrupted.

"The woman, or she and her associates," he resumed evenly, "have literally sent thousands to their death. Apart from several assassinations traceable to her personal beauty, she has been instrumental in emptying at least one throne, and her activities during the World War cost England as many lives as the Gallipoli campaign!"

"Good God, Harley! You appall me!"

"Her presence in London now means that some menace threatens the very basis of the British Empire. The Foreign Office has moved Heaven and Earth to trace her movements. I have been given *carte blanche,* and for weeks past, while you thought me to be out of town, I have actually been at work, night and day, seeking some clue upon which it might be possible to act."

"Harley, who is she? What is her nationality?"

"She is famous in four capitals as Madame de Medici. Who she is, I have yet to learn. Her nationality I suspect, but I am not certain of it. If you have any lingering doubts, Knox, respecting the propriety of my projects—"

"I have none, Harley," I said, aghast at these revelations.

"Then perhaps you will put a kettle on and bring me a loaf."

"Very well."

"And—oh, Knox, at the same time get a poker, red hot, if possible! A clean poker."

"Unpleasantly complicated," muttered Harley as I presently returned, carrying a loaf of bread.

He was seated at the table, studying the envelope, which lay face downward on the blotting pad. As I entered, he reversed it and stared at the large, bold, feminine writing of the inscription. He glanced up at me.

"Have you ever seen writing like this before?" he asked.

"No. It is curiously characteristic."

"Characteristic, yes; but of what?"

"Well"—I studied it with interest—"the writer is certainly not English. She might be French. The figure seven, for instance, is crossed."

"Quite so. But this form is common to quite a number of Continental countries. The outstanding peculiarity, Knox, is the uniform thickness of the plane and the erect strokes."

"Yes," I agreed, "it is curious. She must use a very broad nib."

"Probably a quill," murmured Harley.

He pulled the top off the loaf and extracted a piece of doughy bread, which he proceeded to roll into a large, smooth pellet.

"Once we start," he said, "speed is of the essence of success. Would you mind making one or two of these bread bullets, Knox? Press them firmly, so as to get a smooth surface."

Feeling unusually like a queer sort of lunatic, I obliged my friend, recognizing that this apparent farce had some stern but hidden purpose. When four pellets were completed to Harley's satisfaction, he set them in a row on the blotting pad and gazed meditatively at a number of briar pipes resting in a bowl near his elbow.

"Yes," said he, "these will serve." He proceeded to fit bread balls into the bowls of four pipes. He then pressed each one firmly on the pad to flatten the bulge.

"Good," said he, looking up at me with a smile. "Our experiment proper now begins. The process you are about to see in operation would be of great interest to a dishonest butler, for instance. Fortunately, it calls for a delicacy of touch rarely found among the domestic classes."

Once more he placed the amber-colored envelope face downward on the pad.

"A critical test, Knox!" he said. "A very complex seal, evidently ancient Egyptian, and probably a unique scarab."

The letter was sealed with curious, golden-looking wax, several shades darker than the paper; this was the device impressed upon it:

Harley took up the first pipe, lightly touched the bread surface with his tongue, and then, inverting the bowl, firmly pressed it down upon the seal. He glanced at it, laid it aside, and went through the same routine with the other three.

"Now!" said he.

Something of his repressed excitement had communicated itself to me. With bated breath, I watched him break away the golden wax with a sharp blade from below the lapel of the envelope, leaving intact that actually adhering to the tongue of paper. Every fragment, he carefully transferred to a little copper ash tray. Through a powerful glass that he drew from his pocket, he studied the result of his labors and seemed to be satisfied. Out to where a tin kettle boiling on a gas stove jetted forth steam we went. A small steel poker was wedged between the bottom of the kettle and the bars of the stove.

Very adroitly, Paul Harley steamed open the envelope, I stood at his elbow, watching eagerly as he inserted two fingers and drew out a slip of white pasteboard, of about the size of a *carte de visite.* There was nothing else in the envelope.

But if I was surprised and excited, a quick glance at my friend's face told me that this discovery was one of paramount importance.

"My God, Knox!" he said sharply. "Do you see?"

"I see," I replied, "but I don't understand."

And, in order that I be not hastily accused of stupidity, I reproduce here the figure and writing which appeared on the card.

"Of course," muttered Harley, staring at the card back and front through his pocket lens. "I forget that you know nothing of this business. Well—we have no time to waste. Memorize all details, Knox, for I am about to complete our experiment."

He returned the card to the envelope, stuck down the gum, which remained moist from the action of the steam. "Bring the poker!" he directed.

A strange spectacle, had there been any to witness it, we returned to the study, I carrying the fiery poker.

"Hold it firmly here," said Harley rapidly. "Rest it against the inkstand."

He tipped the fragments of golden wax on to the broken seal, arranging them with a delicate forefinger. This accomplished, he moved the envelope gently to and fro beneath the red-hot point of the poker until the entire seal became fluid. With the wetted end of a penholder, he made the whole fairly even. Then, laying the envelope down, he took up a briar containing one of the bread molds, touched its surface with his tongue and glanced sharply aside at me, smiling grimly. "To be or not to be?" he muttered.

Firmly, he pressed the mold down upon the wax, swiftly raised it: "How's that?" he cried triumphantly.

Magically, the golden seal was intact again! True, the imprint was not so sharp as that made by the scarab, but the sharpness of such impressions varies greatly, and it must have called for a keen eye to detect any irregularity in the complex figure of the snake-wrapped beetle.

"Right the first time, Knox!" said Harley. "I might have spared you the task of making additional bread bullets! However, prudence is a virtue."

He studied the spurious seal through his lens. "Yes," he murmured. "Traces of bread crumb! Unavoidable, of course. A few minutes more and our molds would have become useless—too dry."

He relighted his pipe and sat down in the armchair. Having placed the hot poker in the fender, I extracted bread from one of my own briars and began reflectively to fill the bowl. I could hear the clock of St. Paul's striking midnight. Harley's face had grown masklike, expressionless. His eyes were closed; he began to speak: "You noted the time mentioned, Knox?"

"Two o'clock. It has just struck twelve."

"Yes. I have two hours in which to do—what?"

"I cannot imagine."

"Perhaps to save the world from some new disaster! Good God! It is an awful responsibility! You noted the figure on the card?"

"Of course. It resembled that of a priest in cassock and biretta."

"Think again. I urged you to memorize details."

"I am thinking, Harley."

"Did you ever see a biretta with a feather in it?"

"Ah, good heavens! Of course, something resembling a feather was shown!"

"Did you ever see a mandarin?"

"A mandarin!" I cried excitedly. "That's it, Harley! It was the figure of a mandarin!"

"Undoubtedly. The Black Mandarin."

"The Black Mandarin?" I echoed. "Who is the Black Mandarin?"

But Harley, instead of answering my question, asked another: "Are you following the extraordinary events now taking place in China?"

"Through the medium of the press, yes," I said.

"Have you formed any definite opinion?"

"Well—" I hesitated, "the country is in a very disturbed state."

"Very!" said Harley, suddenly opening his eyes and snapping out the word with almost vicious emphasis. "Hasn't the fact dawned upon you, Knox, that China is in the throes of a new disruption? China is now an integral factor in international politics; all the great nations are mixed up in her affairs—that, indeed, is the root cause of the whole trouble—and the new movement seeks to bring about a reversion to that exclusiveness which formerly was China's greatest strength. The Chinese still believe that the yellow race can dominate the world, and the Oriental mind spells out the means in a manner altogether opposite to Western ideas. A man whose name has never appeared in the press, whose name is unknown even to some of the highest officials in Peking, is the brain at present moving the tentacles of the Yellow Octopus."

"And who is this man?" I asked with rising excitement.

"He is the Black Mandarin."

"But what is his name?"

"A poser, Knox!" said Harley, standing up. "The Secret Services of four nations have been at work all over the East, as well as the West, for years trying to find an answer to that question! He is constantly traveling from capital to capital, undermining the social order of things, destroying the best intellects, and so joining up the delicate threads of a giant cord designed to strangle half the world!"

"But this is unspeakably horrible!"

"The dangerous Madame de Medici is the London representative of the Black Mandarin. We know now that the man, Hebron, is also involved in this business. In two hours or less, he will be—where? Presumably, at the house of Madame."

"Do you know this house?" I asked.

"Quite well."

"And what do you propose to do?"

"First, Knox," replied Harley, "I propose to ask you to step upstairs and to inform Mr. Michael Hebron, if he is at home, that you have a letter for him. I am extraordinarily anxious to hear Mr. Hebron's voice, but equally anxious to avoid being either seen or heard by him."

"It's no good, Harley," I reported. "There isn't a sound from his chambers."

Paul Harley paced uneasily up and down the study.

"Mischief!" he muttered—"mischief somewhere. Associates of Madame de Medici are not so forgetful, Knox; and the fact that so many clever men have drawn blanks for years in all attempts to start up the Black Mandarin would point to the fact that those who know him are also scrupulously careful. Therefore—why is Mr. Michael Hebron not at home?"

"He may not have anticipated such a summons," I suggested.

"What time was it delivered?"

"Shortly before eleven."

"In only giving him three hours' notice, Madame clearly assumed that he would be at home. He was certainly expecting such a summons, Knox, What time is that striking now?"

"A quarter to one."

Harley continued his restless promenade. "Believe me, Knox, the organization surrounding the Black Mandarin works faultlessly. Nothing is left to chance. We may dismiss the idea that this man's absence is due to carelessness either on his own part or on that of Madame de Medici."

"He may yet return in time."

"He will have to hurry. There is barely time now. I will use your telephone, if you don't mind, Knox."

Harley took up the instrument. "East two hundred," he called. Following a short interval, which he suffered with impatience, "Hullo, yes," he said. "Paul Harley speaking. Has Inspector Wessex returned? . . . Ah! Very well. I should be obliged if you would send a messenger to him at once. A close watch should be kept on the house. Anyone leaving must be followed at all costs. Ask the inspector to keep in touch with you, as I shall be returning not later than two o'clock and will advise you where I will meet him. Meanwhile, as I am working against time, would you phone the Yard for a raid squad to start for Limehouse now, and have them send a fast car to wait outside my office, at once? Thanks. Goodbye."

As he replaced the receiver, I heard the clock of St. Paul's strike one.

"Now, for action!" said he, and smiled grimly. "We will give the invisible Mr. Hebron one more chance. Do you happen to know his phone number?"

"No," I shook my head. "But, hold on! Martindale Smith leased those chambers for several years and only gave them up two months ago, when he married. The number will be under his name."

I snatched up the directory, skimmed down the long columns of Smiths, and presently discovered: "Smith, J. Martindale, K.C. . . . Central 24621."

"Good!" said Harley. "Give him a ring."

I obeyed, and found myself being consumed with impatience, doubtless communicated to me by Harley, However, the exchange reported, "No reply," and I hung up the receiver and turned to my friend, whose behavior now resembled that of a caged animal.

"Expected it!" he snapped. "Excuse me, Knox, but I should like to look out of your bedroom window."

"What!"

"Can I obtain a view of any window above from there?"

"Oh, I see! Yes, the bathroom."

"Excellent!"

He hurried from the room. He vibrated nervous enthusiasm and I caught the infection. I divined that this was to be one of those "Baghdad nights"—a term of Harley's—such as I had experienced in his company before. Yet, had I known what the night indeed held in store for me, I wonder if my enthusiasm would have cooled?

Harley came back almost immediately. "Have you a pair of tennis shoes?" he asked.

"I have."

"Please get them for me."

"What are you going to do?"

"I am going to climb up the water spout and into Mr. Hebron's bathroom!"

"Good heavens! But suppose he returns and finds you in his chambers?"

"If he returns, Knox, you will intercept him to give him his letter."

"But how shall I communicate with you?"

"Find a long piece of string, or tie several short pieces together, and I will show you."

He spoke in the rapid, incisive manner of one whose course is clear, but whose time is limited. While he took off his boots and put on the tennis shoes, I hunted out a ball of twine. Just as Harley threw widely open the bedroom window, city clocks were chiming the first quarter. He secured the end of the twine to a buttonhole and climbed out upon the ledge. I saw that, by the aid of the rain pipe, it was no difficult matter to reach the ledge of the bathroom above, and I saw also that the window was half open.

"The moment I am in," he said rapidly, "I shall tie the string to anything handy and suitable and set it somewhere where its fall would make a loud noise. Then you will go out and wait on the landing for the possible return of our man. If he comes, ask him in while you get his letter. Come back to the bedroom and haul on the string until you hear the crash. Give me a couple of minutes after that."

With which he stretched his foot to a joint in the pipe, secured a firm hold upon it, and was very soon perched on the ledge ten feet above. He pulled the window right down and dived recklessly in. The string remained stationary for a while and then ran out another three feet.

I hurried out to my front door, opened it and listened. No sound reached me from above or below; but, almost immediately, this silence was interrupted in an unforeseen way. I heard Michael Hebron's door burst open.

"Knox! Knox!" came a frenzied whisper. "Up! Quickly!"

Utterly at a loss to account for this change of plan, I nevertheless ran upstairs without delay. Paul Harley was standing in the open doorway, a look of absolute horror on his face.

"Knox," he said, grasping my arm, "prepare for a ghastly spectacle!"

He turned and, as I entered, closed the door.

"The first part of our problem is solved," continued Harley. "We know why Michael Hebron did not answer the telephone; and we might have spared ourselves the trouble of duplicating the seal."

I followed him to a room corresponding to that which I used as my study. It was oddly appointed, containing a quantity of Oriental ornaments. The window was closed and the stale air of the place retained a sickly perfume, as if joss sticks had recently been burned in the room. Indeed, I had noted this queer smell at the moment that I entered the chambers. But that which blotted out at the time every other impression, and which brought me up with a cry at the threshold, was the figure of a tall, gaunt man lying stretched upon the carpet!

"Good God!" I said. "What does this mean?"

"It means murder!" returned Harley. "He is dead."

"Why," I muttered, "the carpet is wet with blood!"

I stared down at the contorted face. The man wore a light tweed suit, the front of which was hideously smeared with blood. But the expression upon that agonized face was dreadful. Normally, I thought, it had been a strong, harsh face, the skin rather yellow and wrinkled, the brow high and bony, the gray hair fine and scanty; a face perhaps not without nobility. The hands were clenched. A pistol of unfamiliar pattern lay half under a table near the body.

"Why not suicide?" I asked, pointing to the weapon.

"Because he was not shot; he was strangled!" rapped Harley.

"Strangled! But the blood—"

Paul Harley grasped my arm again. "Come into the next room," he said, "and you will understand."

Dazed, horrified, I followed him to a room that had the appearance of a business office. There was a trail of blood across the threshold.

"Harley!" I whispered, and grew sick. "This place is a charnel house!" A dead man was seated at the desk!

He wore dress clothes. His arms were stretched out across the desk and his head rested sidewise upon an open telephone directory, so that, as we entered, he seemed to be looking up at us, slyly. His left hand almost touched the telephone upon the desk.

For several moments, Harley and I stood looking into that horrible room in silence.

"Which of them is Hebron?" I said hoarsely.

"The other," Harley answered; "the Chinaman—"

"Chinaman! You think the man out there is a Chinaman?"

"I know he is. I knew it after the first glance."

"But," said I, gingerly bending over the dead man at the desk, "this was a very swarthy fellow too, and yellow-skinned—"

"Yes," rapped Harley irritably. "Don't touch him, Knox. We must disturb nothing."

"We must inform the police."

"On the contrary, we must avoid doing so."

"What!"

Paul Harley came nearer to the terrible figure.

"Perhaps a coincidence," he said. "But the directory is open at the page upon which *my* name and number appear! See?"

"Good heavens!" I was unconsciously speaking in a sort of church whisper. "You are right! But what hell's business took place here tonight? If that pistol was fired—"

"It was fired very recently, Knox. This poor devil is shot through the left lung."

"I have been at work all the evening. I could not have failed to hear—"

"The pistol—a Colt automatic—is fitted with a silencing tube, an invention presumably designed in the interests of criminals! Let me think! Let me think! Here, in these chambers, Knox, lies the clue to a mystery that has puzzled some of the best brains of Europe and America! I feel that every moment wasted here may mean a thousand lives in the near future!"

"But, Harley! This ghastly crime calls for—"

"A mere piece of side play!" he cried irritably. "Oh! Don't think me callous; but the murder of this man, Hebron, is no more than—"

He paused. His expression changed. Turning, he ran out into the lobby, and I followed. A dark overcoat and a crush hat lay upon a chair. Beside the chair, a small attaché case was standing.

"Search the pockets of the overcoat!" he cried.

Stooping, he opened the brown leather case, took out a queer-looking black garment, and uttered an exclamation of astonishment. It was a long cowl, such as those seen in pictures of the Spanish Inquisition, having eyeholes, but otherwise made to cover the wearer from head to ankles!

"Nothing else!" he said, peering into the case. "Anything in the coat?"

"Yes," I replied dazedly. "This!"

It seemed that I moved in a land of nightmares. The finding of the black cowl was sufficiently astounding, but what I had extracted from the breast pocket of the overcoat for some reason or another astonished me even more greatly. This was an amber-colored envelope, addressed in the odd, square writing which I knew to be that of the woman called Madame de Medici, and sealed with the scarab seal! The seal was broken, for the envelope had been opened.

Harley snatched it eagerly.

"'Mr. W. Julian,'" he read, "'17 Vale Court, Maida Vale.' We know the name of another of them now!"

"The man who lies dead at the writing desk?"

"No doubt. Make sure of the contents, Knox."

He returned the envelope to me and ran off. Mechanically, I opened it, withdrawing a card identical with that found in the other envelope. Then, his eyes feverishly bright, Harley came running back, carrying over his arm another of the black cowls!

"Do you understand, Knox?" he cried. "The man Julian evidently came here on his way to call for Hebron. They quarreled—"

He stopped speaking. A clock somewhere near was chiming the half hour.

"Thirty minutes to reach the house of Madame de Medici!" he said.

II
The House of Zani Chada

St. Paul's was left behind and we were racing through deserted city streets that, during the day, were all but impassable. The Daimler, which had been drawn up outside Harley's office in accordance with his instructions, devoured miles of East End thoroughfares with gluttonous speed. For the first five minutes or so of our cold, midnight journey, my friend remained silent, and, divining that he was endeavoring to perfect his plan of campaign, I did not disturb him.

"The fact that material for which a dozen men have been scouring the world should have fallen into our hands like this," he said presently, "almost overwhelms me!"

"The long arm of coincidence in operation."

"Coincidence, Knox? Where is the coincidence? That the man known as Michael Hebron should die by the hand of another member of the group tonight is trick of Fate, certainly; but you don't suppose his selection of those quarters above yours was a coincidence?"

"I had counted it one."

"You were wrong. Our association is sufficiently well known, Knox, in such circles to explain it. He chose the set above you in order to spy on me. You wondered, quite naturally, why I made no investigation of the crime committed there tonight. Let me explain. This international quest for the Black Mandarin, for which my own efforts have only been requisitioned in the last two months, has already become with me, as with others before me, a positive obsession. I regard this man's existence as a menace to the peace of the world, although I am by no means confident that his removal would eradicate the evil. Another, no doubt, would assume control of the secret machine.

"But, think of it, Knox—the keenest men of our own, as well as agents of other powers, have focused on this thing for years. The United States is keenly interested, of course. The trail of the Black Mandarin has been laid from coast to coast, and a wave of crime, varying in character almost from day to day, has swept over that country. The most brilliant man that ever came out of Washington, Raymond McCabe, practically broke himself on the problem. He failed utterly to establish the identity of the Black Mandarin, who recently disappeared from the States as mysteriously as he had arrived. That he existed and assuredly controlled powerful diverse groups of criminals and others whose schemes were inimical to American interests is proved without the shadow of a doubt. But, beyond that, neither McCabe nor anybody else could penetrate a yard."

"This society, if it is a society, must be a wonderful organization."

"Undoubtedly, it is. McCabe came into touch with it time and time again, but always with the same negative result, until finally, either in despair or fear, he abandoned the task and retired from the service altogether. But, before he retired, he secured one very tangible clue, which the events of tonight have made specially significant. It came into his possession during a row between rival tongs in 'Frisco, but, unfortunately, several hours too late for it to be of any service. It may have influenced McCabe's decision to retire from the obviously unequal contest."

"And what was this clue, Harley?"

"A card with the figure of a mandarin, in silhouette, upon it, and a time and date written underneath!"

"The same—"

"Exactly, Knox. Imagine my feelings, therefore, when I found an exactly similar card tonight! I had already devoted considerable attention to the mysterious Madame de Medici, who had crossed my path on several occasions in the past and whom I know to have some sort of relations with China. Here came proof positive that she was an agent of the Black Mandarin!"

"Surely, her method of communicating with her fellow conspirators is a careless one?"

"What! A district messenger? My dear fellow, excluding such unlikely possibilities as that which came to pass tonight, no method could be safer! You must know that I employ them regularly in most delicate affairs. No, I continue to regard Madame as above reproach."

"And what are your plans for tonight?" I asked.

We were racing along Commercial Road East, as a glance from the window showed me. In contrast to the daytime activity of this thoroughfare, its present air of desolation was extraordinary. It offered a vista of shuttered shops and blind windows that brought home to me the strangeness of our journey. This, indeed, was a "Baghdad night," and our business was with dangerous, nocturnal creatures.

"Up to a point," Harley replied, "my plans are simple enough. From that point onward—I have no plans!"

"But, explain," I urged, "You have brought the cowls—"

"And I have brought the cards!"

"Am I to suppose that you intend to penetrate to the meeting which, I assume, has been called for tonight at the house of this woman?"

He turned to me, smiling. "You think it madness, Knox?" he said. "But consider the facts. The first is clear as daylight; the members of this organization are known, naturally, to their chief, but not to one another!"

"Why do you think so?"

"Think so! It is evident! Julian and Hebron obviously shared confidences, but if the remaining members were acquainted one with another, why the cowls?"

"Good heavens! Of course! Unless—"

"Well?" he rapped impatiently.

"Unless the gathering were convened to meet some nonmember—"

"A prisoner! A trial!" He cried out the words excitedly; but the next moment, he was shaking his head.

"No, Knox, it won't do. The cowls are as old as the history of secret societies. The practical utility of the device is obvious. But neither Madame de Medici nor her formidable superior could descend to anything so dramatically unnecessary as the trial of a captured enemy." He stared at me significantly. "There would be no trial, Knox!"

I was silent for a moment. "Your first point granted," said I, "you hope to obtain access by impersonating the dead man, Hebron?"

"Exactly."

"But why take the risk? Wessex is here, with a party from New Scotland Yard. Why not simply raid the place?"

"For two reasons," he replied. "First: we have not one scrap of evidence to justify a raid. Second: I could learn more by being present at that meeting than we should ever learn by interrogating prisoners—assuming we could find an excuse for making any!"

"I see. But the second cowl? The absence of Julian might lead to dangerous inquiries."

"Wessex shall be Julian!"

"Wessex shall not!" I said hotly. "You owe this night's business to me, Harley, and this being so—I see it through with you."

"But, my dear fellow—" he began.

"Have I failed you so lamentably on other occasions that you have come to distrust me? Besides, I know some thing of the East; Wessex knows nothing."

Harley brought his hand down heavily on my knee.

"Forgive me, old man," he said. "No thought of distrust was in my mind, and you know it. I simply regarded Wessex as the proper, official person to accompany me. But I admit, now, that you are likely to be of greater service, and if the risk, which I don't disguise, appeals to you—say no more."

"Good enough," I replied. "It's settled. But right at the outset, I see big difficulties. We know absolutely nothing of the methods of procedure usual at these meetings. They may partake of the character of Masonic rites."

"We chance it," said Harley grimly, as the chauffeur turned the car and drew up before Limehouse Police Station. "We have exactly five minutes."

Inspector Wessex, whom I knew well, came hurrying out to meet us.

"I began to wonder if you were coming, Mr. Harley," he cried. "There is something afoot tonight beyond a doubt, but it isn't at the house of Zani Chada—"

"Then where is it?"

"At Kwee's, behind Ropemaker's Fields."

"How far is Kwee's from the house of Zani Chada—and who is Kwee?"

"It nearly backs on to it. Kwee is employed in a dry-goods store in Pennyfields, but we've been watching him lately. Six or seven men, not natives of the district, have gone in there tonight. That is to say, six have been definitely reported by the chaps watching the house."

"How do they arrive—singly? In parties?"

"Singly."

"What sort of men?"

"They all appear to be respectable; in fact, some of them might pass for gentlemen. Several have carried hand bags."

"There you are, Knox!" said Harley excitedly; then, to Wessex: "Have you been able to see who admitted them?"

"No. It wouldn't be possible without attracting attention."

"And no one has gone to the house occupied by Madame de Medici?"

"No one. It is all in darkness."

"Get in, Wessex," rapped Harley, who had conducted this conversation through the open window of the car. "We have less than two minutes! Tell the man to stop at the top end of Three Colt Street, by the church."

These instructions were given, and Inspector Wessex, looking very puzzled, joined us in the car, which immediately started.

"You see," continued Harley, "by a pure accident—a murder, to be exact—"

"A murder?" cried Wessex.

"Yes. But I haven't time to explain," said Harley dryly. "By virtue of this accident, I have obtained the means of penetrating the meeting which is taking place tonight. Mr. Knox is coming with me. The raid squad is posted near the house of Chada?"

"No. They are standing by at the station."

"Get them nearer the moment we have gone in. A pistol shot will be the signal. Ha! Here we are!"

"I take it," said Wessex, as Harley jumped out at the corner of the gloomy, deserted street, "that you have got a strong line on Madame de Medici at last?"

"A very strong line," was the reply. "Wessex!"—he grasped the Scotland Yard man by the arm—"she is the link with the Black Mandarin!"

"Great Scott!" cried Wessex. "For God's sake, be careful, Mr. Harley!"

"You may rely upon it! Bring the attaché case, Knox. Now, Wessex, direct me, and then get back to bring up the others."

"Take the third turning on the left. There is one lamp in it. Well, just past the lamp is a narrow courtway. At the end is a door. That's Kwee's."

A keen breeze from the north was blowing as the Daimler moved off into West India Dock Road, and a church clock—St. Dunstan's, I thought—was chiming the hour of two. There are some people, I doubt not, whom the night aspect of Chinatown would chill with apprehension, but, for me, ordinarily it held no terrors, this jungle of bricks and mortar lying to right and left. The greater part of London's Asiatic colony is harmless enough, and those members who are noxious lurk deep in secret burrows to which the stranger must penetrate if he would toy with the darker side of Eastern life.

Angry clouds drifted across the moon, and there was a wintry bite in the air. The artery of Dockland, as I took is parting glance along it, was by no means deserted, despite the lateness of the hour. Several big steamers were on the point of sailing, and I observed a party of lascars heading for the dock gates. A string of lorries, too, drawn by a puffing traction engine, came rattling along the unevenly paved roadway, leaving a trail of sparks behind, both above and below. There was something cheery in the red glow from the little furnace reflected upon the faces of the two men in the cab.

Fitfully, a pale moon shone upon mean houses, shuttered, dark, seemingly uninhabited. I knew something of the nightlife of this quarter, yet it was no easy matter mentally to people these silent shells of buildings with wakeful Asiatics. Within a hundred yards of me, there were those who gambled, who smoked opium, who waxed riotous on spirits sold on unlicenced premises. Yet, Chinatown seemed to be asleep. In a lull of the wind, sounds reached me from the docks as we set out toward the house of Kwee, metallic sounds, the clangor of engines, the hooting of some tug coming out of the Pool, but from the Causeway area came no voice, no light.

The wind howled, elfin, overhead; a few flying drops of rain touched me and the moon disappeared for good behind a bank of storm cloud.

"Whoever is watching, the place is wonderfully well hidden," said I, perhaps not without apprehension, as we turned into Rope-maker's Fields.

"It is their business to be," Harley rejoined. "I should have liked to change my appearance, Knox, had time allowed. I am wondering why visitors go to this house and not to Chada's."

"Who is Chada?"

"The owner of the establishment at present occupied by Madame de Medici. He got into trouble with the police not too long ago, in connection with the death of a man named Peters—a member of that unpleasant but useful profession, 'copper's narks.' Chada is a wealthy Eurasian, and is now missing. Here is the lamp—here is the court, Knox—and there's the door!"

We looked along the alley beyond the street lamp, narrow, dark and uninviting.

"Why the precaution of the cowls if we have to show ourselves to the doorkeeper?" murmured Harley.

"Perhaps we are supposed to put them on here, before knocking?"

"Ah, quite possibly. Even at the cost of being considered eccentric, let us do so!"

Thereupon, opening the leather case that had belonged to the man Julian, we drew out the two hideous disguises. Both Harley and I wore soft hats, and these we easily crushed into the case.

When, a moment later, in the dimly lighted passage, I surveyed my companion, I could scarcely repress a start of nervous revulsion. Although I knew it to be Paul Harley, this sinister, black figure, whose eyes gleamed at me evilly through the slits of the cowl, was one to chill the most intrepid heart.

"Horrible!" he said, surveying me with a distaste I doubt not as keen as my own. "I fear I shall never thoroughly like you again, Knox!"

It was so characteristic of the man, this light jesting in perilous hours, that the uncomfortable pessimism that had threatened to conquer me fled as by magic. We were about to enter a den abandoned to the uses of those who acted against states and to whom human lives were no more sacred than the blades of grass one crushes underfoot. Perhaps memories of that ghastly shambles in the chambers above my own had been haunting me, but now, reflecting how hotly I had volunteered, and recalling the fact that a raid squad from Scotland Yard would ere long be surrounding the place, I found a new outlook.

Harley approached the door, which boasted two dirty stone steps.

"Have your ticket ready!" he murmured softly, and, raising his hand, he beat one stroke on the knocker.

A curious fact immediately became apparent. The knocker was muffled.

"Ah," he breathed. "What now?"

For the result, I think, neither of us was prepared. A faint sound from above drew my glance upward. And there, descending upon a length of twine, was a little Chinese basket of split cane! Of the one, concealed in some upper room, who lowered it, no glimpse could be obtained.

I grasped Harley's arm, pointing, and we watched the basket descend until it swung gently to and fro in the sheltered alley, about shoulder high. Harley grasped it and looked quickly inside. But the basket was empty.

For my part, I doubt if the meaning of the thing would ever have dawned upon me. But my friend, muttering something under his breath, produced the card bearing the mandarin figure and dropped it in the basket!

At the same time, he plucked at the sleeve of my cowl urgently, and, realizing what was expected of me, I deposited the second card beside the first. As I did so, Harley twitched the string—and the basket was immediately drawn up. I bent to Harley's ear.

"What was it you said?" I whispered.

"I said: 'A device used by the Hip Sing Tong,'" he replied in an undertone. "The door will be opened mechanically, I expect."

His expectation was realized. Faintly was borne to my ears, as if from a subterranean cavern, the booming of a distant gong. Following a short interval, during which I listened for a repetition of the mysterious sound, but heard only that of the wind howling along the Thames reaches and of the muted bombilation of the quarter, there came a sort of rusty creaking, as of some heavy weight being raised. This ceased, but was followed by a metallic click. The door swung open, revealing a pitch-black interior.

I hesitated, whereupon Harley seized my arm and I found myself in the stuffy darkness of the room beyond.

Scarcely had we crossed the threshold when the door reclosed, almost silently, as it had opened. The rusty creaking was renewed while we stood there wondering what to do. It ceased—and an electric lamp became lighted immediately above us.

I was feeling very far from comfortable, and my first impulse was to glance at the door. I learned that, although from outside it had the aspect of a very ordinary, common kind of door, inside it presented a totally different appearance. In the first place, it was extraordinarily thick and heavy, and, in the second, a sort of iron frame, working in metal grooves, had been lowered on chains from above, thus forming a second or inner door.

The room in which I found myself resembled many others I had seen in Chinese houses, except for the presence of the electric lamp and the portcullis. That is to say, it was scantily and tawdrily furnished. An advertisement for somebody's cigarettes ornamented the mantel, and the furniture was mere lumber. The only truly Oriental thing I could see was one of those plaited flasks with bright silken tassels, which hung from a common wooden bracket on which rested a figured mug bearing the legend: "A present, from Southend."

On a table by one wall, I noticed quite a number of small handbags and attaché cases, and, accordingly, I placed there the one that I held in my hand. Nothing further happened, and the room was very silent. There was no window opening on the court, and, staring at the iron-barred door, it became terrifyingly plain that, simple though we might have found it to get into the house of Kwee, to get out, failing the aid of the unseen gatekeeper, was frankly impossible.

Harley, an unrecognizable figure in his unpleasant disguise, was staring about him eagerly. Suddenly, he stood still, jerking his head in the direction of a rough curtain that I took to conceal some opening. A gong hung beside the curtain, the wooden striker attached to it by a loop of cord.

"This is the dressing room, Knox," Harley whispered. "We announce ourselves as soon as we are ready!"

"Do you think so?" I murmured nervously.

"For what other purpose is the gong placed there? At any rate, I am going to risk it!"

Stepping forward, he took up gong and hammer and struck a loud, harsh note, sounding very sharp and staccato in the small room. In the ensuing silence, we both stood, listening intently. Then, from somewhere beyond—from a long way off, it seemed—the signal was answered.

A deep, lingering gong note, amphoric and reverberant, came back to us.

At the same moment, with some slight rattling of the brass rings, the curtain was drawn aside, and I found myself staring down stone steps into a dimly lighted cellar!

"I see!" Harley murmured. "There is a passage through to Zani Chada's! The police have suspected it for a long time; but it is evidently masked very cleverly."

We descended the narrow steps, Harley leading. They led down to a small and dirty cellar in which the invisible Kwee seemed to store a quantity of valueless lumber. Light was furnished by a gas jet projecting from the brick wall. A doorway which possessed no visible lintel or casement, and which I suspected ordinarily to be indistinguishable from the rest of the wall, gaped invitingly. Beyond, I could see a rough tunnel, resembling a mine gallery, its chilly gloom enlivened by the presence of another gaslight set some twelve or fifteen feet along.

Harley entered the cutting without hesitation, and I, perforce, followed him. We had arrived immediately under the light at the time that a familiar rusty, creaking noise caused me to glance back.

The entrance to the tunnel was closed!

Remembering the signal agreed upon, I reflected—and my skin grew clammy—that no sound of a pistol shot fired in this drain would reach the upper world. If suspicion should touch those we were come to seek, or—hideous thought—had already touched them, we should be trapped like rats!

The tunnel, having sloped down to the point at which the light was situated, now sloped upward, terminating in a cellar considerably larger than Kwee's. This contained a great store of wine, was electrically lighted and well ordered. Evidently, we were under the house of Zani Chada. Upstairs we proceeded, thus far having come upon no sign of immediate human presence.

A little pantry gave access to a corridor. At the end, where I had a glimpse of a strangely appointed hall or lobby, a Chinaman, in native dress, was waiting to receive us.

If I was threatened with panic at this moment, I believe that I succeeded in concealing the fact well enough, but I was assuredly grateful of the shelter afforded by my monkish cowl. Harley spoke never a word, but in silence advanced along the corridor to meet the Chinaman. I followed; nor do I scruple to confess that I first assured myself of the possibility of speedily withdrawing from beneath the hampering robe the revolver that I carried.

I had not supposed that Limehouse could afford the spectacle of such a hallway as that in which I found myself. Evidently, the house of Zani Chada was a survival of the days when Chinatown was not—of an earlier generation that rode out to the Essex Flats by chaise or on horseback. It furnishing, however, was unique, oddly blending the manner of a Roman mansion with that of an Oriental palace.

Here were pillars and a painted ceiling, a great staircase softly carpeted, and chairs of Arab woodwork. As we came to the end of the corridor, the servant raised his hand, palm forward, in salutation, at the same time inclining his head.

Paul Harley returned the salute, and I followed his example; at which the Chinaman silently indicated two ornate, carved chairs, bowed, left us, and walked slowly up the staircase, his soft slippers sinking into the pile of the carpet as into moss.

The moment that we found ourselves alone, Harley whispered urgently: "Knox, did you note how he stared at our palms?"

"Our palms? No," I muttered. "Why would he do so?"

"Why, indeed!" Harley murmured.

He began to glance about him furtively. I should say at this point that my friend possessed a sort of sixth sense, by means of which he was sometimes enabled to detect the presence of imminent danger, although there might be no visible evidence to confirm it. As we waited there in that queer hallway, I think this uncanny prescience touched him. I think he was seeking desperately to evolve some new plan of action.

However, if this were so, he failed. Quiet as a phantom, the Chinaman who had met us descended the stairs, his yellow face expressionless, bowed and indicated that we should follow him.

Harley's face, of course, I was unable to see, but, through the slits in his cowl, he flashed me a glance the significance of which was lost upon me. But that he intended to convey a warning of some sort, I was sure. Not knowing what was in his mind, not knowing what flaw he had detected in our daring plan, I followed him up those silent stairs in the carpet of which one's feet sank deeply, with a chill of foreboding at my heart colder than any I had known that night.

The place was perfumed with a faint, incense-like smell, which, as we reached the top of the staircase, I recognized to be similar to that in the chambers of Michael Hebron.

A curtain was drawn aside; we passed along a short corridor illuminated by a golden-shaded lamp in the form of a flambeau upheld by an exquisite ivory statuette. The walls were covered with tapestry and the floor was overlaid with rugs and skins. Our guide rapped twice upon a closed door, opened it and stood aside, bowing.

Harley entered and I followed, to find myself looking upon a scene so grotesque and in some ways so sinister that its reality almost eluded me, and I felt as one who dreamed an evil dream.

We were in a long, low-ceilinged room, an Adam room such is found in old English houses. I think at some time it had been used as a dining room. There were several very fine oil paintings on the wall and the massive furniture was antique and valuable. Around a long council table, a party of ten was assembled, nine men and one woman; at first, I assumed the nine cowled figures to be those of men. All were standing, facing us, hands upraised in the salute with which the Chinese servant had greeted us on our arrival. They had risen from he chairs in which they had been seated, and I found all my attention focused upon the woman who stood at the far end of the long table.

She wore a black robe, so designed as to conceal no line of her perfect white shoulders. By her pose and the curve of her red lips,

I judged her to be beautiful, despite the presence of a narrow mask through which gleamed the most extraordinary amber-colored eyes which I had ever met with in a human being. Her jet-black hair was dressed with classic simplicity; and as she stood there, one jeweled hand resting lightly upon the table, I knew that this was the notorious Madame de Medici; and her power for evil or for good I could no longer doubt. I thought that I had never seen a more arresting figure.

Harley raised his hand and I did likewise; and in the very act of this salute, I observed something, something that seemed to check the beating of my heart, of which at first I did not grasp the entire significance, while realizing that it boded no good.

I have said that Madame de Medici stood alone at one end of the long table, so that, at the moment of entering, I had assumed her to be president of this singular gathering. Now I saw that, facing her at the end of the table nearer to us, was a great, high-backed ebony chair, dragon-legged and golden-cushioned. This, and another chair on the right of it, were the only vacant places at the board.

Palpably, either Harley or I—in other words, either Hebron or Julian—was expected to preside over this meeting!

How I, alone, should have dealt with the situation, I know not, but my fear, already great, was now increased by a sudden, inarticulate murmuring that greeted our return of the salutation. The eyes peering at us through the slits of black cowls seemed to my excited imagination to become like the eyes of wild animals.

I had my hand upon my robe, ready to make a wild plunge for the revolver that lay in my pocket. I think I should have turned and fled, but that the amber eyes of Madame de Medici seemed to hold me hypnotically, seemed to forbid me to move. Never in the whole of an adventurous life, much of its adventure due to my share in Paul Harley's cases, had I known a moment to compare with this! I knew, as certainly as if ten voices had denounced us, that in some way our plans wore at fault. I knew that Paul Harley's sixth sense had told him of this already, so that I was astounded when he walked forward to the throne-like chair, indicating that I should take the place upon his right.

As we advanced, every head around that board turned in the direction of Madame de Medici. She bowed slightly and the whole assembly became seated.

I had never once taken my gaze from her face, or, rather, from her eyes. Indeed, I scarcely felt capable of doing so. I groped for the chair and sat down mechanically. Once seated, however, furtively I pulled the black robe aside and rested my hand upon the revolver in my pocket.

Madame de Medici remained standing. A complete silence fell. Faintly, I could detect a perfume that, later, I was to identify with that diffused by the amber envelope.

The glance of those tiger eyes was directed now upon my friend; and, as if ordered silently to do so, the cowled heads turned once more in our direction, but, this time, their intolerable stares were focused wholly upon Paul Harley. The influence of the beautiful Circe being temporarily removed from me, I became my own master in a measure.

I glanced aside at Harley. His face I could not see, but that he also had his pistol in readiness was a fact that I detected immediately.

There was a large antique clock upon the mantel shelf, registering ten minutes after two, and so seemingly irrelevant are the things which linger in one's memory that I can recall to the present moment the peculiar key in which this clock ticked; a deep, discreetly somber key, mellow with age. Meanwhile, I wondered what was to befall and what we should gain by continuing the farce further, since we were as surely unmasked as if we had stood undisguised among that grotesque gathering. Then Madame de Medici spoke.

Of this extraordinary woman I cannot hope to convey any just impression, but it is well that God has fashioned but few like her. Her voice had a silvern note which must have won for her international fame had she chosen the stage as a vocation. She had languorous; almost insolent, movements; feline, indescribably fascinating. Her entire personality appealed direct to the senses, like incense or barbaric music, or the rhythm of a pagan dance.

"My friends," she said, speaking very softly, but her eyes flashing a lightning message from face to face, "our company is now complete."

A faint murmur interrupted her. The man on my immediate right was breathing heavily, and the fact came home to me in a flash of intuition that if I feared these cowled mysteries about me, their fear was at least as great as my own. At their identity, or even their nationality, I could not guess. But that they were swayed each and every one by the personality of the woman standing at the end of the table was beyond dispute. To her they looked for guidance, in her they counted upon leadership. Ignoring the murmur, she continued to speak. "I propose," she said, "that we adjourn to the lower room in accordance with custom."

Some hidden meaning underlay the words; there was comprehension in the movements of the cowled heads. Something touched my knee, and, glancing swiftly downward, I saw this to be Harley's hand, in which he grasped a pistol. Divining his meaning, I withdrew my revolver from my pocket and held it in readiness below the table.

"If you will follow me," concluded Madame de Medici, "I will lead the way."

Gracefully, languidly, she turned and walked toward a door at the far end of the room. The nine men around the table rose, pushed back their chairs and followed her. Their anxiety to be gone was unmistakable. Harley stood up also. For once, I think, he was momentarily at a loss. He knew that he had made a mistake, but no doubt he counted upon the party surrounding the house, and no doubt also, he felt himself handicapped by the presence of a woman. As the company turned their backs upon us, he whispered: "Did you see how they all stared at our palms?"

"Yes," I returned. "Quick! What are you going to do?"

In the wake of the graceful figure, the nine cowled men had now disappeared from the room.

"We are discovered," he said; "we shall learn nothing. In some way, we have blundered. So—first to get rid of this damned cowl!"

We were now alone in the long apartment, not one of the retreating conspirators having given us so much as a backward glance. Harley threw off the black robe and stood, pistol in hand, looking about him. I also discarded my hampering garment, and was about to speak when an extraordinary thing occurred.

So thickly were the rooms and the corridors of this house carpeted that no sound of footsteps was perceptible, for which reason it was impossible to determine in what direction the party had gone. Now, as we stared at the distant doorway by which they had made their exits, Madame de Medici, her mask discarded, re-entered.

The amber eyes were half veiled by their black lashes; her lips were curved in a mocking smile. She was even more beautiful than I had supposed.

"Well, Mr. Harley," she said sweetly, "will you not present your friend whom you have brought to see me?"

III
As Daylight Approaches

The task of recording the events that immediately followed is one that I approach with hesitation.

I had slipped my revolver back into my pocket at the moment that Madame de Medici re-entered the room. Harley, too, had concealed his pistol. To him, as to me I doubt not, recognition of defeat had come. Legally, we were at the mercy of this strangely beautiful woman, who now, sinking gracefully down upon a cushioned settee, lighted a cigarette and surveyed us through lowered lashes.

Even had Harley been attached to the official police, his position at this moment must have been an unenviable one. The best that we could hope for now was that the men stationed around the house should succeed in tracing some of the members of this mysterious organization as they departed, for the woman's bewildering self-possession had cut the ground from under our feet.

Watching her as she reclined there, I thought that she found amusement in our dilemma; and knowing, for I could not doubt the fact, that she was involved in a grim conspiracy which had taxed the Secret Services of four nations, I realized that beneath this graceful, catlike indolence, a dangerously powerful spirit must lie concealed.

This was no idle masquerade upon which we had intruded, but a scene in a secret drama which one day might involve the whole of the Western world. Long as I had known Paul Harley, I had never seen him so palpably nonplused. He was angry and could not disguise the fact; but he knew himself helpless and reduced to a battle of wits with a woman.

"Well, Mr. Harley," said Madame de Medici, "I shall not offend you by pretending to misunderstand what has brought you here tonight." She paused, glancing at the cigarette that she held between her fingers. "For a long time now, you have subjected me to surveillance. Because, perhaps strangely, I choose to live in this house, you have had me followed when I have visited my friends in the more civilized quarters of London. Tonight"—she smiled, gazing fixedly at me while she continued to address Harley—"you have really gone too far. It is almost absurd."

"It is more than absurd," he returned, watching her. "It is positively offensive. I apologize, Madame de Medici."

She scarcely glanced at him, keeping her extraordinary amber-colored eyes, which now were fully open, turned persistently in my direction. A taunting smile rested upon her lips, and, watching her as she lay there in her lithe beauty, I told myself that Aspasia, Sappho, Faustine, Semiramis, Irene must surely have been such women as this. Yet, I found a joy in contemplating her. Nor did I recognize how completely the details of the scene were fading from my ken; how, little by little, my world was dwindling, seeming to begin and to end in two darkly fringed pools of amber. Madame de Medici continued to address Harley and continued to watch me.

"You have avoided me socially, Mr. Harley, yet you visit my house uninvited."

"And find you entertaining strange company!" rejoined Harley with repressed venom.

"It is a secret society which meets at my house!" she explained coolly, and smiled at me the while.

Suddenly, the fact that the speaker's regard was directed elsewhere seemed to attract Harley's attention.

"Knox!" he said sharply, so that I started as if awakened from a doze. "What was that address in Maida Vale which we were given tonight?"

Indeed, I had the utmost difficulty in grasping what was asked of me. I became conscious of a positive but unfamiliar stupidity, as well as of a disinclination to tax my brain with what appeared to be a weighty problem.

"Try to remember, Knox," Harley added. "It is important."

I cannot recall having once removed my eyes from contemplation of the bewitching face of Madame de Medici from the moment when she had seated herself on the settee up to that when Harley asked me this apparently irrelevant question, A conviction, not wholly unpleasant, that the whole scene was unreal had begun to take possession of me. Fear had gone. I recognized that these people had nothing to gain by harming us. Embarrassment I had experienced when first our equivocal position became apparent to me, but now this had given place to a sort of acute esthetic delight in the beauty of the woman who lay there on the settee, watching me smilingly with those strangely long, amber eyes.

Harley began to speak again, but I scarcely heeded his words. Regarded in retrospect, this apathy that, unchecked, I permitted to steal upon me seems almost incredible. But I was handicapped; I was falling, an easy victim in a contest fought with strange weapons. Today, armed with my new knowledge, I think I should give a different account of myself.

Dimly, I could hear Harley's voice; but, as though I had eaten hashish, he seemed to be speaking from a great distance; while, on the contrary, Madame de Medici seemed bodily to have approached nearer to me, or I to her.

It was all a delusion, of course, as I have since recognized, and in upon it, as my wonder grew and the lure of the sorceress wrapped me more closely about, there burst a sudden sharp cry from my friend. Almost, the spell was broken—almost, but not quite. I clenched my fists as I remember distinctly . . . I heard the sound of a fall.

And now I have to relate how I failed my friend in direst need, for while, in a sort of subconscious fashion, I realized that he was calling upon me for aid, I also realized—and knew a swift, sickly terror—the depth of my subjection to the uncanny power that lay in the eyes of Madame de Medici.

I had experienced it when first she glanced at me that night, but now I experienced it to the full. I could not remove my eyes—I could not turn aside! I was entrapped in some strange magic; knew I was entrapped, resented my impotency, yet lacked the strength to combat the spell cast upon me!

My mentality became sharply divided. I told myself that the perfume in the apartment, which at first had been no more than faintly perceptible, now was grown so oppressive that I was likely to swoon. Never having succumbed to this characteristically feminine ailment, I had no previous experience to guide me. But I had been put under an anesthetic in a military hospital in Singapore, and my present sensations closely resembled those which I had experienced on that occasion—the gradual loss of interest in everything about me, a sensation as though veil after veil were being lowered, slowly obscuring the scene. It was similar.

In Singapore, my last flicker of interest had centered upon a broken button in the surgeon's white operating garment. Now, it centered upon the liquid amber eyes of Madame de Medici. It was strange, this reasoning with myself, while weakly I succumbed to the influence that was overpowering me.

I seemed to be sinking lower and lower in a cloud of incense, and to be looking up as from the bottom of a great pit, through shifting, tenuous vapors, at amber eyes bending over me, far above. Then the unforgettable silver-bell voice called to me softly, and I mounted out of the darkness toward the light, to find myself in a room canopied with cloth-of-gold.

A Madonna, that I knew for an Old Master, looked down compassionately from the wall upon a garishly cushioned divan where Madame de Medici reclined, watching me with that slow smile which rendered her carmine lips so alluring. She dropped her cigarette into a silver bowl on a table by her side and began to speak.

She spoke of the passionate soul of India in revolt; of monasteries placid in the shadow of snow-capped mountain peaks of the heart of China, loyal to a tradition older than the name of England; of latticed rooms and their silken secrets; of the holy Ganges and of the forbidden Purple City. It was a song, a song of eager hearts, of a naming torch leaping from crest to crest, firing the palm and destroying the pine; of the gloom of Himalayan valleys, of the sunshine whitening Damascus.

I heard of rose gardens and of great carnage; I saw the spirit of the Yellow People stand naked before me—and it was a great and a powerful spirit. A curved sword swept down out of the sky, and it cleaved a great ravine in the earth, upon one side of which I saw a great white army, and upon the other an army yellow, brown and black. One of the leaders of the yellow army crossed the ravine and for a while disappeared.

Then, presently, I saw him again, strangely habited, but his face was the face of Michael Hebron. Many times his raiment changed, but always he remained facially the same. Incense and a murmuring like that in an Eastern bazaar ran through all the song, the siren song, and there was amber everywhere, amber and carmine, and the ivory of women's shoulders.

And now, in the ordinary dress of an Englishman, I saw Michael Hebron lying dead at my feet, and the music became a great, tremulous sigh. My other self stirred, questioning this trance that was half delicious and half terrifying. At one moment, I had been in a palace of ivory; now I stood again beneath the canopy of cloth-of-gold, watching a beautiful sorceress coiled, serpentine, amid many cushions.

Another voice, a harsh voice, broke in upon the music. It called my name urgently, insistently; and up from the very deeps of my being burst a sudden strength. Putting forth a giant effort, I cast off the magic and the incense and the amber spell.

"Knox!"

As if my effort had brought death, darkness fell—and I found myself groping amid unfamiliar things, groping toward the voice that called, which now I knew for the voice of Paul Harley. There was a confused sound of knocking, too. . . .

A disk of light flickered in the darkness. Then a shadowy figure came into view. It was Paul Harley, carrying an electric torch,

"Where are you, Knox?" he cried, flashing the light all about us.

Suddenly, he saw me where I stood. Doubtless, I looked like one newly recovered from an opium debauch, for Harley stood still, staring at me with a strange expression in his eyes. I thought that he looked haggard and ill, and wondered why.

Truth to tell, my bemused mind was groping for an explanation of my presence in this room with its compassionate Madonna, its great jade Buddha, its canopy of cloth-of-gold, its mingling of Christianity and paganism and wild riot of color. In the dim light of the torch, it all looked shadowy and mysterious.

"I should have warned you," said Harley, and his voice sounded almost like a groan.

The knocking which I had heard dimly in my trance now proclaimed itself to be a persistent battering upon some distant door.

"What has happened, Harley?" I whispered—"For God's sake, what has happened?"

"Several things," he returned grimly. "Simple in themselves, but collectively damnable. In the first place, the electric light has been turned off all over the house from some unknown switch in the cellar. In the second place, while you stood there drinking in the wicked beauty of Madame de Medici, I was neatly and efficiently sandbagged from behind!"

"My God, Harley, and I never knew it!"

"You were past knowing anything! I should have warned you."

"But," I cried, the wonder of the thing suddenly bursting upon me—"warned me of what?"

"Of the uncanny power of this woman who has tricked us. How far she has tricked us, I have yet to learn. Don't you understand, Knox? Hang it all, man, pull yourself together!"

"I am endeavoring to do so, Harley. What is that crashing sound?"

"Wessex breaking into the house. It will be daylight in ten minutes, and he probably thinks we are both murdered."

"Daylight!" I repeated. "Then how long—"

"Between three and four hours!" interrupted Harley bitterly. "She took a big chance, Knox, even if she has escaped, which we have yet to learn. By this outrage, she has made London too hot to hold her. But I can see why she took the chance. Now that it is too late, I can see many things that were dark to me before."

"But to me, Harley," I protested, "the whole affair has the seeming of a nightmare. You were sandbagged, you say; but why? Her coolness in grasping the situation and dealing with it as she did put us in a hopeless position. She could have had us arrested as burglars!"

"I know, Knox. But she wanted to learn what had become of Hebron and Julian, and she adopted the only means that occurred to her of finding out."

"What means? I don't follow."

"Listen," said Harley irritably. "My head feels as though it were splitting, and in any event, this is no time for long explanations. But your recollections of our interview with Madame probably take you as far as the time when I asked you to recall a certain address?"

"I remember your doing so perfectly."

"I knew the address well enough, Knox! I was merely endeavoring to stimulate your mind to individual action. I could see what was happening to you."

"But," I cried, "what was happening to me?"

"You were being hypnotized!"

"What?" I was confounded.

"You were being hypnotized by the most proficient hypnotist in Europe; a woman who possesses dangerous powers as well as dangerous beauty, I have already hinted at several episodes in her career, but if I were to tell you the whole truth about Madame de Medici, even now I doubt if you would credit it."

"I find it hard to credit even your assertion that I have been hypnotized!"

"Do you?" Harley snapped. "Then perhaps you will tell me of your experience since the moment when I was sandbagged, and when, by the way, you made no attempt to assist me."

"My dear fellow!" I cried reproachfully, "don't remind me of that. Of course, I can see now clearly enough that I was under some unusual influence."

"Very unusual!" he replied. "But, without disrespect, I would add that men of greater mental powers than yourself have fallen under it more than once. But tell me, quickly, what you can recollect of your experience."

I clutched my head, because it seemed to me that tonight I had stepped clear of solid earth, and for a while had moved among phantom things; in a world beyond the boundary of common sense, governed by laws whose very existence was denied by science. Then, haltingly, I began to recount what I could remember of my dream or trance, for, to this day, I cannot define it.

"Right!" said Harley as I concluded. "I suspected it. Knox, all that we know, she knows now. She holds every clue that we hold! She knows that two members of the organization are dead, and, unless I am greatly mistaken, Limehouse will never see Madame de Medici again. Her activities, unfortunately, will be renewed elsewhere, no doubt."

I stared at him haggardly.

"But—"

"Oh, she knows, Knox, she knows!" he cried, "She has sucked your brain empty of every bit of information of interest to her!"

As he spoke, the distant hammering culminated in a dull crash.

"The door is down," he said. "Come on, Knox!"

At that, flashing the light of his torch ahead of him, he walked out of the room, staggering slightly, by which I knew that he was still suffering from the effects of the assault upon him. I followed, and presently my feet were sinking into the thickness of the carpet upon the wide staircase. Below, in the pillared hallway, there were several disks of moving light, and a confusion of voices came up to me.

"Mr. Harley!" I heard, and it was Inspector Wessex who cried the name.

"All right, Wessex!" my friend replied. "We are both safe."

"Thank God!" cried the Scotland Yard man.

"What news, Wessex?" asked Harley, descending the stairs. "You have followed all the men who left the house?"

"All the men who left the house?" came another voice with which I was unfamiliar. "Nobody has left the house—not a soul! Neither this house nor that of Kwee!"

"What?" Harley cried sharply. "Then there is still a chance, but a remote one! Knox, take a party through the passage to the house of Kwee. You know the way. If the doors are closed, post someone there and report to me. We can then break in from the front. Meanwhile, Wessex, spread your men out and search this burrow from cellar to attic. Particularly try to find the main switch and get some light on again."

Thereupon commenced such an overhauling of the house of

Zani Chada as I despair of describing. From foundation to roof, there was not a square foot left unaccounted for. The whole place was queerly and exotically furnished. In the scheme, there was a substratum that was purely Chinese, but in many of the rooms it had become overlaid with a sort of medieval luxuriousness that I suppose reflected the personality of Madame de Medici, so that some of the rooms might have belonged to a Florentine courtesan of the time of Lorenzo the Magnificent. But the outstanding wonder was that, excepting ourselves and the police, no living soul could we find within its four walls!

Kwee's also was empty from roof to cellar, and I had rarely witnessed a more curious scene than that discovered as dawn crept over the roofs of Chinatown, touching grayly the faces of the search party.

"We should never have found the passage from Kwee's," said Harley bitterly, "if it had not been shown to us. Doubtless, there is another by which they all escaped."

"Zani Chada's cellars have had the reputation of being catacombs for some years now," Wessex added.

"Well"—Harley turned to me and conjured up a smile—"where Raymond McCabe failed, I need not be ashamed to do likewise."

"But you have not failed yet, Harley!" I cried.

"No," he murmured, "but I have missed my big chance."

IV

A Definite Clue

We walked back to Limehouse Police Station through the deserted streets. The storm had blown over, but the skies remained gray and lowering. In some subtle fashion, I felt ashamed of myself. I had given important information to the enemy, and the fact that I had been forced to do so by a superior will was poor consolation, especially since the superior will was that of a woman.

"Oh, by the way, Mr, Harley," said Wessex as we came in sight of the police depot, "your secretary, Mr. Innes, phoned several times during the night, and finally, at close upon two o'clock this morning, said that a messenger from the Foreign Office had delivered an important letter."

"What's that? From the Foreign Office?" Harley's face lighted up.

"Yes," replied Wessex. "I explained that we couldn't get in touch with you at the time, and Mr. Innes said, as he expected the matter was of importance, that he would remain at your office until you phoned."

"He'll have turned in by now," murmured Harley, whose chambers adjoined his business premises. "I see the Daimler is waiting, so I need not wake him by phoning. We can drop you and Sergeant Preston at Figtree Court and I will go along to Chancery Lane."

He had already imparted to Wessex details of the gruesome crime which had been committed in the chambers above my own, so that Wessex merely nodded in acquiescence; and when certain necessary formalities had been gone through at Limehouse Police Station, Harley and myself, with Wessex and his assistant, Detective-Sergeant Preston, drove through the empty East End streets on that gray morning, a disconsolate quartet.

We knew no more respecting the identity of the Black Mandarin than we had known at the outset. Except for Madame de Medici, not one name was added to the list of members known to the authorities. Worst of all, they must now be fully alive to their peril. Not only had we failed to achieve anything, but we had also undone the result of much patient work in the past.

When, presently, we were seated in the book-lined study at the back of the office in which Harley ordinarily received his clients during business hours, he poured out two stiff pegs of whisky. Innes brought in the Foreign Office letter and Harley eagerly tore open the envelope and scanned the contents. "Ah," he murmured—"in code. If you will excuse me, Knox, I will decipher it at once."

He set to work, his pipe fuming between his teeth while, at the other side of the room, I outlined to Innes the extraordinary events of the night. Our murmured conversation was presently interrupted by a cry from Harley,

"A message from the legation at Peking! The first definite clue to the identity of the Black Mandarin which has ever come to hand! And an important one!"

Surrounding himself with clouds of tobacco smoke, he continued his task of decoding the message.

I resumed my conversation with Innes. Suddenly, the telephone bell rang.

"Extraordinary!" Harley murmured, his heavy eyebrows raised. "Who the devil can it be? Attend to it, Innes."

Innes nodded, stood up and went out of the study to the outer office, while Harley immediately became absorbed again in his code message. The next moment, he laid down his pencil, stood up suddenly and turned to me. "Knox," he said, "there is someone on the telephone. Have *you* any idea who it is?"

"Not the slightest."

We stood together, watching and waiting. That Harley's extraordinary powers of intuition had forewarned him, I cannot doubt; but, for my part, I started back literally stupefied when Innes, returning, said: "Madame de Medici to speak to you."

"Madame de Medici?"

"At any rate, it was a lady's voice."

The expression on Harley's face I cannot pretend to define. I knew his immovable calm. But this was so totally unexpected that we could only stare at one another. Recovering himself, he proceeded to the telephone. He repeated the conversation to me afterward.

"Madame de Medici speaking," she began. "I must apologize for troubling you at this unearthly hour, but, then, you did not shrink from troubling me." Harley winced under the cutting lash of her words. "I am leaving London almost immediately, and I deeply regret my inability to return your unexpected call. I equally regret my lack of hospitality, Mr. Harley, even if you were an uninvited guest. Last night, a deadly blow was struck at the organization to which I belong. I know everything now. While you and your friends have been making yourselves busy in Limehouse, I have visited the scene of the tragedy. But, with all your cleverness, the end is not yet. We shall meet again, my friend, and it may be that we shall understand one another better."

Then silence.

Harley could think of nothing to say. When he did find words, Madame had gone. He returned to the study and we stood like two carved men. At last, my friend said: "I have met my Waterloo, Knox, and she called me up to gloat over my defeat."

"What do you mean, Harley?"

He did not reply to my question.

"Somewhere deep in my very bones, I admire that woman," he continued: "Within the last eight hours, while we have been making ourselves ridiculous, she has forestalled us every time."

"Harley," I cried, "it is all so incomprehensible."

"It will be clear as day," he assured me, "when we have heard the report of Inspector Wessex. Good heavens!"—he brought his open hand down upon the table—"that that woman could be visiting Hebron's chambers while we were guessing what to do. Have you any idea of the nationality of Madame de Medici? Does she look Italian?"

"Not in the least."

"She has lived in Italy," he went on, beginning to gather up his papers from the table. "Indeed, I think she has lived in almost every country, in almost every capital of the world at one time or another. But, at last, I think I have placed her. Yes—and it explains many things." He stared me squarely in the face. "She is Chinese, Knox!"

"What!" I cried.

"She is Chinese!—a fact which opens up an entirely new line of inquiry. But, truth to tell, I have lost faith in myself. Another peg of whisky is indicated, I think, Knox. And then we will rejoin Wessex."

There was intense but suppressed excitement in his manner; but now, as he gave a final glance at the decoded message, it occurred to me that the information received from the British legation in Peking was really responsible for this.

When, presently, we set out, I was in no mood for the horrors of Michael Hebron's chambers, what with the mad traffic of the night and the chill of the hour of dawn.

However, I mastered my feelings as well as might be, and, presently, found myself standing before the door at that top set where properly our adventure had commenced. Sergeant Preston opened to us, and, almost immediately, I detected that queer, incense-like smell which characterized the chambers. Wessex was standing just inside the lobby, notebook in hand.

"Well, Wessex," said Harley eagerly, "what have you discovered?"

"I think I have reconstructed the affair," replied the Scotland Yard man; "that is to say, I can give you a fairly clear idea of what happened."

"Good!" rapped Harley. "Go on."

"Suppose we talk in here," said Wessex, opening a door on the right. "Then we will go over the ground together and you can check my reasoning."

We entered a plainly furnished dining room, Wessex turning up the light. Frequently referring to his notebook, he outlined the results of his inquiry.

"The divisional surgeon hasn't come yet," he explained, "but that doesn't matter very much. The facts, it appears to me, are these: The man called Julian came here some time during the evening, to call upon Michael Hebron. The exact time I expect to learn by inquiries at the flat in Maida Vale. He was in evening dress and carried a small attaché case which contained, according to your account, Mr. Harley, a black-cowled robe."

"It did," Harley confirmed. "And a similar robe I found folded up in a hand bag in Michael Hebron's bedroom."

"Very well," continued Wessex. "He went into the study and talked to Hebron for some time. I have counted the cigarette stumps, and I have worked it out that he must have been there for fully half an hour. What they quarreled about, we don't know, and probably shall never know–"

"It wasn't exactly a quarrel," put in Harley, "but go on."

"Well, then," continued Wessex, glancing at him questioningly, "from a table drawer, which is still open, Hebron took out a Colt repeater, fitted with a silencer—presumably unnoticed by Julian—and shot him as he sat in the armchair. He probably meant to shoot him through the heart. The bullet was an inch too high."

"I know," murmured Harley. "I saw the wound."

"Julian, who must have been a man of indomitable will, started to his feet, upsetting the ashtray from the arm of his chair, and fell upon his assailant. Hebron must have dropped the pistol when Julian sprang, for Julian evidently got him by the throat, threw him, and, in spite of a ghastly wound, squeezed the life out of him."

"Yes, yes," said Harley rapidly, "I agree with all your conclusions so far."

"I think it is possible," continued Wessex, "but it is for the divisional surgeon to say, that Julian might have recovered from his wound except for the violent exertion of his attack upon Hebron. He was determined to kill him. So far, I am fairly sure of my ground, Mr. Harley. From various clues that I can show to you, I have reconstructed the whole affair. We now come to mere surmises. Julian, having finished the man who had shot him, seems to have staggered into the next room, evidently with the idea of getting to the telephone. He had actually opened the book and almost reached the instrument when a tremendous hemorrhage seems to have finished him."

"He had done more than that," said Harley gravely. "He had given a few more years of peace to a world that was threatened with war. . . . "

"I suggest now," said Wessex, mastering the surprise occasioned by this statement, "that we go into the study and view the body of Hebron, which I have not moved more than was necessary for my inquiry."

"Very well," Harley agreed.

We filed into the room of which I had ghastly memories, and there was the long, gaunt figure stretched upon the floor. I turned, looking at Harley, and, although his face was set and mask-like, his eyes gleamed feverishly, and I, who knew him well, realized that he held a hidden clue to this baffling mystery. He did not speak, however, until Wessex had drawn his attention to the data by means of which he had reconstructed the details of the crime.

"Have you determined the nationality of the man, Hebron?" he then asked.

"Well," Wessex replied, "we may term him an international, but I should say he was Asiatic."

"Asiatic, yes. A Chinaman."

"Likely enough," returned Wessex—"as you say, he belonged to the Black Mandarin group."

"Look well at his face, Knox," Harley invited. "Note the intellectual strength of the brow—the power in every line."

I looked as he directed, but was revolted by the spectacle, for the man had died of strangulation. His throat was discolored and his features contorted.

"This," said Harley, "was, no ordinary man." He turned to Wessex. "His fists are tightly clenched?"

"Yes," was the reply, "he clenched them in his death agony, I suppose."

"Probably," murmured Harley, in a voice so altered that I glanced at him sharply.

Intense excitement, long repressed, now manifested itself unmistakably.

Even Detective-Sergeant Preston, who was engaged in making an inventory of the contents of the room, noted it, for he looked up from his work as Harley drew a sheet of quarto paper out of his breast pocket and began to speak again.

"I have here," he said, "a decoded message which has come through from Peking. I will not read it in detail, but it contains a definite clue to the personality of the Black Mandarin."

"At last!" cried Wessex. "You know who he is?"

"No," returned Harley; "but it is a clue which should enable one to recognize him; it is contained in these words"—he read from his own transcription:

"Owing to some obscure pathological condition, the official denominated *I,"* (he glanced aside to me. "This refers to the Black Mandarin, Knox," he explained, and continued to read) "bears a characteristic mark to which possibly the name by which he has become known may be attributed. In the palm of his right hand is a deep, nearly black, patch or stain, some two inches in diameter."

He replaced the paper in his pocket.

"At last, Knox!" he cried. *"Now* I understand why the palms of our hands were scrutinized so closely tonight when we returned the salutation given to us! *Now* I know what upset all our calculations and brought the whole ceremony to such an abrupt end."

"Good heavens! You don't mean—"

"Perhaps I am jumping to conclusions," he broke in, "but, at least, we can test the matter."

He dropped on one knee beside the body of Michael Hebron, seized the clenched right fist and forced the fingers open. "I was right!" he cried triumphantly, and started to his feet.

In the center of the dead man's palm was a discolored patch resembling a bruise!

"Why, Mr. Harley," said Wessex—and the words came as a mere whisper—"does this mean that the Black Mandarin—"

"It means," interrupted Harley, "that the Black Mandarin, in the name of Michael Hebron, has been living in these chambers many weeks, but, above all, it means that the Black Mandarin is dead! He lies here at your feet!"

"Good God!" exclaimed Wessex. He was incapable of speech.

"We might have known, Knox," continued Harley excitedly—"it was as plain as daylight. Undoubtedly, the meeting at the house of Madame de Medici was convened to meet the Black Mandarin in person! He it was they expected. He it was who should have occupied the presidential chair in which I seated myself! His personality was unknown to his associates, do you understand, as it was unknown to the rest of the world. I thought I was impersonating an ordinary member of the group, whereas I was endeavoring to impersonate the dreaded chief, the man for whom the Secret Services of four countries have been seeking for years!"

"But, Harley," I cried, "one, at least, of the group must have been acquainted with the secret and must have been in his confidence!"

The expression on Paul Harley's face underwent a subtle change.

"You refer to Julian?" he suggested.

"Certainly."

"This is the eve of my retirement, Knox," he continued strangely, and turned to Wessex. "Before we go into the next room," he said, "have you learned anything regarding the other dead man—Julian?"

"Well," replied Wessex, who seemed to have been stupefied by this astounding discovery, "I think, but am not sure, that his hair is dyed."

"Ah!" cried Harley. "Eyebrows and eyelashes?"

"Dyed also, if my theory is correct."

"Anything else?"

"Nothing much," replied Wessex, staring hard, "except that he was certainly not an Asiatic, although, from what we have learned tonight, I gather that he must have been high in the confidence of the Black Mandarin."

"There is no doubt of it," replied Harley, leading the way to the next room. "You noticed, I suppose," he added, speaking over his shoulder, "that the telephone directory was open at the page upon which my name appears?"

"It had not occurred to me," confessed Wessex. "Is there any particular significance in the fact?"

"There is a very great significance!" Harley assured him.

We stood grouped in the doorway, looking at the huddled figure in the chair, for Inspector Wessex had left the body much as it had been found until the divisional surgeon should have made his examination. Harley paused.

"When you go to the flat in Maida Vale, Wessex," he said, "to confirm the time of Julian's departure, I shall certainly accompany you."

"His papers will no doubt be of interest," Wessex admitted.

"I anticipate that they will be of extraordinary interest," replied Harley; "in fact, I am going to phone Scotland Yard immediately to see that Madame de Medici does not anticipate us. She may have anticipated us already."

He looked at me; his eyes were afire with excitement.

"Those premises must be guarded, Wessex. They probably contain information of vital interest to the British Empire as well as to the United States!"

Let me confess that the discovery of my neighbor, Michael Hebron's being none other than the Black Mandarin had staggered me to such a degree that now I was utterly incapable of following Paul Harley's reasoning. I knew not what he implied, or what to anticipate, and I think that Wessex, and certainly Preston, who stood behind us in the doorway, shared my bewilderment.

Then Harley stepped forward, bent, and peered into the ghastly face of the dead man, tilting the lampshade on the table.

"I should have known," he murmured; "I should have known."

At last, I found words, "You should have known what, Harley?"

"I should have known that his hair was dyed," he replied. "I should have understood that a better man than I can ever hope to be had given his life for his country, Knox!"

He stood upright and spoke passionately: "You and I and a million who will never even hear of the things that have happened tonight, you and I, who have paid tribute to those who saved us from the curse of Prussianism, should unite, I think, with every man, woman and child of the white races in doing honor to the memory of one who has averted an even greater evil."

We stood there watching him, Preston, Wessex and I, in our dense stupidity, not comprehending, until, at last, suddenly, blindingly, the light came.

"Harley, Harley!" I said, "I understand—"

He looked at Wessex.

"Do *you* understand?"

"I am sorry, Mr. Harley, but I don't."

"Then I will enlighten you. This is Raymond McCabe, of the American Secret Service!"

THE DYKE GRANGE MYSTERY

I
Ali Mahmoud

"Your complaint that there is a certain monotony about Norfolk's scenery," said Paul Harley, "is not justified by the facts."

I raised my head from the cushion upon which it rested and stared at him. He was contentedly watching the float upon the end of his line, which bobbed gently up and down on the miniature waves of the river. At a spot selected by my friend, we had anchored our boat, the anchors consisting of blocks of stone lowered over the bow and stern. The day was hot and still, and the contents of the luncheon basket from the Cardinal's Hat—a quaint riverside hostelry which was our temporary home—had induced in me a somnolent mood, without in any way diminishing Harley's enthusiasm for rod and line.

So tortuous were the windings of the little stream that one might behold the miracle of a wherry with its great brown sail seemingly traversing a meadow. No other fishers were near us, and except for the periodical passage of the wherries, whose masters, without exception, seemed to cherish a fiendish desire to run us down, nothing had disturbed our placid sport.

"What do you mean?" I said sleepily.

"Look!" Harley pointed downstream.

Resting on my elbow, I stared in that direction and then sat upright, staring even harder.

A man wearing a *tarboosh,* that little red felt cap commonly called a fez in this country, was standing on the river bank a hundred yards below us. He was otherwise attired in European fashion except that he wore a jacket of khaki drill. He was clearly some kind of Easterner.

He seemed to be looking in our direction when:

"Ha!" exclaimed Harley, rapidly winding in his line. "A big one this time!"

He proceeded to land a roach, and I was stricken with the old amazement to note how this man, whose life had been one long adventure, whom I had seen calm and unmoved amidst scenes of panic, now was stirred to childish excitement by the presence upon his line of a flapping fish. "Splendid!" he cried. "The biggest today. I think that will do, Knox. Our Oriental friend seems to be coming in this direction. Suppose we hail him?"

Dropping the fish into the basket that contained his earlier captures, Harley raised one anchor and I the other, so that very gently we began to drift downstream. At a suitable spot I forced the nose of the boat in to the reedy bank as the man in the red cap approached us.

"Salamat!" cried Harley genially.

The brown face of the stranger lighted up at sound of the familiar tongue.

"Esh-halak, Effendim!" he replied.

Harley turned laughing eyes in my direction.

"An interchange of Arab greetings on a Norfolk river bank," he said. "Are you satisfied, Knox?"

He scrambled forward and jumped ashore, entering into animated conversation with the Oriental in what was evidently the latter's native language.

I gathered that the brown man was some kind of peddler—although of a superior sort since he was neatly and respectably dressed. This idea was born out of one more terrifying for, as the two conversed, I saw the man produce from his pocket a dangerous-looking dagger, its hilt thickly encrusted with gems, whether real or otherwise I could not determine. I started, but, seeing him hand the weapon to Harley, recognized that his intentions were pacific enough.

Harley examined the thing critically, shook his head and returned it to the man, speaking to him rapidly in Arabic. Finally a sum of money changed hands and the Oriental, with many expressions and gestures of gratitude, departed whilst my friend rejoined me in the boat.

"Very odd, Knox," he said, scrambling perilously to his place. "That poor fellow's guardian angel must have guided his steps in our direction."

"What is he?" I asked. "An Arab?"

"Possibly has Arab blood," returned Harley, "but he comes from Mitrahna, in Egypt, that romantic village in the palm groves which is all that remains of royal Memphis."

"What on earth is he doing wandering about Norfolk?"

"He is some kind of performer, a member of a combination which came to grief in Cromer recently. The manager did the traditional thing and bolted with all the available funds, leaving poor Ali

Mahmoud and the rest stranded. Ali's case is aggravated by the fact that he has very little English, and he has been wandering about for several days endeavoring to raise enough money to get to London, from which he seems confident he can work his passage home."

"Did he want to sell you that wonderful looking dagger?"

"He did. He uses it in his performance, apparently, and it's the only thing of value which he has left." He stared at me queerly. "I advised him to keep it and gave him the address of a man in London who would offer a fair price for it."

"Is it genuine, then? Are the jewels real?"

"Absolutely real, Knox. It's old Damascus work—apart from which I would say there are a hundred pounds worth of gems in the hilt." He paused, fumbling for his tobacco pouch. "Ali Mahmoud offered to sell it for forty shillings," he added. "I gave him that amount and returned him his dagger."

"Very odd," I murmured, taking the sculls and heading upstream.

Dusk was not far off, and our beer jar had long ago run dry. The day had been an exceedingly hot one, and now the charms of the Cardinal's Hat called to me urgently. Harley began to arrange his tackle and I to pull gently upstream. But another encounter was to come, for, as we turned a bend where a row of pollard willows broke the reedy flatness, there stood a short, thickset man in riding kit, staring intently toward us.

"Sir Joseph Peek," murmured Harley. "As pretty a scoundrel as anything outside Moscow. But I suppose we must be civil."

I had been staring at the man over my shoulder, but now I turned my head again and grimaced at Harley. My acquaintance with Sir Joseph was slight, and I had no desire to improve it.

At this moment, however, surprise was predominant in my mind and my grimace had indicated this, for Sir Joseph Peek, a wealthy landowner of the neighborhood, had accumulated his fortune and subsequently earned his knighthood in the Egyptian Delta, his interests being concerned with cotton.

"Yes," murmured Harley, reading my glance aright. "It's very odd. First an Egyptian juggler and then an Egyptian cotton grower. Complain no more, Knox."

"Hullo!" called Sir Joseph from the bank as I pulled slowly by. "What luck today, gentlemen?"

"Fair," returned Harley, holding up the roach that he had last captured. "Sixteen inches of him. Did you ever see a bigger?"

"No," returned the other, a sardonic smile showing momentarily upon his dark, florid face. "But I don't like roach."

"Sorry," drawled Harley, dropping the fish back into the basket. "In that event, I will keep it myself."

"Ha, ha!" cried Sir Joseph. "One to you, Mr. Harley. But I will return good for evil. May I expect you and Mr. Knox to dinner at the Hall tomorrow evening?"

Harley muttered something under his breath which I was unable to detect, and then:

"Thanks," he said. "It's very good of you. We shall be delighted."

"Pleasure, Sir Joseph," I murmured.

"Cheerio, then," came the heavy voice from the bank. "Seven-thirty tomorrow night."

"Means well," murmured Harley, "but I happen to know too much of his private history to experience any rejoicing. Couldn't very well refuse, though, could we?"

"No," I answered absently as another bend in the stream concealed Sir Joseph from view.

But, nevertheless, I was annoyed at Harley's acceptance, and I pulled on in silence to the little landing stage of the Cardinal's Hat, where we disembarked and walked up the gravel path to the inn.

II

Murder!

"I cannot understand what has become of Wessex," said Harley.

We had dined, and dined well, and now we sat on either side of the little porch, smoking and looking out to where the river whispered gently past the landing stage. It was a still and perfect night, and, save for occasional bursts of conversation from the bar parlor, the silence was unbroken.

This was the sort of solitude in which Paul Harley really reveled—wisely, no doubt, since there could be no more complete change from the stress of a life such as his. But I was as curious as he respecting the absence of Wessex.

Detective Inspector Wessex of New Scotland Yard, an old friend of Harley's, had been investigating a sordid but mysterious tragedy in Great Yarmouth. It was one of those beach murders which sometimes enliven the dullness of a summer season, and Wessex had traced the crime to a member of a highly respectable and religious family, a middle-aged man whose Sunday school activities had instantly aroused the suspicion of the trained investigator.

Wessex had conducted the inquiry very ably, and he was returning to London in the morning, but, knowing that Paul Harley was sojourning at the Cardinal's Hat, he had arranged to dine and spend the night there with us and to outline to the celebrated private investigator the details of the case. His absence was unaccountable, for we know that his official business at Great Yarmouth had terminated early in the day.

Now, as we sat there on the porch, drinking in the freshness of the evening breeze, the hum of a car upon the winding road reached our ears.

"Here comes Wessex," said Harley. "I wonder what has detained him. He is too late for dinner, but no doubt there is cold meat available, and the ale is excellent."

Louder and louder grew the drone of the motor, and presently the car rounded the last bend and the light of the headlamps shone through the hedge on our right. We stood up, crossed the little patch of lawn and walked down to the gate. Inspector Wessex stepped out of the car.

"Mr. Harley!" he cried. "Thank heaven you are here. I have walked straight out of the Great Yarmouth case into one that has simply stunned me."

"What do you mean?" asked Harley. "What has happened?"

"Murder has happened."

"What! Another beach crime?"

"Nothing of the kind. Someone has been murdered at Dyke Grange, not a mile from here."

"But when?"

"Tonight—less than an hour ago."

"What?" cried Harley. "How in heaven's name did you come to hear of it?"

"Simple enough," explained Wessex. "The Norfolk police knew I was here, and when the application came thorough to Yarmouth, the superintendent, knowing where I was bound for, phoned to have me intercepted. So instead of coming to the Cardinal's Hat, I went to Dyke Grange, and I only left there ten minutes ago."

"And you say a murder has been committed?" I exclaimed.

"Undoubtedly. But the circumstances! Gentlemen, I am utterly bewildered."

"Do you want me to look into the matter?" asked Harley.

"I beg of you to do so, Mr. Harley. I don't know what to make of it."

"Come up to my room for a moment, and then we will accompany you."

Wessex agreed, and presently the three of us were seated in the little low-ceilinged room, the lattice windows wide open, so that from where we sat we could see the headlights of the cars in the lane. An oil lamp burned upon the table, and Henry, the solitary waiter of the Cardinal's Hat, had placed a tray of refreshments beside it.

"It's this way," said Wessex, leaning his elbows upon the table and staring across at us. "Dyke Grange is an old Jacobean place, at one time surrounded by a moat. The moat is dry now, however. The property is supposed to be let, and is actually in the hands of a Norwich estate agent. But from what I can gather, the owner places impossible obstacles in the way of prospective lessees."

"Who is the owner?" I asked.

"Sir Joseph Peek."

"What!" cried Harley. "And you don't think he really wants to let Dyke Grange? Why not?"

"Well," Wessex spoke slowly, "a man named Forder and his wife act as caretakers and live in the wing where the servants' quarters are situated. They are a very unpleasant couple, but I don't think they know anything about the crime. The rest of the house is unfurnished, with the exception of a bedroom and sitting room, access to which can be gained by a side entrance. I rather fancy—" he hesitated, staring significantly at Harley.

"What do you fancy?" prompted the latter.

"I fancy Sir Joseph used these rooms at odd times."

"For?" prompted Harley.

"Well—he slept there when he was too drunk to go home, and also arranged interviews there which he did not want to take place at the Hall, you understand?"

"I follow you. The man has an unpleasant reputation."

"He *had,"* corrected Wessex.

"What?"

"I say he had. He is lying in Dyke Grange, stabbed to the heart!"

Harley sprang to his feet excitedly, and I, scarcely knowing if I heard aright, clutched the edge of the table, watching the speaker.

"Old Forder, the caretaker," Wessex continued, "came rushing down to the village constable at Dykeham at about half-past eight—that is to say, about the time that I was due here. In going round to lock up, he had found the dead man. As a result, I was held up just as I came through Dykeham village. We had had a puncture and I was about half an hour late. Otherwise, the news would have reached me here.

"Good God!" muttered Harley. "Good God! And we were speaking to him only this evening. Go on, Wessex, go on."

"Well," continued the detective, "what do you say to coming and seeing for yourself? I have had everything left absolutely as I found it, and the local man is on duty there."

"You are right," said Harley shortly. "Let us start at once. Wessex, it's almost incredible!"

III
Gypsy Peggy

We descended the stairs just as Peggy Gatten, the landlord's daughter, crossed the passage below. She started and turned her head aside, as if to avoid us, but:

"Good evening, Peggy," said Harley genially.

"Good evening, Mr. Harley," she returned, but hurried on without further speech.

I derived the impression that she had been crying, for her fine, dark eyes looked unnaturally bright. She was a handsome brunette, her figure too full for classic beauty, indeed of an Orientally voluptuous mold, so that I had more than once suspected a Gypsy strain in Peggy, possibly inherited from her mother. She was no stranger to the arts of the toilette, but practiced them with so heavy a hand as to mar rather than to enhance her rustic good looks.

Dave Gatten, her father, came of a stock which had bred fenmen in the good old days, a poaching, lawless lot, and I wondered if even his present prosperity had entirely quelled the family spirit within him; for he was an independent fellow, and at times there was a wild look in his eyes which, as Harley had laughingly remarked, lent him a remarkable resemblance to a Stevensonian pirate. His treatment of his daughter was sometimes harsh to the point of brutality; more than once I had overheard him taking her to task respecting her mode of dress. But tonight we had little leisure to consider the domestic life of the Cardinal's Hat.

As we hurried out to the car which waited, a mental picture arose before me of Sir Joseph Peek lying in his blood. I seemed to hear his rather coarse voice crying: "Cheerio, then. At seven-thirty tomorrow night."

As the car moved off:

"What was the weapon used?" asked Harley.

"Well," replied Wessex, "that's the point about which I am so hopelessly puzzled."

"Why?"

"He was stabbed to the heart—so much is evident. And in the next room—not the room in which he was killed—I found a jeweled dagger on the floor."

"A jeweled dagger!" I exclaimed in a hushed voice.

"Yes, a wonderful looking Moorish thing."

"Good God!" whispered Harley. "Do you hear that, Knox?"

"I do."

"But," continued Harley, "where is the mystery—if you say you found a dagger lying on the floor?"

"Here's the mystery," returned Wessex. "There is absolutely no trace of blood on the blade!"

IV
A Cigarette Stump

The car pulled up in a narrow lane beside a low stone wall in which a gate was set.

"There is a path from here," explained Wessex as we descended, "which leads directly into the wing in which the crime was committed. Sir Joseph was in the habit of using this path, and tonight it was probably used by someone else as well."

The path that we were following was a mere grass track, at one point passing through a clump of trees; then, as we came out from their shadows, Dyke Grange lay before us. Built upon a sort of mound, possibly artificial, the Grange, a low rambling building, must be approached from this point through a piece of weedy ground where the path was more clearly defined, and thence through the dry moat, into which and up on the farther side the track led.

"This was the way I came tonight," explained Wessex as we crossed a narrow piece of neglected lawn and approached a curious Gothic window, tall, narrow and pointed at the top.

The room within was dimly lighted by the moon, and the church-like quality of the illumination was enhanced by the presence of stained glass in a smaller Gothic window upon its further side. The floor level was three feet beneath us where we stood, and I could see that there were oaken steps leading down from the window. As the three of us stood looking in:

"This," said Wessex in a rather hushed voice, "was Sir Joseph's private entrance, and the furnished rooms are immediately above."

Neither Harley nor I answered him, for we were both staring at something which lay upon the polished oaken floor some ten or twelve feet from where we stood. It was a jeweled dagger, its blade gleaming coldly in the moonlight and the stones of the hilt glittering like the eyes of venomous serpents.

I looked silently at Harley and he read my glance, nodding his head slowly.

"The same, Knox," he said, "beyond a shadow of doubt! Ali Mahmoud's knife!" He turned to Wessex. "Where are the man Forder and his wife?" he asked.

"They are in their own quarters at the other end of the house. Relations of the dead man, and others, are there as well; and a local officer is on duty in the next room—the room through that doorway yonder. But"—he spoke eagerly—"do I understand that you have seen this dagger before?"

"I have, Wessex! But be patient. Let us go in. This was the way you approached tonight?"

"Yes," replied the inspector shortly, piqued, I thought, by Harley's reticence.

He pushed the leaves of the window and they opened noiselessly.

"No creaking," muttered Harley.

"No," returned the inspector. "The hinges are oiled; I examined them. He used this door pretty frequently, I fancy."

We walked down the steps on to the polished floor. There was a curiously musty smell in the room, not unlike that of a cheap cigar. Harley dropped to one knee, and, bending, stared intently at the dagger. By the light of his electric torch he examined it critically, but without touching it. This done, he raised it, submitted it to further scrutiny, and replaced it. Then:

"Not a stain," he muttered. "Not a stain. It fell a yard from where it lies. The notch is just discernable. It hasn't been touched, Wessex?"

"No; it lies exactly where I found it."

The sound of an interrogatory cough reached us from the room beyond, and:

"It's all right, constable," cried Wessex. "We're coming in."

The communicating door was open and, our footsteps echoing in the big, empty room, we crossed and entered that adjoining. In some respects it was similar except that it possessed no Gothic windows and was lighted from the north. The constable was standing over by the window, watching the doorway through which we had come, and, some distance from him, beside a second, closed door, lay the huddled figure of a man wearing riding kit. He lay half upon his face, one clenched fist shot straightly out before him, the other arm doubled under him unnaturally. A great quantity of blood had stained the oak beneath his body.

We stood for a moment silent, then:

"Anything to report?" asked Wessex.

"No, sir," replied the constable, evidently awed by the intrusion of a great tragedy into his humdrum routine.

"Did you move him?" asked Harley, turning to Wessex.

"Only enough to enable the doctor to examine his wound," was the reply.

"Who sent for the doctor?"

"The man Forder, after he had communicated with the police."

"And he arrived while you were here?"

"He had arrived a few minutes before."

"I see. Was he smoking?"

"Smoking? No. Why do you ask?"

"Sniff, Wessex, sniff!" He turned suddenly to the constable. "You have not been smoking, officer?"

"Certainly not, sir."

"Sure?"

"Quite, sir!"

Harley walked all around the ghastly figure, shining his torch upon the floor and examining the bloodstains. It was a sickening spectacle, and once, when a ray of the torch fell upon the pallid face of Sir Joseph Peek, I reflected how I had disliked his florid complexion earlier in the evening, and I shuddered at the thought.

"Anything of interest in his pockets?" asked Harley.

"Nothing," was the reply. "Keys, cigarettes, a few odds and ends in his note case, but no money."

"No money?"

"No paper money. He had a little silver in his trousers pocket."

Harley stooped and gingerly turned the body on its back.

"Ugh!" he exclaimed at the sight of the bloodstained breast. "A strong blow, Wessex."

"Undoubtedly. And with just such a weapon as—" The inspector jerked his thumb over his shoulder in the direction of the next room.

Harley made a brief examination of the hands, clothing and hair of the dead man and stared critically at the soles of his boots. Then:

"Here's a burned match on the floor," he said abruptly. "Upstairs."

Opening the door, we found ourselves at the foot of a carpeted stair and, mounting this, we entered an elegantly furnished and well-lighted room in which the pictures, statuettes and decorations spoke eloquently of the tastes of its departed owner. There was a vague smell of tobacco in the stale air of the room and Harley, staring about him, said slowly:

"What sort of cigarettes were in Sir Joseph's case?"

"Algerian," replied Wessex. "Similar to French Caporals."

Harley turned to me.

"That is the smell in the room below!" he said.

He pushed open a door and walked into a tastefully appointed bedroom, glanced rapidly around, shrugged his shoulders and came out again. Silk shaded lamps burned in both rooms. One of the drawers of a large writing desk was open. In an absent fashion, Harley began to examine the contents. He came upon a number of photographs. Turning his head, he glanced over his shoulder at me quizzically.

"There are two points to be decided," he said.

"What are they?" I asked eagerly.

"First, where Sir Joseph dropped the cigarette which he lighted and partly smoked in the room below; and, second, which, if any, of these fair but frail ladies—" he tossed the bunch of photographs upon the desk—"was here tonight?"

"Good God!" said Wessex. "What makes you think a woman was here?"

From a little coffee table standing beside a deep settee, Harley took up a china ashtray and held it out toward Wessex. It contained the stumps of three tiny, gold-tipped cigarettes.

"Choice Egyptian," he said. "Hadjes Nessim. A man with a palate for these could never smoke Algerian!"

Wessex stared rather stupidly.

"But," he began, "a man may have been here—the man who murdered him. Why"—his face lighted up excitedly—"the clue of the knife is strengthened, Mr. Harley. The man who smoked these Egyptian cigarettes was the owner of the Oriental dagger!"

"If the dagger is the property of a man," returned Harley, "then its owner certainly did not smoke these cigarettes."

"I don't follow you," Wessex declared bluntly.

Between finger and thumb, Harley took up one of the gold-tipped stubs and held it directly under a shaded lamp.

"Examine it closely," he invited.

Wessex and I bent forward, staring curiously.

"Do you see the faint red stains upon the gold?" asked Harley. "Lipstick, Wessex; lipstick!"

V
Theories

"Well," said Inspector Wessex, walking into our sitting room at the Cardinal's Hat on the following morning, "we've got the Arab; he was arrested an hour ago at Norwich."

"Good!" said Harley, standing up and crossing the room to where his tobacco pouch lay upon a seat beside the window. "You are making progress. What statement did he make?"

"He will have to be more fully examined through an interpreter," replied Wessex. "But he has denied all knowledge of the crime. Nearly eight pounds in paper and silver money was found upon him, and you will remember that Sir Joseph's case was empty."

"Did he explain how he had come to lose the jeweled dagger?"

"Yes." Wessex frowned thoughtfully. "He declared that he had sold it to Sir Joseph for five pounds!"

"Ah!" Harley looked up suddenly. "When and where did the sale take place?"

"Apparently a few minutes after his interview with you on the river bank—or so he declares. He says that Sir Joseph spoke to him in his native tongue," continued Wessex, "and that in this way the deal came about. It is a rather thin tale, however, and very suspicious his coming out pat with the name of the murdered man."

"Why?" asked Harley. "My two pounds and Sir Joseph's five, together with the few shillings already in Ali's possession, would account for the sum found upon him. Evidently, Sir Joseph gave the man all his ready money."

"Well, Sir Joseph's reputation in Egypt was a pretty bad one. I've learned that. Here's a native of that country, haunting a lonely part of Norfolk, most mysterious behavior, and the dagger, known to have been his property, is found almost beside the body of the murdered man. Papers or other incriminating evidence had obviously been taken from the drawer of the table above, and, lastly, Egyptian cigarettes had been smoked in that room."

"By someone whose lips were painted," murmured Harley tonelessly.

"Yes," agreed Wessex. "It's an awkward point, I must admit."

"Very awkward," said Harley. "Then we have the extraordinary circumstance that the knife, admittedly once the property of Ali Mahmoud, exhibits no traces of blood."

"He may have cleaned it."

"Why, having done so, leave it behind? Then you must remember my discovery of the Algerian cigarette stump near the gate opening upon the lane. Have you considered this, Wessex?"

"Yes, and I know it's your idea that Sir Joseph had walked down the path with someone to the gate and stood there for a moment, smoking, and had then dropped the cigarette end. You think he was followed back?"

"Well, mention an alternative."

"He may have been waiting there for someone. And this person may have murdered him as they entered the house."

"Meaning by 'this person,' Ali Mahmoud?"

"Who else?"

"Listen, Wessex: the Algerian cigarette was lighted in the room where the dagger was found. Evidence: the burned match and the smell. He smoked there for a few moments and then walked to the gate. He was almost certainly accompanied by the woman who had been to visit him. After she had gone, the murderer came! Have you traced the originals of any of the photographs?"

Inspector Wessex shook his head.

"Not so far," he admitted, "but then I've had very little time." He glanced at Harley. "Do you believe the Forders' story that they were unacquainted with the identity of any of Sir Joseph's callers?"

"Yes," replied Harley promptly. "The man was an artist in intrigue. I don't believe for a moment that he would have taken these people into his confidence."

"But you are convinced that there was a woman with Sir Joseph last night?"

"I am."

"You think she came back and murdered him?"

"Oh, no, I don't. No woman's hand struck that dreadful blow."

Wessex sighed wearily.

"In other words, Mr. Harley," he said, "your theory leads us nowhere. Mine, shaky in places, at least points to a possible culprit."

"And the motive?" asked Harley. "Do you suggest robbery?"

"Well, he seems to have taken all the ready money which Sir Joseph had upon him."

"And left behind him a piece of property possibly worth two hundred pounds," murmured Harley. "No, Wessex, I prefer your theory of a private vendetta. But even that leaves me very cold. The woman has no place in it—or I cannot fit her into one—and, further, I don't doubt that the Egyptian's statement is absolutely accurate."

"Do you think this man Ali was not at Dyke Grange last night?"

"I doubt if he knew of the existence of the place."

"Hm!" Wessex scratched his chin perplexedly. "At any rate, he is in custody."

VI
The Net Closes

We walked downstairs together and into the porch. The Cardinal's Hat seemed to be deserted in the morning; no one was about in any of the rooms. We lingered there for a while in thoughtful silence, staring at the spectacle of great brown sails apparently jutting up from the middle of the meadows, when something dropped lightly upon my hat brim and then fell at my feet. I looked down, and:

"Harley!" I whispered, glancing up at an open window over the porch. "Harley, look!"

I stooped and, raising the object that had dropped from above, held it between finger and thumb for his inspection.

It was the gold tip of a tiny Egyptian cigarette!

"Ah!" He snatched it from my hand and peered at it closely. Then: "Lipstick!" he muttered. "Lipstick!"

There were faint red stains upon the gold.

Harley grasped Wessex and myself each by an arm and drew us back into the inn. Stepping into the little bar parlor, he rang the bell. His eyes were very bright and his face was very grim. Presently, Henry, the ancient and melancholy waiter, appeared, and:

"Could I speak to Miss Peggy for a moment?" asked Harley.

"I'm afraid not, sir," was the reply. "She's been lying down all morning, suffering from a very bad headache."

"Is that so? The news of the tragedy in the neighborhood has upset her, doubtless?"

"It has upset us all, sir."

"There is something I want to ask Miss Gatten," said Harley after a moment's hesitation. "I should like you to take a little note to her. I will write it now, if you will bring me paper and envelope."

Five minutes later, Peggy Gatten came into the sitting room where Harley, Wessex and I awaited her. Her appearance rather shocked me, although she had obviously attempted, by the employment of devices of the toilette, to conceal the fact that her usually fresh color had deserted her. There were shadows beneath her eyes, telling of a sleepless night, and her expression puzzled me.

"Ah, Peggy," said Harley genially, "sit down, won't you? I am sorry to worry you when you are obviously far from well, but I must ask you to tell me where you get those little gold-tipped Egyptian cigarettes that you smoke."

Peggy had seated herself at his invitation, but, hearing those words, she leaped to her feet, wide-eyed, clutching at the back of a chair.

"All right," said Harley gravely. "You need not answer. I know now. Tell me what happened at your interview with Sir Joseph Peek last night."

The girl moistened her lips and seemed to be seeking for words with which to reply, when there came a dramatic interruption. Unheard by us, so intent were we upon this strange scene, Dave Gatten, the landlord, had approached the door. Now it burst open and a rugged, fierce figure, swarthy and menacing, he strode into the room.

"I'll tell you!" he shouted. "I'll tell you!"

"You!" came in a whisper from Peggy. "You!"

"Yes! Who else!" shouted the man, his eyes lighting up madly. "I'll do no good by trying to conceal what's bound to come out at the trial. I might as well tell the truth now and take my chance."

Harley was standing by the window, his face quite expressionless, but I saw the light of a sudden understanding dawn on the countenance of Inspector Wessex. Rising from the chair in which he was seated, the inspector came forward.

"Dave Gatten," he said, "I arrest you for the murder of Sir Joseph

Peek at Dyke Grange. Anything you say will be used as evidence against you."

"Let it be!" cried the man truculently. "Let it be!"

He folded his arms, glaring around from face to face.

"I've watched and I've wondered," he continued, addressing himself to the pale-faced girl who now crouched back against the wall of the room, staring at him glassily. "Fine dresses and silk stockings, aye, and jewels, too! They never came out of your savings, Peggy! It was easy, but it was going too far. And last night I followed you. You talked so loud up in that room above that I heard almost every word, and I can answer the question you have just asked her, sir!

"He told her he was through with it all, that it must finish before things were discovered. Then"—Gatten turned to Harley—"I saw the black-faced dog light a cigarette in the room below. I saw him come out, smoking it, and walk down to the gate with my girl. I lay flat behind a bush, waiting for him to come back. When he did and walked in through the open window, I followed him! He heard my footstep on the steps and turned.

"I don't know what he read in my face; I don't know what I had in my heart. But there's something in my blood, as there was in my father's blood before me, that just drives me mad at times. His ugly face seemed to be grinning at me through a red mist. I struck at him and he dodged the blow. I leaped upon him and picked him up in my arms."

Gatten illustrated the act, his movements exhibiting that gigantic strength which I knew him to possess.

"He knew he was outmatched, but he wrenched one arm free and got it into his pocket. I saw the glitter of a long blade and I threw him off and fell back a step. He came for me, as mad now as I was, and then—" Gatten paused. "Well, then I remembered the big clasp knife which I always carry—always have carried. I can prove it. And the next I knew, I had it in my hand with the blade open.

"He struck at me. I caught his wrist, twisted it, and the dagger fell. The light was very dim, there in that empty room, but I could see enough of him to know that he had read his death sentence in my face. He turned and ran, and I followed him. Halfway across the inside room I caught him and threw one arm around his neck. He twisted about, squealing like a hare, and reached up to my throat. Then I struck at him with all my strength."

He stopped abruptly and brushed his sleeve across his brow, which was streaming with perspiration.

"I dropped the clasp knife, still open, into my pocket," he resumed, "and stood listening for a moment, looking down at him where he lay at my feet. The red madness was gone for the moment and I could think coolly. I had heard you"—he turned his glaring eyes upon Peggy—"I had heard you ask him for certain things of yours which he had, and I had heard him refuse to give them to you. I found my way upstairs. You had said over and over again: 'Open that drawer; I want my letters.'

"I found the drawer and I opened it, and I found your letters and some photographs. I didn't know if I had everything, and I might have looked further, but just then I heard a door bang somewhere in the house and I hurried back down the stairs and out through the open window, which I closed behind me. I forgot the dagger, or I might have brought that, too. But what I want to say is this—he attacked me, the black-hearted mongrel. And except for the last blow, all I did was to defend myself."

He squared his broad shoulders.

"I feel better," he said, "now that I've got the story off my chest. When I heard you'd sent for Peggy, I knew it was only a question of time. You can do as you like, gentlemen. What I've done, I've done, and I'm not sorry for it."

Uttering a low moan, Peggy sank down, insensible, to the floor. Her father did not even glance aside.

"I've burned what I brought away," he concluded, "and I have cleaned my clasp knife. But the lining of my coat pocket is still stained with blood. I've spoken because I'd rather face the music now in my own time and in my own way than skulk like a rat in a hole waiting to be dragged out. It was sure to come, sooner or later."

"It has come," said Harley gravely.

Inspector Wessex was raising the unconscious girl, and I saw my friend's glance fixed upon her face, its pallor throwing into ghastly prominence the unnatural scarlet of her painted lips.

RED MIST

"I am going to make a very extraordinary request, Knox," said Paul Harley.

He stared for a while at the card in his hand whilst I waited for what was to come. Then:

"Mr. John Tresmond, of Stone Lacey, Devon, is waiting outside," he continued, "and I have every reason to believe him to be a very worthy country gentleman. This is what makes the matter difficult." He fixed his keen gray eyes upon me, and: "You know I have a reason for my seemingly maddest actions, Knox," he said. "Very well—from now onwards, I wish you to be Harley, and I will become Knox!"

"But, my dear Harley!" I exclaimed, "this is incredible. It is the Salterton Abbey case, is it not?"

Harley nodded.

"Following his letter," I went on rapidly, "Mr. Tresmond has come to town, and probably he wants you to go down to Devon to investigate the mystery. Do I understand you to suggest that I should take your place in this matter, that I should impersonate you? My dear fellow, firstly, it would be a shocking violation of Mr. Tresmond's hospitality, and, secondly, I fear the imposture would be discovered at the very outset!"

"You are wrong, Knox. Mr. Tresmond does not know me; you and I are about the same build, both clean-shaven; and in regard to your behavior in Devon, I shall have ample time to coach you."

He strained across the table eagerly.

"Knox," he went on, "I mean it. You know what we have been discussing. You know that I am up against a big crisis in my career. Listen! Schulameyer is still in England! It is imperative that I leave London tonight."

"Schulameyer!" I cried. "Then why take up this case?"

"If I assure you that I must," he said, "will you consent? At the worst, it means a week in Devon. The country is delightful, the trout fishing is good. I have no doubt that Mr. Tresmond will prove to be an excellent host; and when the ruse is discovered—" he shrugged his shoulders. "It means a lot to me, Knox."

To say that I was mystified would be inadequate, but his earnestness was unmistakable, and my time was my own for three weeks ahead.

"Very well," I said, not a little reluctantly. "I am going to be dreadfully embarrassed, but if it means helping you—why, I'll do it."

"Good!" said Harley. "You are a real pal!" He pressed a button on his table, which meant that the waiting client was to be admitted.

A moment later, Mr. John Tresmond of Stone Lacey came into the room. A very typical English country gentleman, fresh colored, clean-shaven and stockily built, his hair gray at the temples and his manner possessing that direct simplicity which disarms unjust suspicion, but often leads to the undoing of crookedness, being the armor of an honest man who nevertheless is no fool. A moment he paused, looking from face to face, and:

"Mr. Paul Harley?" he inquired.

"This is Mr. Harley," said Harley, indicating myself. "My name is Knox; I sometimes assist—in a modest way!"

I felt a flush rise to my cheeks, but:

"Please sit down, Mr. Tresmond," I said, quite unable to check a reproachful glance in Harley's direction. "You are here to give us some further particulars respecting the Salterton Abbey mystery?

"Precisely," said the visitor, seating himself in the armchair that I had pushed forward. "You were expecting me?"

Unseen by Mr. Tresmond, Harley nodded.

"Yes," I replied, "I was expecting you. I have read your letters with very great interest, but, if I may say so, the case appears to be rather one for a psychic specialist than for myself. I am a criminologist, you see, and the matter which has brought you to London is rather in the nature of a ghostly manifestation, I gather."

Mr. Tresmond nodded.

"It is," he admitted; "or, at least, apparently it is."

He stroked his chin reflectively whilst I studied the man whose hospitality I was doomed to accept under false pretences.

"The legend of Salterton Abbey, as I have informed you, is that of a black-clad monk, enveloped in a cloud of flame, whose appearance presages disaster to the ruling baron—for, of course, the abbey dates back to feudal times. Needless to say, there is no ruling baron today."

He smiled almost apologetically. "But, nevertheless, I am, so far as I am aware, directly descended from the race which in the old days exercised undisputed sway over the lands of Stone Lacey."

Unconsciously, he was addressing his remarks rather to Harley than to me, but now he turned his frank blue eyes in my direction, and:

"You will find us in the Doomsday Book, Mr. Harley," he said; "but the modest estate which I administer to the best of my ability today is a shadow of that which belonged to my family at the time of the Conquest. My wife is Irish on her father's side and somewhat superstitious. I had believed myself immune from ghostly fears. I am perhaps something of a materialist. I regret to say that I pooh-poohed her story when first she told me that she had seen the black monk and the red mist in the valley below the Abbey. This"—he pointed to an open letter lying on the table—"I have mentioned."

Harley nodded, and, recollecting my part:

"Quite so," I said hastily, "I remember."

He regarded me silently for a while, then:

"Mr. Harley," he said, "on Wednesday evening last, I, myself, from my study window in Stone Lacey, saw the black monk in the valley. He was surrounded by a red vapor!"

"An effect of the sunset," Harley interjected.

"Nothing of the kind," said Tresmond sharply. "It was a stormy night. I watched him through field-glasses from the window, pacing slowly along beside the little stream which runs through the valley. The red mist seemed to follow him. Then, in a clump of trees, he disappeared, and I saw neither the monk nor the mist any more. Now"—he squared his jaw—"I don't believe in ghosts, Mr. Harley. I have spent hours exploring that valley since I saw the apparition, but I have discovered nothing to confirm my secret suspicions. You say you are not a psychic investigator, but a criminologist, and this is why I have come to you!

"Let me confess that your name was not familiar to me. I heard of you from a neighbor. But I am convinced, sir, that this thing has a material basis. It is a plot. Its end I cannot even dimly imagine. But if I am not a wealthy man, I have certain financial resources. My wife is panic-stricken—my servants threaten to leave me. I, myself, am uneasy in mind. I am here, Mr. Harley, to ask you to visit Stone Lacey and to unmask the impostor who has disturbed the peace of my household. I think the case may prove to be much more interesting than you surmise."

There was a moment's silence; then:

"I am inclined to agree with Mr. Tresmond," said Paul Harley.

I drew the curtains aside, opened the window, and leaning out, studied the moon-bathed landscape.

The quarters allotted to me were immediately above Mr. Tresmond's study, from which he had witnessed the apparition of the monk. Below me, the ground fell away into the valley, where the trout stream purled over its rocky course. Stone Lacey was a low, granite-built house of barrack-like appearance, although, as is often the case with these unprepossessing homesteads, delightfully comfortable as a residence. Part was of great age, but the west wing, in which I was housed, was modern; indeed, late Victorian. It had been added by the grandfather of my host. The room that I occupied was one not usually allotted to a guest, but since it commanded a view of the valley and of the ruins of Salterton Abbey, Tresmond's half apologetic explanation had been unnecessary.

An August moon lighted the room magically. I looked down to where the little stream in the deep valley lost its turbulence and followed almost sluggishly an S-shaped course, one loop embracing the former grounds of the abbey, where, doubtless, on many a Thursday of long ago, diligent monks had fished till dusk that the refectory table might be well graced on Friday.

I could see the ruins very clearly, distance lending them an appearance of delicate black lacework. Trees cloaked the farther slope, but above them, a mysterious silhouette against the blue sky, a tor stood out to show that before Christianity had claimed this valley for its own, champions of an older faith had been laid to their rest there.

No ghostly manifestations disturbed the serenity of the night and, reclosing the curtains, I lit a cigarette and sat down in an armchair to consider my position. It was a false position to which I could not entirely reconcile myself; yet Harley's reasons for this impersonation he had made evident enough.

At this time perhaps the most famous criminologist in Europe or America, he had accepted from the Foreign Office the task of tracing one of the most brilliant and elusive criminals of modern times, Isaac Schulameyer, an international with big financial backing, whose mission was to disorganize the industries of England. He had undertaken to make the British Isles untenable for Schulameyer, and apparently he had succeeded. Then, an hour before Tresmond's visit, information had reached Harley that proved that his task remained unaccomplished. The enemy of industrial England was still in our midst. Worse, he knew the identity of the man who had undertaken his downfall.

Nevertheless, since there was nothing mercenary in Harley's disposition, the big fee offered by Mr. Tresmond for the solution of the Stone Lacey mystery could not satisfactorily account for my presence in Devon; Harley had had some deeper motive; and this—which I resented—he had not seen fit to confide to me. I wondered how I should reconcile myself with my host when the imposture was discovered. But my belief in Harley had never been shaken, and whilst far from comfortable, I nevertheless trusted to my friend to see me through, recognizing that he must have seen in this ghostly business something of greater importance than was apparent to me.

* * * * *

Puffing at my cigarette, I reviewed the events of the evening since my arrival just before the dinner hour up to the present time. I had met Mrs. Tresmond and had endeavored to study her character as Harley would have done. Of her two sons, she had lost one in the war, the other was in the Indian Cavalry. Her daughter had recently married and had gone with her husband to Canada.

Stone Lacey, I determined, had lost its charm for Mrs. Tresmond. Sweet-natured she was, and charming, but looked older than her years. The memory of those who had gone was an insupportable sadness. She heard their voices in the orchard and saw their phantom figures crossing the lawn.

A dear fellow was John Tresmond, but utterly lacking in imagination. This terror that had come unbidden had shaken the fortitude of the once light-hearted Irish woman who had lived and wrought loyally beside him in Stone Lacey, never regretting the gaiety she had left behind. But now her outlook was changed. I was conscious of the tension. Tresmond would have been well advised to shut up Stone Lacey and to set out with his wife upon a protracted tour, touching Canada in the West and India in the East. Her life had become empty and she was ill-prepared to sustain the apprehension which this traditional horror had brought to life.

It had touched the entire household. The servants were frankly panic-stricken. Indeed, I foresaw several desertions in the near future. The place was lonely, and the scanty news that I had gathered of the neighbors had done little to disabuse my mind of the idea that few visitors disturbed the lonely lives of this elderly couple.

Only one other residence was in sight from Stone Lacey, and this not from the modern wing—a queer, low-pitched Jacobean place known as the Lych House, standing upon part of John Tresmond's land and tenanted by a Mr. Degas, a retired Anglo-Indian engineer, I understood, and apparently one of the few visitors to the house. It was by him that Tresmond had been advised to consult Paul Harley; for this reason, it must be my special task to avoid meeting him.

I threw my cigarette stump into the grate and began to undress. Already the West Country air had laid hold upon me; sleep was an urgent necessity. Before retiring, I pulled back the curtains and opened my window widely.

My last thought, as I laid my head upon the pillow, was not of the monk and the red mist, but of a vague idea which had pursued me through the sunken lane by which, in Tresmond's car, I had been driven from the station that night—of someone, the idea was not definite, who had followed me. Indeed, before turning in, I had taken a final survey of the moon-bathed landscape, expecting to see not the figure of a black-clad monk, but some other figure—a furtive figure—lurking under the shadows of the trees, perhaps not far off, perhaps near—watching my window.

In the morning, I set out soon after breakfast, not sorry to escape for a while from my false position. Harley's instructions as to my behavior had been fairly definite, and, so far, I thought, I had followed them closely enough. The best that could come of the whole business, in my opinion, was that I should be in a position to confirm the existence of the apparition.

That I should succeed in accounting for it, I regarded as a very remote possibility.

England was gasping under the visitation of a heat wave at this time, and I wore a somewhat distinctive Palm Beach suit of Harley's and a wide-brimmed, soft felt hat boasting a pugaree band; a costume which I had often thought rendered my friend unduly conspicuous in warm weather.

I was counseled to avoid meeting any of the neighbors if possible—notably that Mr. Degas, who presumably was acquainted with Harley. The wearing of a costume so unusual in England did not seem consistent with this policy, but that Harley was in deadly earnest, I could not doubt. Therefore, hoping for the best, I set out on this blazing August morning to inspect the scene of the alleged apparition. I shall now briefly relate what befell me.

In the first place, as I turned out of the grounds of Stone Lacey into one of those sunken lanes characteristic of the neighborhood, I immediately became aware of that same unaccountable idea of being followed.

I ascribed it to a natural fear of detection by someone in the neighborhood acquainted with the appearance of the real Harley, and pursued my way towards the valley in the grateful shade of overhanging trees. Mr. Tresmond had indicated what my route should be, and his wife, solicitous for my comfort, had wished to send the car to meet me at a certain point, in order that I should be back in time for luncheon. This offer I had declined, however, as it did not fall into line with certain of Harley's instructions.

At a point in the hedge where a footpath led one past heaps of boulders, over a shoulder of the moorland, and thence steeply down into the valley where the trout stream pursued its way, I paused and looked about me while I loaded my pipe.

A sudden sound, as of stumbling footsteps, brought me sharply about.

Someone, I determined, who had secretly watched my approach, was scrambling down the bank on the opposite side of the lane!

Ten seconds later, I had sprung to the top and was peering

through a gap in the thick hedge.

A little moor pony was galloping away like the wind!

Everywhere about me were evidences of pre-historic man—stone rings and fallen boulders. Far above on the right, the tor stood out against the almost tropical blue of the sky. Left, upon the other slope, I could see the gray front of Stone Lacey, and so clear was the air this morning that I believed I could see Mrs. Tresmond's white frock and sunbonnet as she moved about in the kitchen garden, doubtless supervising, as was her housewifely habit, the selection of vegetables for luncheon.

I pressed on, passing the boulders, and beyond them paused, looking down the steep slope patched with gorse into the rocky valley where the stream ran. At points its course was hidden from me, but as I scrambled down, new aspects constantly opened up, so that presently, under the shadow of an outjutting rock, I became aware of the presence of a motionless figure.

Harley's instructions leapt to my mind. It was a man who stood there, but because of his position, he could not possibly have seen me. Therefore I stepped aside and dropped down behind some bushes, peering out cautiously.

The distance was too great for identification, but I saw that the stranger wore a rough tweed suit and a tweed hat, the brim pulled down over his eyes. He was fishing, for, as I watched, I saw him make a throw, the sun glittering brightly upon the running reel. This set me thinking. I wondered if it could be a coincidence that the fisherman was planted at a point I could not very well avoid passing in pursuit of my original plan; namely, to follow the stream in the direction of Salterton Abbey to the spot, closely described by Mr. Tresmond, at which the apparition traditionally appeared.

I had dropped down behind the bush to reflect upon my next move, and now, raising my head, I made a second and startling discovery.

The fisherman had vanished!

At first, I could scarcely believe the evidence of my senses. I thought he must have moved downstream and was temporarily obscured from sight by one of the many upcropping boulders. It was not so, however. I crouched there for fully ten minutes, watching intently right and left; but the figure did not reappear. He had vanished as though the earth had swallowed him up.

Reviewing my mental impression of his appearance, frankly, I began to wonder whether he, too, had not been an apparition. Even at the risk of meeting him—if he had ever existed outside my imagination—I determined to pursue my original course.

With this idea in mind, I got upon my knees and was about to stand up when suddenly I paused, spellbound with astonishment.

Not twenty paces away, but below me on the slope, a man had risen as I had done, from a clump of bushes, and was peering down cautiously in the same direction as myself!

He, too, had been watching the fisherman!

Instantly I dropped back, removing my hat and keeping my head sufficiently raised to enable me to see what this second mysterious stranger was about. In attire, he was not unlike the phantom fisherman, but nevertheless, it was not he. Indeed, it was physically impossible for the other to have reached that spot unseen by me.

I had not long to wait. Taking advantage of every cover that offered, the watcher on the slope below me crept down into the valley. Moving from time to time to keep him in view, I studied his movements for fully half an hour, and that he was searching for the missing man with the rod became perfectly obvious. He moved away in the direction of Salterton Abbey, which was hidden by a clump of trees, and at last I lost sight of him.

As I stooped to pick up my broad-brimmed hat, I became aware of a distant rumbling. I looked back over my shoulder. So absorbed had I been by the mysterious comedy in this valley that I had failed to note both the passage of time and the coming of an ominous thundercloud, which now had cast its shadow over the farther slope, backing the tor with a grandeur of ebony banks and creeping ever onwards. Point after point became mantled, so that, even as I watched, more than half the valley grew overcast.

"Oh, ah! 'e be marked down, be Squire Tresmond!" said my acquaintance, whilst thunder boomed over the inn and such torrents of rain fell as almost to drown the sing-song voice.

"Has the mist ever appeared before in your time?" I asked.

"No, no. But my gran'father, 'e did remember it in 'is days, an' old Squire Roger—'im they called Red Roger—'e went to 'is long rest, 'e did."

We drank in silence for a while, then:

"I saw someone fishing in the Abbey stream about an hour ago," said I, "a tallish man wearing a tweed suit. Would that be Squire Tresmond?"

"No, no," declared the moor farmer emphatically. "Tweed suit—rough like? Oh, ah! That might 'a been—well, who might that 'a been, George?"

George, the landlord, suggested Mr. Dickinson of Tawlish East.

"Oh, ah!" my acquaintance mused, "that be likely, too. Or maybe Mr. Degas of the Lych House, or Major Openshaw of Trennerton. Ah, likely enough!"

So presently I tramped back to Stone Lacey through a countryside refreshed. The smell of damp earth was in my nostrils. The air, electrically purified, was heady as wine. I had lunched well, if roughly, at the moor inn. The storm had lasted a good two hours, and now returning, I sought to arrange in my mind the facts that I had accumulated from the taciturn landlord and the more communicative moor farmer.

One thing was certain—the reappearance of the traditional ghost of Salterton Abbey was known throughout the length and breadth of the countryside, and it was accepted as a fact beyond dispute that John Tresmond's days were numbered. It was an omen that had never failed to portend disaster.

Sorrowfully this information had been imparted to me, for John Tresmond was a popular idol and his wife beloved by all who knew her.

Since I had undertaken to make a daily report to Harley, the compilation of my first presented serious difficulties, and my humor towards my friend was not of the best as I pursued my lonely way back to Stone Lacey.

As "the red mist," the thing was known, for the reason that the appearance of the monk was always preceded by a phenomenon resembling a blood red vapor trailing across the little stream winding around the abbey grounds.

First, the mist was seen. Then, sometimes, but not invariably, the figure of the black-robed monk. Finally, the mist vanished.

This corresponded so closely to the statement of Tresmond that my thoughts inclined more than ever to an acceptance of the supernatural nature of the manifestation.

The eternal Shakespearean line kept time to my steps as I tramped along the hard road, but the crowning mystery, the mystery which baffled me, was that of Harley's motive in taking up a case strictly within the sphere of the Psychical Research Society.

I had plunged into the valley and was mounting the other slope towards Stone Lacey. Above me, from interlocking branches, drops of moisture sometimes fell. A dwindling rivulet pursued an irregular stony course down the lane. Then, in upon my meditations burst a sudden outside influence.

Once again I became acutely conscious of being watched.

Remembering the episode of the moor pony, I paused, listening, looking about me and wondering. Then, dramatically, the justness of my suspicions was placed beyond doubt.

Out from a gap in the hedge, where, I think, she had waited to waylay me, a woman came. Wild-eyed, she tumbled down the steep bank and confronted me!

She was past her first youth, but still possessed a sort of tragic beauty; dark, with somber southern eyes, lithe and sinuous in her movements, a passionate creature who held up her hand as if to check me. She was dressed appropriately enough in a simple walking habit and wore an unadorned felt hat. But, for some reason that was not clear to me at the time, I pictured her otherwise adorned.

Despite the vital animalism that glance and movement betrayed there in that Devon lane, I thought of a crowded room, of tobacco smoke and the vague smell of perfume, of stuffiness, light and laughter, bare arms and glittering jewels. It was pure intuition, no doubt. For a moment the mantle of Paul Harley had actually fallen upon me. Then the woman spoke, and I determined that she was Russian.

"Mr. Harley," she said, "stop for one moment and listen to me."

I stared at her—strangely, no doubt, and:

"Give me your word," she went on earnestly, "that you will never tell any living soul you have met me."

She spoke impetuously, passionately.

"Quick!" she urged; "promise!"

"Very well," I said, "if you wish, but what have you to say to me?"

"This." She looked quickly about her. "Pack your bag. Leave Stone Lacey. It is easy for you to give an excuse. There is a train at eight o'clock. Take it, I beg of you, for my sake, if not for your own. I have risked more than you know to tell you this. It means more to me and to you than you know. I beg of you, I beg of you, Mr. Harley, do as I ask."

She spoke rapidly, her great dark eyes fixed upon me, so that I was carried away by her vehemence.

"No one is in danger," she went on, "no catastrophe will come to Mr. Tresmond or anyone belonging to him. I promise you this, I give you my solemn word, I swear it. Only go. Do not spend another night in that house."

Now her hands were clasped together feverishly. She appealed as one whose life is at stake.

"But," I began hesitantly, "I don't even know your name, madam, although you appear to know mine."

"You are not to know it!" she cried. "You are not to know it!" and stamped her foot upon the wet gravel. "This meeting you have promised is to be secret, is to be sacred. Do I seem as one who jests? Listen to me; do as I ask. Tell me you will do as I ask."

But now, through all my embarrassment and confusion, common sense was beginning to return, a vague recognition of errors into which I had nearly fallen, and recognition, too, of duty to my friend, for whom how blindly I had undertaken this mission.

"Madam," I said, "I am very deeply indebted to you, for I do not doubt your sincerity. But, unless you will consent to tell me who you are and in what way you can possibly be interested in my remaining at or leaving Stone Lacey, I fear I can give you no such promise."

My studied coolness had a singular and unexpected result. She clenched her hands and stared at me for a while as one who has received a death sentence, or is about to deliver it. Then:

"Very well," she said, and the tone of her voice had changed. "You fool! You poor fool!"

Suddenly she was contemptuous.

"I have done all that is in my power," she concluded, "and I bind you to your promise. No one must know that we have met."

"Madam," I replied, "no one shall ever know."

A moment longer she stared at me strangely, then turned, climbed up the bank and disappeared.

That night brought fleeting clouds to obscure the moon and a restless wind that moaned eerily around Stone Lacey. Dinner had proved a dismal business. I thought that the electrically charged air might be responsible in some measure for a nervous tension which characterized not only my hostess and the habitually stolid Tresmond, but those of the servants with whom I came in contact.

Part of my report to Harley I had compiled before dressing, but my difficulties proved to be even greater than I had anticipated. With Tresmond, I had arranged that he should watch from the study window below whilst I made certain notes in my room above. A tired look that I had observed in his eyes had been explained by a chance remark during dinner, which had led me to suspect that latterly he had spent many hours of every night in just this fashion.

Twenty times I had all but betrayed myself—the last when I had begged permission to retire to my room to complete the report.

"Report to whom, Mr. Harley?" Tresmond had asked.

My wits had awakened in time, and:

"To Knox," was my reply, "I make it a custom to record all my impressions of a case whilst the facts are fresh in my mind."

Since this indeed was a custom of Harley's, I counted the lie a white one, and so at last reached my room still unmasked.

The extraordinary interview with the foreign woman in the lane had upset all my preconceived theories. The legend of the red mist dated back to the days of the first Crusade, when a Tresmond had done violence to a wandering friar on pilgrimage to the abbey—in those times the resting place of holy relics. In what way could this woman, or any other human being, be concerned in my investigation of the reborn mystery?

Never possessed of a facile pen, I sat, pipe in mouth, racking my brains for adequate words, forgetful of the passage of time, oblivious of the wind moaning mournfully among the trees. "The fact that someone else was interested in the fisherman," I had written, "may have no bearing whatever on the case."

At these words I was staring, stupidly, when I heard soft but rapid footsteps in the corridor outside my room. As the door was flung open, I sprang to my feet.

John Tresmond stood on the threshold, his usually florid face looking pale in the lamplight. He wore a dressing-gown over his night attire and held a pair of field glasses in his hand.

"It's there!" he said, speaking in a hushed voice. "Thank God, my wife is asleep; but the red mist is in the valley!"

Instantly I tilted the lampshade, crossed to the window and, drawing wide the curtain, beheld a sight which filled me with awe.

More clearly visible when the moon swam free of clouds, but dimly to be seen even in the shadows, a thin stream of red vapor poured along the valley below, following the course of the rivulet and resembling in a ghastly way, viewed from so great a distance, a trickle of blood!

I turned to face Tresmond, and, as my purpose became clear:

"You will never find your way in the dark!" he said, his suppressed tones revealing intense excitement. "I will arouse Edwards. You know why I may not join you; my wife has exacted a solemn promise. But I feel—"

"Arouse no one," I interrupted. "I know the way, I only fear I shall be too late."

"You are armed?" he asked as I made for the door.

"Yes," I nodded, wondering why every man experiences a sense of protection, even from ghosts, when he carries a lethal weapon.

Half an hour John Tresmond gave me to reach the valley, but more nearly an hour had elapsed when at last, from a spot not twenty yards from that where I had hidden to watch the fisherman, I looked down upon the little stream.

Traces of red mist were still visible. The sky had grown more overcast and the distant abbey ruins were backed by angry clouds, but elfin wisps of vapor floated above the water, appearing and disappearing like marsh-lights. Nearer I crept down, and nearer; and now, as if my coming had been noted, this unnatural mist grew more dense, more red—or such was my impression.

A man is made of curious complexities. For my own part, I was, frankly, more terrorized than curious; it was as Paul Harley's representative alone that I pursued the uncanny business to the end.

Then, as I crept around the boulder that had sheltered the fisherman, I saw the black monk.

It seemed to me, literally, in that moment, that my blood grew cold. All the deliberate courage that had thus far sustained me—because I acted for another and not for myself—deserted me utterly. I watched the ominous figure pacing slowly beside the stream, not twenty yards from where I stood rooted to the ground. The red mist, in serpentine coils, floated between us.

Yet, so narrow is the dividing line between courage and panic, that, as I watched, I suddenly regained entire command of myself; that sickening supernatural dread left me; I became all at once master of my emotions.

I had seen the monk stumble!

In an instant I was running towards him, revolver in hand, heedless of the red mist as of the other apparition, now that a common accident had convinced me that I found myself in the presence of some evil imposture. For a phantasm does not stumble.

The figure turned, looking back, but the black cowl quite obscured his face from my view.

A great excitement claimed me—the thrill of the chase. I should have something more definite than I had dared to hope to report to Harley. I cried out in a loud voice. The vapor moved like red smoke over the ground almost at my feet, when:

"Stop!" came imperatively. *"Stand still, Knox, for your life!"*

I pulled up in full stride, as though a solid obstacle had checked me. The voice had come from ahead—at first I thought from the lips of the monk. Then I saw the latter pause, fall back and hesitate. My mind in a turmoil, my ideas chaotic, I heard:

"Go back! Go back—back from the mist!"

And I knew that the hidden speaker was—*Paul Harley?*

Then events moved hot-foot to a swift climax. I drew back urgently from the moving vapor, which only a moment since I had been prepared to brave. I heard the moan of the wind and became aware that the breeze had changed direction.

The monk faced about, uttering an exclamation in some guttural tongue unfamiliar to me. I think he had seen Harley, although I could not see him. A moment longer he hesitated. Then he began to run towards the abbey ruins as a shrill-voiced gust of wind came sweeping along the valley. It carried a dense cloud of red vapor right across the runner's path. He threw up his hands, stopped dead, turned—and seeming to discern the fact that the tail of the mist which lay between him and myself was less dense than elsewhere, he came racing suddenly in my direction.

"Hold him!" I heard vaguely.

Then, whipping a fold of the robe around his face as a protection, the monk turned again and plunged into the patch of vapor.

I raised my revolver.

But even as I did so, the man—his vision obscured, I suppose, by the robe—stumbled, half recovered, stumbled again and, uttering a hoarse, choking scream, fell forward into the moving clouds of smoke.

The wind howled more loudly. Serpentine coils of red mist were borne hither and thither. A tweed-clad, bearded man appeared from the undergrowth, beyond the stream.

"Up the slope, Knox! Run back up the slope!"

The speaker's appearance was totally unfamiliar, but the voice was undoubtedly the voice of Harley!

Gray dawn was stealing up beyond the abbey ruins, and I peered wonderingly into the bearded face of my companion.

"A fairly good makeup, Knox?" he said grimly. "It had to be. I was dealing with a clever man."

"But I fail to see," I began, when:

"Surely, it is clear enough," Harley went on. "It came to me intuitively, not three minutes before Tresmond was shown into my office that day. I needed time to arrange my ideas. I needed free access to the scene of the mystery. And I knew, or I believed, that my appearance was unfamiliar in this district. I have been staying, as 'Mr. Gough,' an enthusiastic mineralogist, at the Hare and Hounds, Trennerton.

"So confident was I of my disguise that I remained quite ignorant of your presence behind me yesterday on the moor, as I lay watching Mr. Degas, fishing."

"Mr. Degas! Then he was the mysterious fisherman?"

Harley nodded.

"Very mysterious fisherman—since he was not trying to catch fish! Yes, had he been a superlative artist, Knox, he would really have baited his hook! As an old hand myself, I immediately noticed the novelty!

"Nevertheless, he tricked me. I had to return after nightfall to find out how he had disappeared. But I was successful; I discovered the cache. It is a partly natural and partly artificial cave-dwelling. At this end, nearer the slope, it terminates in a narrow fissure too small for entrance or egress, but admirably adapted for the purpose of releasing the red mist."

"But what is this red mist?"

"The vile thing, Knox, which prompted my plan to send you down here. It is the deadly 'S Vapor,' possessed by a certain government and named after its inventor, Dr. Isaac Schulameyer! It requires a steady, prevailing breeze for its use—hence the appearance of the apparition tonight. No fewer than fifty cylinders are stored in the cave. His several experiments have destroyed the vegetation in patches all around the neighborhood of the fissure."

My bewilderment grew only the greater.

"But," I cried, "what was the object of all this?"

"*I* was the object!" Harley replied grimly. "Hiding down here in Devon under an assumed identity, Schulameyer saw, in the legend of Stone Lacey, a possible instrument for my destruction. Tresmond was never in danger, Knox. His fears, and the fears of his wife, were merely used to get me on the scene!"

Harley stared at me. Through the unfamiliar disguise, I could detect a quizzical expression that I knew of old.

"You are perhaps wondering," he went on, "about the identity of the woman who intercepted you in the lane?"

"But, Harley!" I exclaimed. "How can you possibly know—"

"My dear double," said Harley, "I overheard every word! I have been watching your slightest movement since the moment you arrived! The lady is Schulameyer's renegade companion—*the cidevant* Countess Natinov."

"Good heavens! Then it means that the monk—"

"The man you saw die in such agony when the red mist touched him is the man known locally as 'Mr. Degas.' That man, Knox, was Dr. Isaac Schulameyer! At last, my job is done."

PUBLICATION HISTORY

"The Voice of Kali" copyright 1923, Doubleday, Page & Co. From SHORT STORIES, December 10, 1923.

"The House of the Golden Joss" copyright 1920, P.F. Collier and Sons Company. From COLLIER'S, THE NATIONAL WEEKLY, August 7, 1920.

"The White Hat" copyright 1920, P.F. Collier and Sons Company. From COLLIER'S, THE NATIONAL WEEKLY, November 13, 1920.

"The Man With the Shaven Skull" copyright 1920, P.F. Collier and Sons Company. From COLLIER'S, THE NATIONAL WEEKLY, September 18, 1920.

"The Black Mandarin" copyright 1922, P.F. Collier and Sons Company. From COLLIER'S, THE NATIONAL WEEKLY, November 4, November 11 and November 18, 1922.

"The Dyke Grange Mystery" copyright 1922, Cassell & Co., Ltd. From THE STORY-TELLER, February 1922; text taken from the *Chicago Tribune,* May 28, 1922.

"Red Mist" copyright 1924, Cassell & Co., Ltd. From THE STORY-TELLER, October 1924.

The Sax Rohmer Library from Black Dog Books

THE GREEN SPIDER
SAX ROHMER

13 rare mysteries, including 4 tales previously unpublished in the US!

With an introduction by Gene Christie.

- A prominent scientist killed by a gigantic green spider . . .
- The mysterious mummy that looted a London museum . . .
- An "impossible" murder on the English moors . . .
- The modern pirates who plundered the idle rich of Southborne . . .

And more tales of suspense await the reader.

"Fine, creepy stuff!"—*Mystery Scene*

THE LEOPARD COUCH
SAX ROHMER

13 works by the incomparable Rohmer, including 4 tales previously unpublished in the US!

With an introduction by F. Paul Wilson.
Lifetime Achievement Award recipient from the Horror Writers of America.

- The leopard couch of eternal memories . . .
- The severed hand of a desert sheikh—and its frightful vengeance . . .
- The mysterious black cat that knew too much . . .
- The vampiric nobleman who terrorized London . . .

And more tales of mystery are found within.

Scan with your phone

Follow us!

Twitter.com/blackdogbooks1
Facebook.com/blackdogbooks1

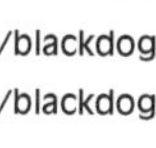

Black Dog Books

www.blackdogbooks.net | info@blackdogbooks.net

UNMASKED

Tom Roberts (ed.)

The forgotten origins of Hollywood's most famous Western heroes: The Cisco Kid, Hopalong Cassidy, Zorro and The Lone Ranger.

198 pages / $19.95

"[A] fascinating glimpse into these characters' early development stage."
—Western Clippings

"There are lots of western fans out there who will enjoy these tales."
—The Nostaglia League

"A must read. Highly recommend!"
—Amazon (Five Stars)

"Should most definitely be added to all Western fans' collections."
—Western Fiction Review

"Highly recommended."
—Rough Edges

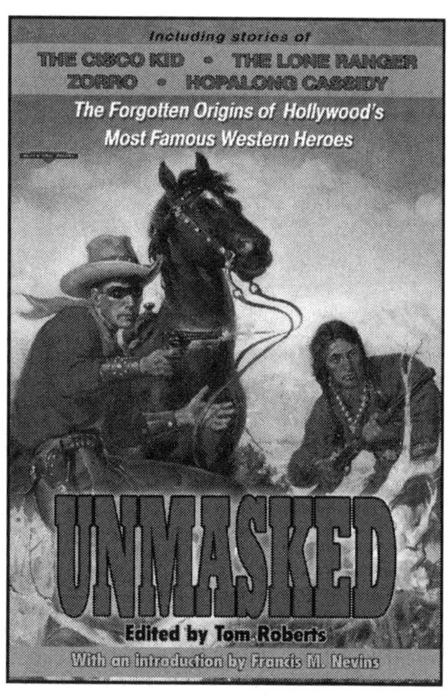

DEAD MAN'S BRAND

Norbert Davis

230 pages / $22.95

"The best collection of Western stories published this past year!"
—Dispatches from the Last Outlaw

"An excellent and much recommended pick, not to be missed."**—Midwest Book Review**

"A superb collection."
—Western Fiction Review

"Some of the best-written Western tales you'll ever read. It gets my highest recommendation."
—James Reasoner, author of *Redemption, Kansas*

"These Western short stories will leave you wanting more."**—Troy D. Smith,** Spur award-winning author of *Bound for the Promise Land*

"Without a doubt better than some of the best Westerns I've read from any era."
—Peter Brandvold, author of the Lou Prophet Ben Stillman and Cuno Massey series

"Any reader who has enjoyed Norbert Davis's mystery and detective fiction should find these Western tales equally satisfying."**—Bill Pronzini**

Scan with your smartphone

www.blackdogbooks.net | info@blackdogbooks.net

LESTER DENT LIBRARY

Before he began to chronicle the exploits of Doc Savage, Lester Dent produced scores of novels, shorter fiction and articles spanning the range of pulp fiction genres—tales of two-fisted action, mysteries, aviation adventures, war stories, romances and Westerns. Unavailable for decades, these works have been collected and are now available for the first time in book form!

DEAD MEN'S BONES
Trade paperback
239 pages / $24.95
Eight thrilling air-adventure stories.

THE SKULL SQUADRON
Trade paperback
227 pages / $24.95
Eleven thrilling tales set against the backdrop of World War I.

HELL'S HOOFPRINTS
Trade paperback
237 pages / $24.95
Eighteen wild West tales!
"A GOLD MINE in reading!"—**Amazon**

FISTS OF FURY
Trade paperback
278 pages / $27.95
Four novel-length adventures of two-fisted Curt Flagg.

Order these and other titles through our website:
www.blackdogbooks.net

Made in the USA
Lexington, KY
04 June 2015